# A FOUND FAMILY AT THE CORNISH COUNTRY HOSPITAL

JO BARTLETT

Boldwood

First published in 2024 in Great Britain by Boldwood Books Ltd.

Copyright © Jo Bartlett, 2024

Cover Design by Alexandra Allden

Cover Illustration: Shutterstock

A CIP catalogue record for this book is available from the British Library.

Paperback ISBN 978-1-80483-950-8

Large Print ISBN 978-1-80483-951-5

Hardback ISBN 978-1-80483-952-2

Ebook ISBN 978-1-80483-949-2

Kindle ISBN 978-1-80483-948-5

Audio CD ISBN 978-1-80483-957-7

MP3 CD ISBN 978-1-80483-956-0

Digital audio download ISBN 978-1-80483-954-6

Boldwood Books Ltd
23 Bowerdean Street
London SW6 3TN
www.boldwoodbooks.com

*This book is dedicated to Julia and Claire, two friends whose journeys to create families of their own took the road less travelled, and offered up the most beautiful of destinations as a result xx*

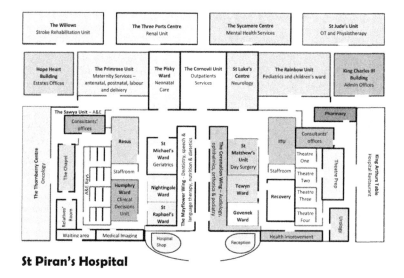

# St Piran's Hospital

# 1

Isla had spent far too many hours researching how to mark her father's sixtieth birthday in a creative way, but when even Google couldn't come up with an answer, she had to accept defeat. After all, you could hardly hold a surprise party, or arrange a hot air balloon trip, for a man who'd been dead for more than five years.

The list of things suggested to commemorate the milestone birthday of someone who had passed away was easier to navigate. Visiting the grave had been top of the list, but she did that regularly anyway, and it didn't seem nearly enough. One of the suggestions had been to go to a place her father had loved, but Nick Marlowe always insisted that nowhere could beat his beloved Cornwall. And, since Isla already lived in the same area where her father had been born, that also took visiting the place where he'd started his life off the list. And she already made a regular donation to the Huntington's charity, the disease that had taken her father from her when Isla had been nowhere near ready to let him go.

She wasn't sure she'd ever have been ready, but her mother's decision to shield her from the rapid progression of his illness, while she was studying all hours in the final year of her degree, had made it even more shocking when the end had come. Isla's student accommodation had only been half an hour away from home, but her mother had played down the doctors' concerns about how quickly her father's health seemed to be deteriorating. It was only when it had become clear that he wasn't going to pull through this time, that Isla had finally been called to her father's bedside. Her mother had said it was merciful that the final stages of his illness had been hastened by a bout of pneumonia he couldn't recover from, because he'd have hated for them to have to watch him become someone else entirely. But Isla had felt robbed of so much and, even now, it was impossible to see any part of it as a blessing. When he'd been forced to give up work just after his fiftieth birthday, as the disease became more advanced, her father's consultant had said he probably had ten to fifteen years left. Instead, he'd got four. And as much as everyone had tried to comfort the family by talking about how he'd been spared from losing any more of who he was, Isla had desperately wanted to hold on to whatever tiny part of him was still left, for as long as she possibly could.

'Are you ready?' Noah, the vicar at St Jude's, gently touched her arm, startling her far more than it should have done. She'd been expecting him at any moment, but she'd been lost in her thoughts, back in those last days at her father's bedside, when he hadn't been able to speak, and she wasn't sure he'd understood her when she'd told him how much she loved him, or even realised she was there. 'I'm really sorry, I didn't mean to make you jump.'

Noah had been so kind since she'd contacted him with her request, and she hated the thought that he might feel even the tiniest bit responsible for how emotional she was being, so she shook her head. 'I've been like this all week. It should have been such a milestone for Dad. All he ever wanted was to make it to sixty, to give him a chance of being able to walk me or my sister down the aisle, and maybe even see his first grandchild. Sixty wouldn't quite have given him grandchildren, but he'd at least have known that Lexi was expecting the twins, and he'd have been able to be by her side when she married Josh. He always said his girls, Mum included, were his life, and he made so many sacrifices for us. I just wish he could have had a tiny bit longer, so he got to hold his grandchildren in his arms. Even if it was only once.'

She hadn't meant to say all of that, but Noah's kindness had opened up the floodgates more than once, and there wasn't really anyone else she could talk to about just how much her father's sixtieth birthday was affecting her. It had been obvious how guilty Isla's mother, Clare, felt about not being able to come back to Cornwall to mark her late husband's birthday. But with Lexi having had a number of complications in the first four months of her pregnancy, her mother didn't feel able to leave Mount Dora, the small town in Florida where she'd grown up, and where the vast majority of Isla's family now lived. Despite almost thirty years in the UK, Isla's mother had told her that returning to her hometown had felt like the only way to save her sanity after losing her husband. Everywhere she looked in Cornwall reminded her of the man she'd loved, and it was just too painful. Lexi had been more than happy to accompany her and had met her husband Josh within six months of arriving. Clare had begged Isla to 'come home' to be with them, but despite how often she'd visited Mount Dora, and how beautiful it was, Cornwall was the only place that had ever felt like home. Even living in Truro, when she'd worked at the hospital there, had felt like a wrench. So getting a job at St Piran's hospital, in the area of Cornwall where she'd been raised, had been a dream come true. She missed her mum and her sister terribly. But even if Cornwall hadn't had a hold over her soul, she could never leave her grandparents. Her grandmother had already lost her only child, and Isla wasn't sure she'd have been able to live with herself if she'd left Grandma Joy without any of her grandchildren either. But the truth was, Isla would have missed her grandparents every bit as much as they'd have missed her.

'Your dad sounds like a wonderful man from everything you've told me.' Even Noah's tone was gentle, and when she'd first approached him with an idea about how to mark her father's birthday, she'd got the sense that he'd also faced a difficult loss of his own at some time. There was just a level of empathy that could only come from understanding those emotions personally. 'Are you ready?'

'I think so.' Isla put her hand in her pocket, checking for the twentieth time that the letter was still there.

'I dug the hole this morning, and James from the garden centre delivered the tree about an hour ago, so everything's ready if you're sure you are?'

'I want to get it done before my grandparents arrive.' Isla turned and smiled at Noah, determined not to cry before they'd even planted the tree she'd bought in her father's memory. He'd always loved the colours of autumn, and his favourite tree had been the mountain ash. When Isla had approached Noah about planting a tree in St Jude's churchyard, where her father was buried, he'd been really enthusiastic about the idea, especially after a storm the previous winter meant he'd been forced to take the decision to have a couple of the mature trees cut down. What had taken Isla longer to ask, was whether Noah would be okay with her putting a letter to her father in amongst the roots of the tree when they planted it. Somehow saying it out loud felt ridiculous, even though she'd loved the idea when she'd come across it online. Isla wasn't sure she believed the words would ever reach her father, but she'd needed to write them all the same. To tell him everything that had happened since he'd died, and to thank him once again for making the unselfish decision he had, so that his children never had to face discovering whether or not they had the Huntington's gene he'd inherited from his own father. Nick had discovered he was positive for the gene back in the early nineties, in the year testing had first become available. And when he'd learnt there was a fifty-fifty chance that he'd pass it on to his children, it was a risk he just wasn't prepared to take. Just a year later, Clare had given birth to their first daughter, with the help of a sperm donor. Four years after that, Isla had arrived. Her parents had got their longed-for children, and they were *their* children, wholly and completely, regardless of where half of their DNA had come from.

When Isla had finally found the courage to ask Noah about the letter, he'd told her he thought it was a wonderful idea, which had helped more than he'd ever know. It didn't seem silly any more, and it made it easier for her to believe that her father would finally hear the things she'd tried saying to him in the last days of his life. She'd spoken to her mother and grandmother about a lot of the things in the letter, but Isla wouldn't have wanted anyone else to read the whole thing. Some of the words were for her father alone.

'Okay, it's just up the path. I chose the empty spot that has a view of the sea. I know you said your father loved being on the water.'

'He did, and Nan always used to joke that he should have been born with webbed feet.' For a moment, Isla had to swallow hard against the tears that had been threatening all day. If only her father had been born with something as easy to live with as that, instead of the genetic timebomb that was Huntington's disease. But this wasn't a moment for dwelling on could haves. Planting a tree that might easily live for four or five hundred years was part of the legacy she wanted to create to mark her beloved father's sixtieth birthday.

There was something else she wanted to do, but she hadn't spoken to anyone about that yet. Not even Noah's kind disposition was enough for her to feel able to confide in him. She had other people she needed to talk to first, and she had no idea how they were going to react. Although she had a horrible feeling they might not like it.

* * *

Between Isla and Noah, they'd managed to lift the eight-foot pot-grown mountain ash into the hole Noah had dug, and she pushed the letter under the root ball, before they filled in the hole. April showers had threatened all day, and it had been overcast until the moment she'd let go of the letter, and then the sun had come out. It was just a coincidence, but that didn't stop Isla feeling happier than she had in days as the sun warmed her skin. It was the closest thing she'd ever get to a hug from her father, and it meant she was ready to face her grandparents when they arrived to visited their son's grave.

'Hello my love, you're still looking far too thin.' Isla's grandmother enveloped her in an embrace that smelt of Lily of the Valley and Deep Heat. They were Joy's signature scents when she was suffering from the back pain that was the result of a slipped disc more than twenty-five years before. It was quite the combination, but it was strangely comforting to Isla.

'I weigh exactly the same as I have for the last three years.' Isla shrugged. The number of steps she took every day at work meant she could still fit into a size twelve, despite a passion for biscuits that bordered on an obsession. But she definitely wasn't in any danger of fading away.

'I just worry about you, that's all.' Joy narrowed her eyes as she looked at her granddaughter. 'Although you look really happy, almost glowing. Have you met someone?'

'No Nan, I haven't.' Isla laughed again. It was the same question her grandmother asked her every time they met, her voice full of hope that this might be the time when the answer would finally be yes. As far as Joy was concerned, a happy relationship was all she wanted for her granddaughter. Isla was pretty sure she knew what was at the root of it. Her sister Lexi meeting Josh meant there was no chance of her returning to Cornwall, and Joy was probably hoping that the reverse might be true for her youngest granddaughter. Isla could understand her grandmother's logic, but partner or no partner, she had absolutely no intention of leaving Cornwall. 'I just had a moment, when I felt as though Dad was *really* here, and that makes me happier than anything else.'

'I love it so much when I get moments like that.' Joy put an arm around her granddaughter's waist. 'Me and Grandpa are always smelling your dad's favourite aftershave around the house, aren't we, love?'

Her grandmother turned towards her husband, who nodded. They were the kind of couple who still held hands, almost twenty-five years after they'd got married. Grandpa Bill was her grandmother's second husband, but Isla couldn't remember a time before him, because she'd only been eighteen months old at their wedding. Joy's first husband had died of Huntington's disease five years before that. From what Isla's father had told her, his parents had been devoted to one another before the illness took him bit by bit, so Joy hadn't just found true love once, but twice over. It was no wonder she saw it as the most important thing in life.

'There's a robin who comes into the garden, every time I'm out there working too. And I'm sure that's Nicky.' Bill's tone dared anyone to try and tell him that wasn't the case. He'd come into his stepson's life when Isla's father had been in his early thirties, but they'd always had a close bond, and Joy and Bill had both called him Nicky. He'd been an only child and Bill had never had any children of his own, which meant their lives had revolved around their son and his family. Losing him had hit them incredibly hard and, when the rest of the family had moved to Florida, Isla had become even more aware of being the light in their lives. They worried about her all the time, calling to make sure she'd got home from work okay if it was raining hard, or God forbid, on the odd occasion it snowed. They were so proud of every tiny thing she achieved too, and Joy told everyone she met about her granddaughter 'the nurse'.

'I'm sure he visits Clare and Lexi in Florida too, although that's a lot of flying for a little robin.' Joy winked at her granddaughter. There was no bitterness in her voice, even though it must have broken her heart when half her family moved over four thousand miles away.

'What time did you arrange to do the video call?' Isla glanced at her watch. It was almost 7 p.m. and the light was changing to a honey-coloured glow, as the sun slowly began to dip lower in the sky. It wouldn't set for more than an hour, but the day was clearly on its way out and her father's sixtieth birthday would soon be over.

'Half seven our time, and one-thirty for them. I thought dinner for us and lunch time for your mum and Lexi was the best plan; I just needed to be here for six fifty-five. It's when Nicky arrived in the world.' Joy was explaining it to Isla like she'd never heard the story before, but her grandmother had relived every detail of her father's birth on numerous occasions, everything from it lasting for twenty hours, to the fact that the midwife's name had been Barbara Nicholas, and she'd refused to leave Joy's side until her son was safely delivered. 'I've got everything ready to go. All your dad's favourite foods, and your mum's made the same for them.'

'Dad would have loved the idea of us all getting together, even if we are on opposite sides of the Atlantic.' The lump was back in Isla's throat. Technology made it much easier to see her mother and sister, even if it wasn't in the flesh, and it had also allowed her to be there for the big moments of Lexi's pregnancy, like when the sonographer had confirmed, just the week before, that she was expecting one daughter and one son. But it wasn't the same as them all being together, and right now it seemed like a lifetime until they would all be together again. Isla had booked three weeks off work and bought the tickets to fly out with her grandparents a week after Lexi's due date. They'd talked about going earlier, because there was a good chance she might give birth sooner than expected with twins, but Lexi would need time to bond with her own little family too. Life was moving on for Isla's big sister, and she was incredibly happy for her, but sometimes the changes in Lexi's life made the gulf between them feel far bigger than the number of miles that separated them.

Isla didn't speak again until a few minutes after they'd reached her father's grave, waiting until her grandmother had had the chance to whisper the words she needed to say to her son at the very moment he'd been born. 'When Dad arrived, did you love him instantly, or did it take a while to feel that way?'

She stopped breathing as she waited for her grandmother to answer. What Joy said next could change Isla's life. 'I would have done anything to protect him. I felt that from the moment I set eyes on him and the truth is that love grew a hundred-fold over time.'

'Joy, long time no see!' A woman of a similar age to Isla's grandmother bustled up the path towards them, not seeming to take in the fact that they were standing by a grave. If she had noticed, it clearly wasn't going to put her off her stride. 'It must have been ten years since I last saw you, mustn't it? I moved back to Port Agnes a few months ago, to be closer to my grandchildren, and I decided to join the bell ringing group. We practise every Wednesday at seven-thirty, and I offered to open up this week. I might be eighty-two on my next birthday, but I'm determined to stay active.' The woman barely seemed to pause for breath, but Isla's grandmother eventually got the chance to respond.

'You're right Jan, it must have been at least a decade, but it's great to see you.' Joy had obviously decided not to mention the reason why she was standing by her son's headstone, as she hugged her old friend. 'The bell ringing must be great fun and nothing beats being close to your grandchildren.'

'Well, I'd have been able to tell this was one of yours, even if you weren't together.' Jan stepped back and gestured towards Isla. 'She's exactly like you, back when we first met. The boys were at primary school then, weren't they?'

'They must have been.' Joy suddenly looked uncomfortable, and Isla wasn't sure whether it was because Jan didn't seem to have any idea that she'd lost her son, or because of her friend's insistence that there was an obvious genetic connection between Isla and her grandmother. It wasn't the first time someone had said it, and Isla had always put it down to the fact that her parents had shared similar colouring, which mirrored Joy's and her own. All of them had the sort of olive skin that tanned easily, dark hair and brown eyes. Isla would undoubtedly have picked up on some of Joy's mannerisms over the years, too, given how much time they'd spent together.

'No one can give me a greater compliment than telling me I'm like Nan.' Isla leant into her grandmother, an unspoken understanding passing between them. There was no genetic link between Isla and her grandparents, but she couldn't possibly have loved Joy or Bill any more than she did, and she knew without a doubt they felt the same way about her.

Glancing at her watch again, Isla gave Joy a gentle nudge. 'I think we'd better make a move soon if we don't want to be late for the party.'

'Oh yes.' Joy straightened up. 'Sorry Jan, I've got to dash off, we've got a family birthday party to get to. But do enjoy your bell ringing.'

'I will and maybe we can catch up for a cuppa now I'm back in the village?'

'That would be lovely.' If Isla hadn't known Joy so well, she'd have been fooled by her words, because to anyone else they'd have sounded completely genuine. But there was just the tiniest hint, a flicker in her eyes, which made Isla suspect that her grandmother had absolutely no intention of meeting up with Jan. And she was right.

'Her son was Nicky's best friend at primary school, and he must have told her about him dying when it happened.' Joy grumbled the words under her breath as they headed down the path towards the church gate. 'She didn't even care enough to remember it, and I'd rather spend an afternoon scraping seagull poo off every beach hut in Port Kara than meet up with her. She can stick her cuppa up her ar—'

'We don't need someone like her to remember Nicky,' Bill cut his wife off, taking hold of her hand as they reached the gate. 'All the important people will never forget him, and we don't want anything to spoil the celebration.'

'Nothing can spoil it when I'm spending it with all my favourite people.' Joy looked from Bill to Isla, before pushing open the gate. 'And that cheese and pineapple hedgehog isn't going to eat itself.'

A warm glow of contentment enveloped Isla for the second time that day. The people she loved most in the world were the perfect example that 'family' was something no one could create a single definition for. Her parents had been given a gift that could never be repaid, and the least she could do was to help another couple create the family they were dreaming of too by becoming an egg donor. She just had to wait for the right time to break the news to her own family, and hope they saw it the same way.

## 2

Aidan had been an A&E nurse for more than fifteen years, but there were still some days that could take him by surprise. The team at St Piran's had an ongoing contest to share their most weird and wonderful encounters with patients, and he was almost certain he was going to be able to top the list after the morning he'd just had.

'God, I need a coffee.' He let out a long sigh as he reached the desk where two of his colleagues, Danni and Esther, were reviewing the test results of one of their patients.

'What's up?' Danni was an A&E doctor, who'd also become a good friend over the eighteen months they'd worked together at the hospital.

'I've just had a life and death case; I honestly wasn't sure if she was going to make it.' Aidan looked at Danni, and then turned to Esther, another of the nurses in the team, who he also counted as a close friend. Life in A&E could be tough, but it built enduring friendships, and he felt lucky to be surrounded by some of his favourite people every day at work. 'It was seriously touch and go.'

'What was it? Her heart?' Esther's eyes were round with concern, but Aidan couldn't keep a straight face for any longer.

'Hiccups.' He rolled his eyes so hard he was in danger of detaching his retinas. 'She'd had them for over two hours before coming in apparently. I mean, can you imagine suffering in silence for that long, before getting yourself to hospital? I told her she should have called an ambulance, because she wouldn't want to end up being triaged behind someone with a broken neck.'

'You didn't!' Danni laughed, but he was already nodding.

'She made her boyfriend drive her in, too. Poor sod had been on a twelve-hour night shift and then had to come and sit in here with his drama queen of a girlfriend. I told him to blink three times if he was being held hostage.'

'I'm not even going to ask if you did that, because I already know that you did.' Esther grinned. 'The only question was whether or not he blinked?'

'No, but I'm certain he wanted to.' Aidan looked at his watch. 'Only an hour into the shift and I've got a contender for stupidest reason ever to visit A&E.'

'I'm not sure anyone will ever beat paper-cut guy.' Danni raised her eyebrows.

'Paper cuts can be very painful.' Aidan shrugged. 'And it was on his scrotum.'

'We officially have the weirdest jobs in the world. And I can't help feeling a bit hard done by that my mum and dad are on a cruise, now that his active treatment is over, and they didn't even think to invite me and give me a break from all this madness.' Esther shook her head, but she was smiling the way she always did when she mentioned her parents lately. Her father's cancer diagnosis had set them on a rocky path, but everything seemed to be looking up now. 'So the very least I think we all deserve, is a decent cup of coffee. I'll go and get us one while it's so... Let's just say, while there's time.'

It was an unwritten rule, which every member of the team followed, not to mention when a shift was quiet. It was such a rare occurrence in the emergency department, that it seemed only right to have a proper cup of coffee from the Friends of St Piran's Hospital shop, instead of one of the grey, tasteless ones from the vending machine.

'You're a star.' Aidan planted a kiss on top of Esther's head. 'Don't forget, I'm on the skinny lattes.'

'Still?' Esther looked surprised, but as much as he could have killed for a mochaccino, he still had four pounds to lose before he hit the target he'd set with his husband.

'Jase has already lost the stone he wanted to lose, but I've got a bit more to go and he's insistent we need to be in peak physical condition when we have the baby.'

'Have you found a surrogate already?' The excitement in Danni's voice was obvious and he almost felt guilty for shaking his head.

'We've got a meeting with one of the agencies next month and Jase is convinced that us being at goal weight will make a difference.' Aidan might be making a joke out of it, but nerves gripped his insides whenever he thought about the meeting. If the agency was willing to take them on, it would be the first big step on their journey to becoming parents, but there was so much that could happen to derail their plans at every stage. They had to get accepted first, then be matched with a surrogate, find the right egg donor, all before even starting treatment. Becoming parents was all they wanted, but there were no guarantees, and if they didn't hold onto the fact that it might never happen, and consider a plan B, there'd be no way of putting their broken hearts back together. 'Thank God we'll have the chance to go to another one of the meetings with the infertility support group before then, so we can be as prepared as possible. Some of the others in the group have already been through the process and they can let us know what to expect.'

'I'm sure the agency will love you and Jase.' Esther gave his waist a squeeze. 'Do you know what—'

The shrill ring tone of the red phone on the desk cut off her question. It meant there was a life-threatening emergency on the way, the very opposite of what Aidan had dealt with so far that morning, and he picked up the phone instantly. His heart sank as the paramedic team relayed the details, and he suddenly found himself wishing that he could have stuck to dealing with hiccups and paper cuts all day long.

Turning towards Danni and Esther, he grimaced. 'We've got a two-year-old boy coming in with breathing difficulties, and a high fever, who's become increasingly unresponsive since the paramedics arrived.'

'Let's get ready.' Danni was already moving away from the desk, and a tiny bit of the tension left Aidan's spine. Dealing with critically ill children was the scariest part of the job, but there was no one he'd rather face that with than the team he worked with, who'd leap into action the moment the little boy arrived. And he was already praying that would be enough.

* * *

By the time Felix arrived with his terrified parents, who the paramedics had introduced as Corinne and Jack, everything was in place to try and identify what was wrong with the little boy as quickly as possible, and to give him the treatment he needed. Felix had already been given oxygen by the paramedics, the paediatric team had been alerted and one of the consultants was on her way down. Isla had also joined Aidan and the rest of the team who'd be providing Felix's initial care.

'Do you know what's wrong?' Corinne looked almost as pale as her little boy, as she turned towards Aidan. He had a gut feeling what was making her son so poorly, but he wouldn't have given her his best guess, even if it had been his place to do so. There were certain words that were capable of striking fear into the heart, and meningitis was one of them.

'We're going to run some blood tests, but it would help if you could tell us a bit more about his symptoms. I'm Aidan, and this is Danni, one of the doctors.' Even as he spoke, Esther and Isla were busy attaching monitors to Felix, who hadn't stirred despite being transferred onto a different bed.

'He had a bit of a temperature, and I just thought it was a cold at first, but then he started to get really restless and wouldn't let me comfort him. I called 111 and they said to take him to the out of hours GP, but he went really floppy, so they sent an ambulance instead.' Corinne was crying and her partner put an arm around her shoulders.

'That's when his breathing went funny; fast and shallow. Like he was trying his hardest to get more air in, but it just wasn't happening.' Felix's father looked from Aidan to Danni. 'I googled the symptoms. It's meningitis, isn't it?'

'It's too early to say, but we are going to be testing for it. We can get the results really quickly and, if it is that, we can give Felix the right treatment as soon as possible.' Danni had a knack for making it all sound so simple and Aidan had seen how reassuring that was to patients and their family members. Even if things turned out to be far tricker than that, it was what people in the midst of a traumatic situation needed to hear. 'We'll also give Felix a top-to-toe check over, to see if there are any other symptoms we need to take into consideration.'

'I'll make a start.' Aidan moved closer to the end of the bed, turning back towards Danni within seconds. 'Felix's feet are very cold.'

'I'll check his hands.' Danni moved further up, but before she could even give her verdict, Aidan caught his breath, spotting a sign that made his heart sink all over again. Just below the bottom of the little boy's pyjama trousers was the start of an obvious rash.

'Danni.' Keeping his voice low, he shot her a look and pulled Felix's pyjama leg up slightly higher.

'Okay, we need to organise a lumbar puncture and a CT scan.'

'I'm on it.' Isla was already on her way out of the cubicle, and Corinne started to sob.

'We're going to lose him, aren't we.' She turned towards Felix's father. 'We're going to lose our baby.'

'No, we're not.' Jack looked at Aidan. 'I was right, though, it's meningitis, isn't it?'

'It looks like it, but the lumbar puncture will tell us what kind and how it needs to be treated.' Aidan kept his tone level, despite the emotion pulsating in the air.

'Is it going to hurt him?' Corinne's question was punctuated with shuddering breaths after each word, but Aidan could at least give her some reassurance about that.

'Felix will be given a local anaesthetic and he might feel a bit of pressure, but he won't feel any pain, and you can stay with him during the procedure.'

'Good, because neither of us are going anywhere.' Corinne moved to the side of Felix's bed, with Jack just behind her, and Aidan knew that nothing on earth could have moved them from their son's side. This was what parenting was all about. Seeing it, even in the toughest possible moments like this, Aidan was more certain than even that he wanted to share that experience with Jase. And he'd do whatever it took to make that happen.

* * *

The Friends of St Piran's shop not only served the best coffee in the hospital, it also had a couple of bistro tables outside, making it almost like a pavement café. It was part of the reason why it had become the place where the A&E staff would go to unwind at the end of a shift. The other reason was that the shop was run by Gwen, a retired midwife, and unofficial agony aunt to anyone who walked through the doors of the hospital – whether they were patients or staff.

The lumber puncture had confirmed that Felix had bacterial meningitis and he'd been put on IV antibiotics and fluids. He'd been moved to the children's ITU, and Maxine, the paediatric consultant, had seemed confident that Felix would make it, much to everyone's huge relief. There was no way of knowing yet whether there'd be any complications, and his parents had obviously made the mistake of consulting Dr Google again, once the diagnosis had been confirmed.

Aidan had seen them in the corridor outside the children's ward, when he'd gone up to get an update. Corinne was leaning on Jack's shoulder, her body shuddering as she sobbed, looking every bit as emotional as she had down in A&E. Fearing the worst, he'd briefly considered turning around and going back down the corridor. Felix's parents hadn't seen him, and he didn't have to face their naked grief, but he'd never been that kind of person. And he certainly wasn't that kind of nurse.

'Jack.' Aidan said the other man's name softly. He didn't want to intrude, but he had to find out what was going on and whether there was anything he could do to help; even if it was getting in touch with the hospital counsellor, or one of the team from the chapel. It barely seemed possible that at the worst moment in someone's life, the actions of hospital staff could make a difference, but he knew from experience that they could.

'I was going to come and find you.' Jack still had his arms around Corinne, but they both turned slightly in Aidan's direction. 'It's because you spotted the rash and got Felix's test results so quickly that we're eventually going to be able to take our little boy home with us again. And I just wanted to say thank you.'

'I'm so glad he's going to be okay.' Aidan's whole body felt as if it had slumped with relief. He'd been almost certain that things had taken a turn for the worse, and he was still confused about why Corinne was so upset. Although maybe it was no surprise given what Felix's parents had been through. 'It's been a hell of a day for you guys and you must be exhausted. I know you won't want to leave Felix, but have they said anything about you using the parents' accommodation?'

'They've said we can, thankfully.' Jack breathed out slowly. 'It's Corinne I'm most worried about; she's five months pregnant with our second and she didn't sleep at all last night. Felix only wanted his mummy, until he got too poorly to even know what was going on.'

'You really should try and get some rest.' Aidan's voice was gentle but insistent, as he looked at Corinne. 'The team on the children's ward are brilliant, I promise they'll call you if there's any change; and you'll only be five minutes away. Felix needs you to look after yourself too, so that you can be there for him.'

'I just keep thinking I should have brought him in sooner.' Her face looked blotchy and sore, like she'd been crying all day, which she probably had. 'It says online there's a chance he might have lost his hearing, or have some other kind of irreparable damage. If I'd acted sooner there might have been less chance of complications.'

'You don't even know if there are any complications yet.' Jack tried to comfort her, but she didn't seem capable of hearing him.

'But if there are, it will be my fault!'

'No it won't.' Aidan put a hand on her arm. 'He's going to be going home with you, because the two of you knew your baby well enough to spot that something wasn't right early on, and you made sure he got the help he needed. As for any complications, you can deal with them if and when they arise, but whatever they are you'll adapt. My husband was born with profound hearing loss as a result of an infection his mother was exposed to during her pregnancy. He's never let it hold him back from doing anything he wanted to do, and he's the best person I've ever met. Whatever complications your little boy has, if there are any, he's still Felix and you're all going to be okay. I promise.'

'I needed to hear that, thank you.' Corinne pulled away from Jack and threw her arms around Aidan. 'I know I'm being ridiculous, and I should just be glad we're not going to lose Felix, but I looked at what the complications could be, and I felt so guilty. But you're right, whatever we have to deal with, we'll do it as a family, and he's going to be the same special little boy he's always been, either way.'

'In my experience, the people who have to deal with the biggest challenges in life are often the most amazing.' Aidan had meant every word he'd said about Jase; his husband really was the best person he'd ever met. It was why one of the questions they'd been asked to think about in preparation for their interview with the surrogacy agency had been easier to answer than it might be for most people. And they knew exactly what action they'd want to take if they conceived a child who might be born with a disability of any kind. Aidan would never judge other people for those kinds of decisions, but he was certain that – with Jase by his side – they could cope with whatever life threw at them.

'Thank you again.' Jack clapped a hand on Aidan's back. All that mattered was that Felix had made it through, and whatever complications did or didn't arise, it was going to change the family's life forever, the way only a life-threatening incident ever really could. Nothing would ever be taken for granted again, and sometimes that could be a very good thing.

After he'd spoken to Jack and Corinne, Aidan had been able to see Felix, before going down to meet the others at the hospital shop, where Danni immediately set down a drink on the table in front of him. The engagement ring that her fiancé, Charlie, had given her just a few weeks before, caught the light as she did. 'Here you go, you've finally got the skinny latte you asked me for an hour into your shift! Although I also got you a king-size Twix, because I know they're your favourites and it's been a hell of a day.'

'Dan, I think I might actually love you. And if I wasn't gay, and already married, I'd get down on one knee, right here, right now.' He ripped open the packet and dunked half the Twix into his coffee. 'Just don't tell Jase I'm cheating on the diet, because I honestly think he'd take it harder than if I was cheating on him.'

'We won't breathe a word.' Esther mimed zipping her mouth shut, as she sat down opposite Aidan, with Danni and Isla either side of him.

'It was Gwen's suggestion anyway.' Danni grinned. 'She said you look like you couldn't fight your way out of a paper bag, and that a skinny latte wasn't going to put any lead back in your pencil. Her words, not mine. So it was a choice between the Twix, or one of Gwen's ten-minute motivational shake up and wake up routines.'

'The Twix was definitely the right choice. Last time Gwen tried to get me to do one of those she said it was to sort out my posture, so I didn't end up with a hunch back.' Aidan shook his head, but he couldn't help laughing. 'I mean I love Gwen to bits, but sometimes she can be too honest.'

'She can but she's still who I want to be when I grow up.' Esther smiled, but suddenly her expression changed. 'How's Felix doing? Did you get to see him?'

'Yes, and he's doing remarkably well, thank goodness. Even after all these years it amazes me how resilient kids can be.' Aidan dunked the Twix into his coffee for a second time. 'Although I'm not sure the same can be said of his mum and dad. They were completely wrung out.'

'That's parenthood for you. From the moment a baby is conceived it's nothing but worry.' Danni's tone was casual, but Aidan wasn't buying it. He hadn't missed the look she'd exchanged with her best friend, either.

'Have you got something to tell us?'

'No, of course not, I...' Danni exchanged another look with Esther, and then a huge smile spread across her face. 'Oh sod it, I know you're supposed to keep these things quiet for the first twelve weeks, just in case, but how can I not tell you guys? If anything goes wrong, I'm going to need all the support I can get. It's very early days, though, so I'd like to keep it to just us for now and I'll tell the rest of the team after the first scan.'

'Congratulations, that's amazing!' Isla got in first, jumping to her feet and moving past Aidan to give Danni a hug. 'Although I feel like I shouldn't be listening to the conversation, when I haven't been in the team for as long as nearly everyone else.'

'In this place we all know each other's secrets really quickly.' Danni shrugged. 'And some people just fit in and feel like old friends straight away, like you have. Although you are going to have to be willing to share all of your secrets with us too.'

'Oh I promise I will, as soon as there's anything interesting to tell.' Isla smiled.

'That's amazing news, Dan. I'm so happy for you, and you and Charlie are going to make the best parents. But I still can't believe it's happened so quickly.' Aidan really was delighted for them, even if he was trying to push down the tiny bit of envy that was in danger of rising up inside him. He'd had no idea Danni and Charlie were even thinking about parenthood, and yet they were already expecting a baby. It was the only thing he and Jase seemed to have talked about for almost a year, and nothing about the process was going to be easy for them. He was thrilled that such a lovely couple would soon become a family, but he desperately wanted it for him and Jase too. He could already picture a little one running around, with Jase's curls, and the same smile that could light up a room. But it wouldn't bother him one bit if they didn't look like Jase, or share Aidan's sandy blond hair, blue eyes and year-round freckles. All that mattered was that the child would be theirs, and he just had to hold on to the hope that they'd get there somehow.

'The only reason I didn't tell you sooner was because I felt guilty about how quickly it happened, when you and Jase are going to have to jump through so many hoops to get there.' It was almost as if Danni could read his mind, as she reached out to touch his arm. 'I didn't think it was going to be easy for us. I'm nearly forty, and we knew we couldn't hang around. So we decided to start trying once we got engaged, thinking that would give us six months before the wedding, and then we could ask for some help straight afterwards, if we needed it. I didn't even let myself imagine it happening this quickly, so it was all a bit of a shock, and we've got a long way to go.'

'Don't you dare feel guilty on my account!' Aidan pulled her into his arms, not even caring when the second finger of his Twix got knocked onto the floor. 'No one deserves their happy-ever-after more than you do, and what kid isn't going to love having a children's author as a father, not to mention a mum who can make every scuffed knee or grazed elbow better?'

'It's going to happen for you soon too, I know it.' Danni's tone brooked no argument and he hoped to God her certainty wouldn't turn out to be misplaced. 'I'm not facing those scary parent and toddler groups on my own. I'll need you for company.'

'It's nice to know what you want me for!' Aidan laughed, but he couldn't admit just how much he hoped they'd get to hang out together, doing that sort of thing. He had to hold on to the idea that it might not, but it was getting harder and harder to imagine a life without children, with each step he and Jase took towards fulfilling their dream.

'Have they said how long it might take to find you a match once you're approved by the surrogacy agency?' Esther made it sound as though approval was a foregone conclusion, but it was just one of the many barriers they needed to negotiate.

'I don't think there's any way of knowing. We need to find a surrogate who's willing to be a host for donor eggs, because when we looked into all the options, that felt most right for us. Having someone carrying our child, using their own eggs, seemed like we'd be doubling the risk of them developing a bond they couldn't let go of. That might not be true, but it's just the way it felt to us. Although even deciding what to do about the egg donation is another dilemma. They've talked to us about egg sharing with a woman who's trying to get pregnant herself, to keep the costs down, but I don't know if that's the right route for us. What if we get a baby at the end, and she doesn't? I don't know if that's something we'll be able to cope with. There's the option of an unknown donor through the clinic, but any child we had would be able to trace the donor in the future if they want to, and I'd prefer to know a bit more about that person than the clinic would be able to tell us. It's a minefield, and if it wasn't for Jess's infertility support group, I think I might have given up by now.'

'I'll be your donor.' When Isla spoke, the words just seemed to hang there, and for a few seconds Aidan thought he'd imagined them. But she was looking at him so intently he knew he hadn't. As tempting as it was to take her at her word, and believe it really could be as simple as that, he couldn't. People could be incredibly kind and their friendship had developed quite quickly in the past six months or so, but she had no idea what she was promising.

'That's so sweet of you, but it's not the kind of offer you can make without really thinking about it. There are long-term implications, now that donors aren't anonymous any more, then there's the whole can of worms with DNA websites. It's a complicated issue.'

'I know, because I've been looking into it for almost a year, and I've joined all kinds of forums.' Isla was still holding his gaze, and he wasn't sure he'd have been any more shocked if she'd suddenly peeled back the skin on her face and revealed an entirely different person underneath. 'I said I didn't have any interesting secrets, but I suppose there is one. My dad was born with the gene that meant he'd eventually develop Huntington's disease and he had a 50 per cent chance of passing it on to any children he had. So, when he and Mum decided to start a family, they chose to use a sperm donor to conceive me and my sister. It would have been Dad's sixtieth birthday this week, and I've been thinking for the last year about how I wanted to mark it. And I decided a while back that donating eggs to someone who might be in a similar position, or who was struggling to conceive, would be a lasting legacy for my dad, something that repays the debt and honours the choices he made. I know all the implications and all the risks, but I still really want to do it. My only concern was not knowing who'd be raising any child that might be conceived, or how I'd navigate a relationship with the parents, if the child wants to get in touch when they reach adulthood. But, if it was you and Jase, that last barrier would be taken away. I knew you were going to use a surrogate, but I didn't know until today that you were planning on using donor eggs. I wish I could be braver and offer to be your surrogate, too, but the women on Mum's side of the family always seem to have horrendous labours! I really want to donate my eggs and, if you'd be okay with using mine, I'd love to do it for you and Jase.'

'Oh my God, yes!' All through her explanation, Aidan had been reminding himself not to get carried away, and to talk to Jase first, but the adrenaline had been running through his veins so fast he could hardly catch his breath. This could be everything they'd hoped for and more, the answer to a huge part of their prayers, and suddenly he was nodding, and crying, and pulling Isla in for a hug all at the same time. There was still a really long way to go, and finding a surrogate was probably the biggest part of the jigsaw. But knowing that someone as sweet and kind as Isla wanted to be a part of the process, suddenly made it feel like it really might happen. He just had to hope that Jase would be on board with the idea too.

# 3

Isla had been so close to telling her mother and sister about her plans to be an egg donor on her father's sixtieth birthday. Her grandparents had gone out to the kitchen to open a bottle of champagne for the toasts, and Lexi's husband was doing the same on their side of the Atlantic. So it was just Isla and her mother and sister on the video call for a few moments. It was the perfect opportunity to have the conversation she wasn't even sure why she'd been putting off. But then Lexi had said something during the virtual celebrations that had stopped Isla in her tracks.

'You'll never believe what's happened to one of the women in my antenatal exercise class.' Lexi had been balancing a paper plate with a piece of cake on it, on the top of her already obvious baby bump, when she spoke. 'She agreed to be a surrogate for her best friend, but the friend has now split up with her husband and has decided she doesn't want to be a single mum. She doesn't want the baby and now Misty is seven months pregnant, and has no idea what to do.'

'Oh my God!' Their mother, Clare, clearly hadn't heard the story before either. She might have been thousands of miles away, but her shock had been tangible. 'How could anyone turn their back on a baby like that?'

'It's even more complicated because carrying the baby automatically makes Misty the mother, as far as the law is concerned, even though she doesn't have a biological link to the child. It's such a mess.'

'I'm just so glad the law was different when we had the two of you.' Clare had taken Lexi's hand, reaching out to place her other hand against the iPad screen propped up in front of her, as if she could physically connect with Isla too. 'I never had to worry about the donor being a part of our lives. It's so much trickier now. I admire anyone who's willing to be a donor, but I'm not sure we'd still have done things the way we did, if the law had been like that then.'

Lexi had nodded in agreement, and revealed more details about just how devasted her friend, Misty, was. The news that Isla had been so desperate to share had died in her throat. She couldn't tell her mother that she was planning to donate her eggs after what she'd said. It was a world away from being a surrogate, but Clare had always been a worrier. She'd done her best to wrap both girls up in cotton wool their whole lives, terrified that she might lose them, especially when she'd known she was going to lose the love of her life. Clare had asked the girls to promise they'd never join a DNA website that might uncover who their biological father was. Sperm donation had been anonymous at the time of their conception, so a site like that was the only possibility of discovering where half their genes came from. It had been an easy promise for Isla to make, and she was pretty certain it had been just as easy for her sister. Nick Marlowe was their dad, and Isla had no desire whatsoever to discover the man who'd helped him become a father. Now things were different, and she could understand her mother's concerns, but being an egg donor was nothing like as much of a commitment as being a surrogate. She'd just have to wait until another time to mention it, when Misty's story wasn't so fresh in her mother's mind.

Isla had been sent a health assessment by the fertility clinic, and was due to have a session with their counsellor to discuss the implications of egg donation in the next week. If the counsellor signed her off as being ready to donate, there'd be a screening process with blood tests for genetic conditions and infections. It had felt like she was already a long way into her journey with the clinic she'd chosen, but the conversation with Aidan had thrown all of those plans into question. She hadn't hesitated in making the initial offer. It had seemed so natural, such an obvious solution to Aidan's dilemma, and something that might even calm her mother's fears. Her friendships with the whole A&E team were growing quickly. She'd built a particularly good relationship with Amy, one of the other nurses, but Aidan was someone everyone wanted to be around, and he'd made sure she felt welcome in the team from the beginning. He was funny, even on the toughest days, and could find something positive in every situation. It must have been so hard for him to hear how easy it was for Danni to fall pregnant, but he didn't let it show, and the joy he had for his friend had been obvious.

But, by the time she'd got home, she'd started to wonder if maybe she'd been too hasty. Fertility treatment was hugely demanding physically and emotionally, which could put strain on any relationship – let alone a new friendship like hers and Aidan's. She couldn't imagine him blaming her if it didn't work out, but no one could really be sure how they'd react in a situation like that. Then there were the implications if Aidan and Jase were lucky enough to become parents. Would they want Isla to have some part in their child's life? Or would they cut her out completely, not wanting to risk a bond developing that they might feel uncomfortable with. Those were all the things they should have spoken about, long before she opened her mouth and made an offer it now felt impossible to take back. But it was too late for that, and all she could do was hope that she wouldn't live to regret it, anywhere near as much as Lexi's friend had.

Fortunately, work provided the perfect distraction from all her worries, as it almost always did. And, two hours into her shift, Isla had decided she was getting too far ahead of herself, worrying about things that would probably never happen.

'Sarah Vardy is in again.' Amy frowned as the double doors that separated the waiting area from the rest of A&E closed behind her. 'It's retinal cancer this time, apparently. She's been triaged and told to wait until she's called, but she's refusing to move away from the reception desk, and she keeps knocking on the glass, telling them she needs to be seen before she goes blind.'

'Oh God. What are her symptoms?' Isla could guess even before Amy answered that there'd be a very long list. Sarah Vardy was one of their 'regulars'. Every emergency department had them, and every ambulance crew did too. The root of the issue for most regulars was poor mental health, and Sarah had health anxiety and carcinophobia: a crippling belief that she was suffering from cancer, which no amount of tests seemed to alleviate. Her records showed regular visits to A&E throughout her adult life, but the carcinophobia seemed to have escalated at around the time St Piran's had opened, and Sarah came in at least a couple of times a week. She was under the care of the

mental health team, and the problem seemed to have got worse
after she'd lost her elderly mother to colon cancer. Mostly she
seemed to think she was suffering from either that, or lung
cancer. So retinal cancer was a new one.

'She says she's got wiggly lines in her vision and a lump on
her eyelid.' Amy pulled a face. 'There is a lump there, although it
looks more like a gnat bite than anything sinister. But you know
Sarah; that won't stop her believing she's dying, and nothing I
said in triage helped. Even telling her that retinoblastoma is
almost unheard of in adults just seemed to stress her out even
more. I'm going to put a call into The Sycamore Centre now, but I
don't know when they'll be able to send someone down.'

'Shall I give it a try?' Isla looked at her friend, who nodded.
The Sycamore Centre was the hospital's mental health unit, but
the demand for their services seemed to be getting greater with
every passing week. As a result, A&E often had to deal with
patients who needed specialist help for far longer than was ideal.
For some reason, Sarah had taken a shine to Isla, and she seemed
more willing to listen to her than the other nurses. Maybe it was
because Isla had confided how much losing a parent had
affected her too. None of the team dismissed Sarah's fears. Just
because they were irrational, it didn't mean they didn't feel real
to her. But it was hard sometimes, with a backlog of people
needing urgent treatment, and the resulting frustration had a
way of coming to the surface for Isla's colleagues at times. It was
different for her. She'd seen firsthand what living with the fear of
a deadly disease could do to a person. Some people couldn't just
push the fear of something like that to one side and get on with
life, whether they'd been diagnosed with an illness or not. It
consumed Sarah's whole life, and Isla was happy to help in any
way she could.

'You're a star.' Amy was already opening the door out to the waiting area. 'I think she's in danger of having a full-blown panic attack, but hopefully you can get through to her.'

'I'll give it my best shot.' Isla moved past Amy and through to the waiting area, Sarah's head turning towards her, as soon as she heard the doors open.

'Oh thank God!' The older woman ran a hand through her hair as she spoke and it would have been easy to believe she was every bit as unwell as she believed herself to be. Her hair was thinning, to the point of being able to see her scalp in places, and her mouth was set in such a grim line that her lips seemed to have disappeared altogether. She looked pale and exhausted too, but the truth was that she spent so much of her time worrying about her health that she'd stopped taking care of herself in other ways. Sarah had admitted before that she sat hunched over her laptop for hours on end, convincing herself that every tiny twinge she experienced was the cancer taking hold. She'd had ten times more scans and tests than most people would experience in their lifetime, but the relief of a negative test never lasted long. 'They won't listen to me Isla, but everything I've read online proves I'm right. I've got cancer in my right eye and, if they don't treat it soon, it'll spread and I'll go blind, or even die!'

The desperation in Sarah's voice wasn't an act, or a way of seeking attention. She genuinely believed she was going to die if someone didn't take action soon. Other patients were looking in her direction, a couple of whom were laughing at how melodramatic she seemed to be. But it was clearly making some other patients anxious. 'Okay Sarah, let's get you through to a cubicle so that I can take a proper look at you, and we'll take it from there.'

'Thank you.' Sarah's body slumped with relief and, if Isla hadn't put an arm around her, she had a feeling she'd have fallen to the floor.

'Are you okay to walk?'

'My heart feels like it's beating twice as fast as it should and I keep going dizzy. I'm terrified it's because the cancer is already spreading.'

'I think it's because you've been so worried, but I'm going to get a wheelchair to take you through to the cubicles. Just in case.' Thankfully there were a couple of wheelchairs available in the waiting area, and Isla quickly helped Sarah into one. But even after she was sitting down, her whole body was trembling. 'It's okay Sarah, I'm going to get you the help you need, I promise.'

'Thank you.' The older woman grabbed hold of Isla's hand for a moment, pressing it against her cheek, before letting her hands drop back down onto her lap. The kind of help that Isla was going to get might not be what Sarah was expecting. But, either way, she was determined that when her patient left the hospital she wouldn't be feeling anywhere near as awful as when she arrived. A cure might not be possible, but there were things that could help, and the hospital's mental health team had already been alerted. Isla just had to try and keep Sarah as calm as possible until they arrived.

* * *

Joe Carter, one of the consultant psychiatrists from The Sycamore Centre, had come down to see Sarah, and had given Isla an update on the plan for further treatment. Joe was Danni's older brother, and Esther's boyfriend, so Isla had got to know him quite well in the time they'd both been working at St Piran's. He radiated kindness, and it made Isla feel much better to know that Sarah had someone like him to turn to for support.

'She's been having CBT for a couple of months, but I think we need to look at something else. She's been keen to avoid medication in the past, because she thinks it will increase her chances of getting cancer, but she can't go on like this. Otherwise, she could be at risk of having panic attacks on a regular basis, and her anxiety could get really out of hand. She's already missed out on so much because of it, but it seems to be getting worse.' Joe kept his voice low. 'You did a really good job of making her feel heard, and helping her calm down. If you ever fancy a change from A&E, we could always use nurses like you in my department.'

'It's something I have thought about, and I want to do a Master's eventually, so maybe I could look at specialising then. Although I'm not sure I could bear to leave emergency medicine completely.'

'Esther's the same.' Joe smiled. 'I think it turns you all into adrenaline junkies working here.'

'You're probably right, although I'm sure your department has its share of drama.' The previous autumn, one of Joe's patients had experienced a psychotic episode and had abducted Esther. Thankfully no one was hurt, but it had been terrifying just hearing about it, let alone what it must have been like for Esther and Joe to go through it.

'None of us go into this for a quiet life, do we?' Joe gave her a wry smile, and she nodded.

'We certainly don't. Sarah's carcinophobia definitely feels like it's escalating. She was ranting at one point about how unfair it was that she'd ended up with cancer of the eye, when she'd made sure to find glasses that didn't contain any plastic. She seems paranoid that everything is capable of causing cancer. She said she stopped using any sort of deodorant, shampoo or washing powder last year. And I don't want to be rude, but I don't think she's found an alternative that works.'

'No, she hasn't.' Joe sighed. 'Looking at her history this has been going on for well over fifteen years, and her behaviour was already making her isolate herself, but even if she goes along to one of the support groups I recommended to her, I think the hygiene issues are going to make it hard for her to develop any relationships.'

'It's really sad.' It was obvious how lonely Sarah was and, from the way she spoke about her late mother, it was also clear that she was still grieving. She'd talked about how her mum had told her to go out and live her life before it was too late, but she'd been left with no one once her mother had gone. Sarah had cried when she'd recounted that story, and how true it had turned out to be. Her mum seemed to have been everything to her, and it was no surprise that her existing hypochondria had spiralled into something that was now affecting her ability to live a normal life. Thank God for people like Joe, who she was certain wouldn't give up on Sarah. 'Do you think you'll be able to persuade her to try some medication this time around?'

'I hope so. I've promised to go through the side effects of all the medications with her, talking through any risks. I'm also hoping she might be willing to try EMDR.'

'I don't think I've come across that?' One of the things Isla liked best about working in A&E was that, once they'd dealt with the initial emergency, they directed their patients to treatment with other specialists, which allowed her to get some insight into the work of so many other departments.

'It's a kind of therapy that involves the patient moving their eyes in a way that helps their brain to process traumatic experiences. I think it could help Sarah to work through her feelings around her mother's death, and some of the other issues that have contributed to the decline in her mental health.'

'That sounds fascinating and, from what Sarah has told me, her mother's diagnosis came much later than it should have done, which made an awful situation even more traumatic.' Isla knew firsthand how losing a parent could change someone. Witnessing the progress of her father's disease had changed her in so many ways – some obvious, others less so. It was the reason she'd become a nurse, because she'd wanted to give back. And it was the same reason she'd decided to become an egg donor. But there were other things she deliberately kept to herself, because of what she'd been through. Like however worried she was about something, she'd never share that fear with her mother. Her mum had been through more than enough for anyone, and Isla had become her protector when she'd still been at secondary school. She'd never told her about the bully who'd stolen her trainers or taunted her on the bus. She'd put on a brave face when she wasn't sure she was going to get a place on her chosen degree course, and she'd never admitted how much she wished her mum had stayed in Cornwall, instead of moving back to Florida. She wasn't a martyr, but there was no way of knowing for sure whether she'd have been as careful around her mother if she hadn't watched Clare go to hell and back, losing her husband in the way she had. It was what made it so easy for her to understand why Sarah had been as affected as she had been by her mother's death.

'The good news is she's agreed to be a voluntary in-patient for a couple of days, and even better news is that we've got a bed available immediately, which is pretty rare these days. So there'll be a chance to talk to her about all of her options, and I hope this time she might be willing to try something new.'

'Me too.' Isla could have chatted to Joe all day about his work, but waiting time in A&E was already at over two hours for non-urgent cases. 'Thanks again for coming down so quickly.'

'I would say any time.' Joe gave another wry smile. 'But we both know it's impossible to make that kind of promise, and I make it a rule never to say I'll do something unless I'm sure I can keep my word.'

'That's a good rule, and I think it's one everyone should try and stick to.' Isla might have been talking to Joe, but she was thinking about Aidan when she said the words. She'd made him a promise, and it wasn't one she was prepared to go back on. As long as he could promise her one thing in return.

# 4

The Cookie Jar café in Port Agnes had always been one of Aidan's favourite places to go for lunch. There was a deli counter, a small bakery section, and they also bought in a wider range of cakes and pastries from Mehenick's Bakery, on the harbour. It was a good job he lived in Port Kara, about five minutes from the hospital, because if it had been possible to walk to either The Cookie Jar, or Mehenick's Bakery, on a daily basis, the chances are he'd have been at least three stone heavier. It was all well and good promising Jase he'd lose the weight he still needed to shift, in order to get back down to the twelve and a half stone he'd been when they met, but he was only human and a salted caramel brownie was not something he was equipped to resist on the best of days. As it was, he was stress eating, because it was the last meeting of the infertility support group before he and Jase had their interview at the clinic.

The group met after The Cookie Jar had closed to other customers, and this week there were so many questions Aidan wanted to ask, but he was terrified he was going to forget something. Jase was running late from work and there was a chance he might not make it at all, so it was up to Aidan to gather all of the information they needed to give them the best chance of success. It wasn't just the interview on his mind either. When Isla had first offered to donate her eggs, he'd felt as though someone had offered him the moon on a stick. But then doubts had started to creep in.

Knowing the donor personally could make things complicated down the line, especially if they wanted to maintain their friendship and continue working together. Isla might have strong ideas about how he and Jase should do things, and the thought of being part of some kind of throuple when it came to parenting sounded like hell. There was also a risk that the clinic they'd chosen wouldn't support the idea, and it had taken them so long to find somewhere they felt comfortable with. All of which meant Aidan hadn't even told Jase about Isla's offer, and he'd been doing his best to avoid her at work for the last couple of days. He felt like the worst person in the world for even thinking about turning her down when she'd been so kind, and especially when she'd told him why she wanted to do it, but he still had no idea if saying yes was the right thing to do. Or how Jase would react to the fact that he'd all but accepted the offer without even talking to his husband about it.

'Are you okay? You look like you're training for a competitive eating competition the way you're shovelling that in!' Caitlin, one of the other members of the group, looked at him and laughed. 'My three-year-old is like that if he gets his hands on a brownie.'

'I think this is what they call mindless eating.' Cakes were without question Aidan's favourite food group, even if none of the dieticians were willing to give them their own slot on the nutrition wheel. But he'd barely even tasted the one he'd just demolished. 'I don't even think I'd notice if Harry Styles had served the brownie up to me, wearing nothing but a smile.'

'I would have noticed him for you, trust me. So come on then, what's up?' Caitlin gave him a gentle nudge. She'd had her little boy through IVF and had already had three more rounds trying for a second baby. The kinds of stories that were exchanged at the infertility support group left no room for shyness, and she clearly wasn't going to let him off the hook about what was bothering him.

'We've got the interview with the surrogacy clinic in four days' time and it's all I can think about. There's no plan B if they turn us down.' He couldn't risk telling Caitlin about Isla's offer, because it would be very hard to explain why she couldn't breathe a word of it to his husband. One thing he knew for certain was that he was never going to have an affair. Keeping secrets wasn't his strong point; it was just a shame that stress didn't burn calories, otherwise he'd have been able to eat as many brownies as he liked and still have had a body like a Greek god. At this rate, all the comfort eating was more likely to result in him ending up looking pregnant, and that was the kind of irony he could definitely live without.

'They're not going to turn you down; you and Jase are great.' Just like Esther had, Caitlin made it sound like a certainty and he wished he could believe that, but he'd done enough research to know that something could disrupt their chances of becoming parents at every stage of the process.

'I mean, you know that, and I know that.' Aidan smiled for the first time, when she laughed. 'But even if we manage to convince the clinic of that too, they've still got to find us a match. Who's going to put down on their preferences that they want to help a middle-aged gay couple, one of whom has a ridiculous phobia of balloons, which is going to make celebrating our kid's birthday an exercise in hysteria. And another of whom still can't ride a bike, or catch a ball, and will have to hope that any offspring prefers Irish dancing to sport.'

'I didn't know you could do Irish dancing.' Caitlin looked him up and down, her eyes settling at more or less the same spot as the brownie had.

'I'm not a stereotype!' Aidan feigned indignation, trying not to laugh. 'Jase is the one who did Irish dancing from the age of eight; I swear to God he was only interested in me at first because of my heritage, thinking I might share the same passion. And I'll have you know I've been riding a bike without stabilisers since I was twelve.'

'*Twelve*?' Caitlin shook her head, both of them laughing again and it felt so good to be able to do it. The desire to have a baby had fast become all-consuming, but Aidan hated the thought of it robbing him and Jase of their sense of humour. Laughter had been what had bonded them together from the start.

They'd both had their challenges in life. Jase had been bullied at school, when the need to lip read had marked him out from everyone else. He'd told Aidan that one of the reasons he'd loved Irish dancing so much, was because he'd been able to feel the rhythm pulsing through his body. But it was hardly the sort of hobby that had helped him blend in with most of the boys at his school, and the bullying had been pretty much relentless. Jase had refused his parents' offer to take him out of mainstream education, and he'd thrived academically, despite the challenges he faced and the impact of the bullying. It wasn't until much later that he'd been given a life-changing cochlear implant. He still used lip reading to help him in busy environments, or when lots of people were talking, but he was now head of the best primary school in the area. He was a brilliant and empathetic teacher, with a particular patience for supporting children who had SEND challenges of their own. What he'd been through had made him the man he was, but Aidan still felt as though his blood was boiling in his veins when he pictured the bullies who'd taunted Jase as a child.

Aidan's own challenges had been closer to home. Growing up in a household where heterosexuality and old-fashioned masculinity were the only things that defined a man, meant he'd felt like a square peg in a round hole for as long as he could remember. For a long time, he'd been in denial, before eventually finding the courage to be proud of the person he truly was inside. Except all the things that made Aidan who he was, had been seen by the people who should have loved him most as something to overcome, or to hide away, like the shameful little secrets he'd been told they were. There'd been times, before they met, when there hadn't been much laughter for either Aidan or Jase, and he never wanted to go back to that. If he had a habit of making a joke of things, that was just his way of trying to make sure they never did.

'It might not be the age that Olympic cyclists make it on to two wheels, but Jase would still need a trike even now!'

'Okay, so that probably isn't the most impressive list of attributes.' Caitlin gave him a pointed look, suddenly much more serious than before. 'But surely you don't really have to put any of that on the forms?'

'No, but if we get matched with someone, we'll meet up, and it's going to be like a blind date and I'm liable to blurt out all the worst things possible. The last time I had a date like that, I was so nervous, I kept laughing for no real reason. At one point I laughed so hard I started choking on my food, and a pea shot out of my nose and landed on my date's shirt cuff.'

'It'll certainly make an impression if you can repeat that trick!' Caitlin grinned, before reaching out to put her hand over his. 'But anyone who meets you is going to want to be your surrogate. I know I would if I didn't have a womb that expels embryos almost as fast as your nose fires out peas.'

Even as they started laughing again, he knew they probably shouldn't have been, because there was nothing funny about losing a longed-for pregnancy, or not being certain if you'd ever be able to have a baby at all. But one thing Aidan had learnt in life was that sometimes, if you didn't laugh, the only alternative was to cry. He might be longing to swap lie-ins for sleepless nights, and his two-seater MG for a people carrier, but he wouldn't ever be willing to swap laughter for tears. Whatever happened, he and Jase had to find a way of surviving this and coming out the other side as the same people they'd been before, even if they didn't have a baby in their arms.

The Port Agnes midwives had decided to set up the support group when a couple of them had begun their own infertility investigations and had discovered there weren't any groups in the Three Ports area. It seemed ironic to Aidan that women whose whole careers centred on pregnancy and birth ran an infertility support group, and even more so that Jess – the midwife who now headed up the group – had never managed to have a biological child of her own. But it was also what made the group so inclusive. Jess had eventually adopted two children, and there were members who were hoping to become parents by a whole range of means – from IVF and surrogacy, to fostering and adoption. The process wasn't what bound them together, it was the common outcome they were all desperately hoping to achieve.

'Okay everyone, if you can just listen up for a minute please.' Jess addressed the whole room, as the babble of chatter ebbed away. 'As you all know, from time to time, I manage to get an expert to come in and talk to us about a particular issue related to infertility and I'm thrilled that today is one of those days.'

'If you're bringing in the woman who does the sperm counts at my clinic, to tell us she could count my swimmers on the fingers of one hand, then I'm out of here.' Kane, who'd been undergoing ICSI with his wife since discovering that his sperm count was almost non-existent, raised his palms up to the ceiling. He was just one more member of the group using humour to try and make it through an incredibly difficult situation.

'You'll be pleased to hear it's not her, Kane.' As Jess scanned the room, her gaze settled on Aidan for just a fraction longer than it had seemed to settle on anyone else. 'Instead, we'll be joined by Jacinda, a graduate of the group who is now expecting her second baby with the same surrogate who carried her son. Jacinda will be talking to us about her experience of using an overseas surrogate from Georgia. I know there are a couple of members of the group currently pursuing surrogacy, and several more who might consider it, depending on the outcome of their current treatment. So I thought it would be great to hear what it was like for her. Welcome Jacinda, and thanks so much for coming along.'

Jess hugged the dark-haired woman who'd got up from a chair to her right, and Aidan muttered under his breath as he glanced at his watch. 'Please hurry up, Jase, I don't want you to miss this.'

It was five-thirty and the final bell had rung at his husband's school over two hours before, but as a headteacher, the end of the day didn't coincide with the children going home. The school was overdue an Ofsted inspection, and Aidan just hoped the inspectors wouldn't coincide their visit with the run-up to the interview at the clinic. Although he had a horrible feeling they would.

'As Jess said, I'm Jacinda.' The woman smiled. 'And it feels really weird being back here. For a long time, I thought I was never going to graduate from the group and it was one of the reasons why I wanted to come along tonight. Even though public speaking would make my ovaries shrivel, if I still had any!'

'She's one of us.' As Caitlin leant closer to Aidan and whispered the words, he knew exactly what she meant. Jacinda had the same gallows humour almost all of the group possessed.

Normally Aidan would have shot back a jokey comment, but he didn't want to miss anything Jacinda said, and she was looking in his direction as she spoke again. 'I was born without a womb and, unfortunately, that wasn't the end of my bad luck. I suffered hyperstimulation during treatment, which resulted in ovarian torsion.'

'Ovarian torsion is when the ovary, and sometimes the fallopian tubes, twist. It cuts off the blood supply, which in Jacinda's case unfortunately resulted in the loss of her right ovary.' Jess reached out and squeezed Jacinda's arm. 'But if you're going through IVF and you're worried about hyperstimulation, ovarian torsion is a very rare side effect.'

'Yep, with odds like mine, I should have won the lottery, but instead I've got a built-in noughts and crosses grid on my belly from all my surgery scars.' Jacinda shrugged, but she couldn't stop the slight catch in her voice. 'After that round of treatment, I was really nervous about trying for egg collection again, but we got an amazing twenty-five eggs the second time around. Those little pieces of hope turned out to be even more precious than I imagined they would be, because six months later I suffered a burst cyst and lost my right ovary. Thankfully, by then, we'd managed to freeze nine good quality embryos and we were trying to get pregnant, with the help of our wonderful surrogate.'

'Can I ask how you found your surrogate, and how you knew

she was the right person?' Aidan was open to the idea of finding a surrogate from outside the UK, but he knew Jase had a lot of apprehension about it, which was another reason he wished his husband was there.

'We wanted to keep our surrogacy journey private, because we were concerned about the reaction of some of our family members. That was part of the reason we decided to use an over-seas surrogate, but the main motivation was the availability of UK-based surrogates. I couldn't bear the wait to find a match here and, by widening the net, I felt like I could do more to make it happen.' Jacinda took a deep breath. 'As for how we knew she was right for us, it's hard to explain. All I can say, is that when we first met, I knew I could trust Olena. That was the biggest thing for me. I was putting my chance of having a baby into this woman's hands and entrusting her with my precious embryo. I've got friends I've known for years, who I wouldn't have felt able to place that kind of trust in. If you asked me to list the reasons why I felt able to do that with Olena, I don't think I could come up with something that would make sense to anyone else. I just felt it in my bones.'

'Is it okay to ask something really personal?' Louise, another member of the group, who was in her late forties and who'd been trying for a baby for over a decade, put up her hand as she spoke.

'Of course.' Jacinda smiled. 'You know what it's like once you start this journey. No topic is off limits.'

'You're so right. I've been asked everything from how often I'm having sex with my partner, to whether I knew I had a bulky uterus!' Louise shook her head. 'So I'm really sorry that I'm asking this, but did both of your pregnancies result from the embryos you got, or did you have to go down the egg donation route in the end? I've finally had to accept that the age of my eggs is probably not going to result in a successful pregnancy, and so the next stage is deciding on a donor. And I wondered if that's something you had to do too?'

'Both pregnancies ended up being from those embryos I had frozen, but I wanted to be prepared to make that decision if none of our embryos had resulted in a successful pregnancy. My best friend had offered to donate eggs, and there were lots of reasons why that appealed, and some things that made me terrified about the idea. In the end, we didn't have to pursue it, but I guess the biggest decision is whether you choose a known or anonymous donor. You also need to bear in mind that if you're having treatment overseas, some countries don't allow the use of known donors. Then there's the question of whether anyone you know will be generous enough to make the offer in the first place.' Jacinda breathed out slowly. 'Despite my fears, I'm almost certain I'd have accepted my best friend's offer, because any child I had as a result would know how much love had gone into creating them. Not just between myself and my husband, but between me and Aisha. But only you can know what feels right for you.'

Everyone turned to look, as the door to the coffee shop swung open, and Jase crashed through, knocking over a chair with his laptop bag as he did. Aidan might have an always-late, clumsy-as-hell husband, but Jase was the only person in the world he wanted to raise a child with. And suddenly he was just as certain that he wanted to take up Isla's offer to donate her eggs, even if it meant moving clinics and delaying the prospect of finding a surrogate for a bit longer, because of the potential complications of using a known donor. As Jacinda had said, sometimes you just knew. He'd never been more certain of anything in his life, and he couldn't wait to tell Jase that they might be a step closer to fulfilling their dream. He only hoped his husband felt just as sure.

# 5

---

'I don't know how Gwen has persuaded me to do this.' Aidan looked at his reflection in the mirror and shuddered. 'Plaid plus fours, a green and yellow polo shirt, and a *let's par-tee* golf visor... there's no one else on earth who could ever have persuaded me to wear this outfit. When I was at school, I used to think I was going to be the next Jean Paul Gaultier. That bloody art college has got a lot to answer for, not letting me in.'

'But then A&E would have missed out on one of its finest.' Jase put an arm around his shoulder and grinned. 'Although describing you as one of the finest while you're wearing that is a bit of a stretch.'

'You're not allowed to be rude, when I'm wearing this outfit to raise money for charity.'

'*Charity*? I thought you were wearing it for a bet!' Jase ducked out of the way, but Aidan still managed to catch hold of him, circling his arms around his waist.

'You know full well that Gwen designated whacky golf outfits as the dress code for this year's hospital fundraiser, and this charming ensemble has got me a lot of sponsorship.'

'It'll get you a lot of funny looks too.' Jase grinned again. 'But I love you, even if you do look like you got dressed in an Oxfam shop, during a power cut.'

'You're going to pay for that comment.' Aidan pulled him closer, but he couldn't keep the smile off his face.

'Oh yeah, how?'

'I'm going to wear this every time we go out for the next six months.'

'Lucky I've got a thing for a man in plaid then.' Jase raised his eyebrows.

'Oh, have you now?'

'Yes, but only when that man is you.' The way Jase was looking at him, Aidan knew without a trace of doubt that he meant it. He could be wearing an old potato sack and Jase would still find a way of making him feel good about himself. Back home in Ireland, when he'd realised that the attraction he had to other boys wasn't something that was ever going to change, he'd wondered if he'd ever feel that way. Neither of his parents had accepted it easily when he'd eventually come out, but his mother had come round fairly quickly in the end. It was his father, Sean, who still behaved like he'd time-travelled from the 1950s, and still couldn't bear to acknowledge that his son had married another man, despite the fact Jase made Aidan happier than he'd ever been. His father's catholic faith made the idea of having a gay son unthinkable, and when it had become increasingly obvious to everyone that's who Aidan was, long before he'd come out, Sean had used the most derogatory terms possible to describe same-sex couples. It had made a little part of Aidan curl up and die every time the words had come out of his father's mouth. It was a big part of the reason why – when Aidan had been turned down by the art college – he'd hopped on a Ryanair flight to Stansted and eventually drifted into studying nursing instead.

Even though his father hadn't completely rejected him after he'd come out, their relationship was incredibly strained, and Aidan still couldn't look at the group photos from his wedding without feeling sad. His father had claimed to come down with a sickness bug the day before his parents were due to fly over for the wedding and had said the last thing he wanted to do was to spoil their big day by risking it and becoming the centre of attention for all the wrong reasons. After a few glasses of champagne, Aidan's mother, Anne, had confided that it was all for the best, because his father would have had a face 'like a slapped arse' in all the photographs, if he'd decided to come. But the truth was, there was a painfully obvious gap in the pictures from the wedding, every bit as noticeable as a missing tooth in the middle of a smile.

Aidan didn't want to think about any of that now, though, or what his father's reaction to the idea of him and Jase having a baby might be. There was something he needed to talk to his husband about. Something he'd been trying to find the perfect words to say, ever since they'd left The Cookie Jar, three hours before. But there were no perfect words, no way to phrase this that would guarantee Jase would be delighted by the news. He just had to put it out there and hope for the best.

'I'm afraid I'm going to have to ask you to rein in your appreciation for a man in plaid for a little while, and not just because I don't want to get creases in my plus fours before tomorrow's fundraiser.' Taking hold of Jase's hand, Aidan pulled him down to sit side by side with him on the bed. 'There's something I need to talk to you about.'

'You know conversations that start with lines like that terrify me.' Jase widened his eyes. 'You're not about to tell me you're running off with your caddy, are you?'

'Sorry, but there's no way you're getting rid of me that easily.

Or ever, in fact.' Aidan curled his fingers around his husband's, feeling the smoothness of the wedding band that Jase hadn't taken off since the moment Aidan had put it there.

'I'm glad to hear it, because I could never let you go. But I knew there was something big on your mind, you've got that look you always get.'

'The gormless one?'

'No, the one I know is about to change my life in one way or another.' Jase held his gaze and Aidan couldn't put it off any longer.

'I think I've found the perfect egg donor. She's bright, kind, with a similar kind of colouring to you, and most of all she understands what it's like for a child who's been born as a result of a donor's kindness, because her parents had her with the help of a sperm donor.'

'She sounds amazing.' The smile on Jase's face mirrored his words. 'Did the clinic put you in touch with someone? I didn't think anything would happen until after the interview.'

'No, I know her in real life, we both do.'

'Who is it?' The smile on Jase's face had only wavered slightly, but the wide-eyed concern was back too.

'Isla.'

'From work?' Jase had adopted an unreadable expression as Aidan nodded. 'She's great, but she's so young. Are you sure she knows what she's getting herself into?'

'I am, because of what her parents did, and because she was already going through the process of having the checks and undergoing counselling, before she even knew we were looking for a donor.'

'Oh my God, really? She'd be great, wouldn't she?' Excitement definitely seemed to be winning the battle now. 'But what are the clinic going to say, if we want to use our own egg donor? Do you think it might affect how hard it is to get a match with a surrogate?'

'I've got no idea and that's why I didn't know whether to tell you at first, but also because having a known donor comes with its pros and cons. Although I don't think I'd have any issue with Isla being a part of our lives for the long haul, if she wants to have some kind of relationship with the baby. As long as we get the right balance. I'd be a lot more nervous about doing that if I didn't know her history, but I really think she understands and that this could be the best of both worlds for the baby as a result, knowing where they came from and being able to reach out if they want to, but understanding that their parents are the people who've raised them.'

'I've discovered so many things I love even more about you since we started this process, and the fact you always talk about our baby like it's a certainty is one of them.' Jase pressed his lips against Aidan's for a couple of seconds.

'That's because I know it's going to happen. Just like I was certain, the night we met, that we were going to end up getting married. I knew we were going to be a family from that moment, I just didn't know exactly what that would look like.' Aidan might have had his doubts in the past that they'd ever get their dream, but he wasn't just saying those things to reassure Jase anymore, he was really beginning to believe it.

'I'm kind of glad you didn't admit all of that straight away, or I might have headed for the hills!'

'Yeah, yeah, of course you would.' Aidan pulled a face. 'You know you're the luckiest man alive and you have done since that night too.'

'I have.' Jase nodded, and Aidan felt it again, that overwhelming sense of love and acceptance he got every time his husband looked at him the way he did. Whatever happened, they were already a family, and even if he didn't want to contemplate the idea of them not having a child, he knew they'd make it through if it came to it. They'd just have to get more pets, and take up hobbies like golf for real. As long as he had Jase, Aidan would even be willing to wear matching plaid plus fours. And if that wasn't the definition of love, he had no idea what was.

* * *

Isla was beginning to think she'd misunderstood the brief Gwen had given for 'whacky golf outfits'. She looked more like a clown, with her oversized bow tie and baggy tartan trousers with braces. She should just have gone through Grandpa Bill's wardrobe. He and her nan loved golf, and played most weekends, and she knew for a fact that he had his fair share of garish outfits. Normally she wouldn't have dreamt of wearing anything like that and, unlike Gwen, she didn't enjoy being the centre of attention. But she was happy to do almost anything for a good cause, even if it meant making a fool of herself in front of her colleagues. It was just as well that her crush on Zahir, one of the doctors she worked with, seemed to have petered out, or she might have worried that she was blowing her chances. It wasn't because of anything he'd done that her feelings had changed, but it would be too complicated to explain to anyone she might date that her top priority right now was becoming an egg donor. Not everyone would be on board with the idea, and the thought of telling someone she'd just started dating wasn't remotely appealing.

She was no expert on dating at the best of times. Seeing how much it had hurt her mother to lose the man she loved had made Isla wary. Even if all the stars aligned, and she somehow found her soulmate in this great big world, there was a chance she could still lose them far too soon. That fear had settled somewhere deep inside her, and the thought of actively seeking out something that had the potential to hurt her so much seemed like madness. So she'd decided to leave it to fate. If she was ever going to take that chance, it would be because fate had put someone worthy of that kind of risk in her path. She wouldn't go searching for him in a bar, or on a dating app. It meant she'd been single since her father's death, with just a handful of dates that had ended up going nowhere at all.

'Does your bow tie revolve?' Esther laughed as Isla made her way over to where the team representing the A&E department were standing. Gwen headed up the Friends of St Piran's Hospital, a group which organised a series of fundraising events throughout the year. The spring event was going to be the biggest so far and Gwen had persuaded the management of the Three Ports Golf Club to host a charity golf tournament on their beautiful links course, which stretched along the coast just outside Port Tremellien.

She'd also got permission to use the practice area, which didn't need to be treated as carefully as the rest of the course, and the Friends had set up a sports day track, with lanes marked by small cones and an inflatable finishing line and start posts. Although the hospital teams had all been asked to wear the most garish golf attire they could find, most of them were taking part in the sports day rather than the golf competition. The tournament itself was open to both hospital staff and supporters, with all the entry fees going to the Friends' fundraising efforts. Participants had also been encouraged to get sponsorship to wear the most tasteless golfing-related outfits they could find, and Gwen had promised a prize for the person she deemed to be worst dressed. Looking around, Isla realised she had no chance of winning a prize, but Aidan was definitely in with a shot. Joe had gone all out too, and was dressed from head to toe in bright orange.

'Unfortunately, the bow tie is very boring.' Isla turned towards Joe. 'Although I'm not sure I could ever have hoped to compete with an outfit that can be seen from space.'

'The worst part about it is that I already owned every single item of clothing you see before you.' Joe shrugged.

'I'm just glad he's never worn them all together before, and has no intention of ever doing it in the future.' Esther laughed again. 'You did promise me that, didn't you?'

'Okay everybody, thanks for coming.' Gwen's announcement over the sound system cut off whatever response Joe had been about to give. 'We're almost ready to start the inaugural St Piran's sports day and I just wanted to set out a few rules for the six teams competing.'

As well as the A&E department, there were staff representing The Sycamore Centre, where Joe was a consultant, The Thornberry Centre, where the hospital's oncology department was based, and staff from King Arthur's Table, the hospital restaurant. They all faced stiff competition from the team who worked in the maternity department, and the occupational and physiotherapy team from St Jude's Unit, who'd been trash talking for weeks about how they were going to take everyone else down.

'The rules are as follows: no cheating will be tolerated.' Gwen was holding the microphone with a stern expression on her face, but then she laughed. 'At least not if we catch you doing it! Either way, the judges' decisions are final, and the overall losing team will be performing a forfeit. As will anyone I feel hasn't made the effort to follow the dress code for today. When I was at school, if you forgot your sports kit, you were expected to take part wearing your knickers and vest. But believe me, what I've got in store will make doing the egg and spoon race in your pants seem like a dream come true. Let's just say I'll be gifting the outfit I've bought for the forfeit, for Sexual Health Awareness week in September, once the sports day is over.'

'Bloody hell, I'm glad I went all in now.' Aidan pulled out the side of his plus fours and did a little curtsey. 'There's no way Gwen can accuse me of not looking a total prat. Knowing her, she'll make anyone she doesn't think has made enough effort dress as a giant scrotum.'

'I'm starting to worry that the bow tie and tartan trousers won't be enough.' Isla really didn't like being in the spotlight, and the idea of being singled out by Gwen did not appeal in the slightest, especially not if Aidan's prediction about the costume she'd have to wear was right.

'Stick with me, kid.' Aidan put an arm around her. 'With the amount of clashing patterns we're wearing between the two of us, Gwen won't be able to focus for long enough to even work out who we are. In fact, no one from A&E is going to be getting the forfeit. We're a team and we're all in this together. It's us against the rest of the world!'

Aidan might have been hamming it up as he raised his fist into the air, like he was reenacting a scene from *Braveheart*, whilst the rest of their team cheered. But his words made Isla's eyes prickle with tears all the same. *It's us against the rest of the world* were the words her father had always said at the toughest of times, and she'd always believed their family of four could face anything as long as they were together. Only now her dad was gone, and the other half of that foursome lived thousands of miles away. But if she got the go-ahead from the fertility clinic, she'd be part of a team again, with Aidan and Jase. She just had to hope her family would want to cheer them all on, too. Otherwise running the three-legged race dressed as an intimate body part would be the least of her worries.

## 6

The hospital fundraisers always drew a crowd and the idea for a sports day had grown out of a tug of war event at a previous summer fair. It had got the spectators on their feet and cheering for their chosen team and, according to Danni and Esther, the midwives had made short work of the A&E team on that occasion. This year the crowd were even more partisan, and the trash talking was no longer confined to inter-departmental rivalry. There was even a chant about the hospital cafeteria that got louder and louder every time they seemed to be doing well in one of the races. '*Two, four, six, eight! Who makes food taste out of date?*'

Despite the rivalry, there was a brilliant atmosphere and it looked certain that the fundraiser would be a huge success. The teams and supporters had been charged entrance fees, and there were a few stalls selling refreshments, as well as a tombola. Gwen's husband Barry was even running a sweepstake on picking the individual who got the most points for their team overall. There was no way it was going to be Isla. She'd finished second to last in her first race, and right in the middle of the field in her second race. Although the way her grandparents had cheered when she'd crossed the line, anyone would think she'd just won an Olympic gold. As it currently stood, according to the results recorded on an old whiteboard propped up against a chair, Zahir from A&E, and Angela from The Sycamore Centre – who everyone called Chooky – were in the lead. As an Australian, who'd only moved to the UK and joined the mental health unit the month before, there'd been some good-natured ribbing about Chooky being a ringer, who'd been brought in just to guarantee The Sycamore Centre victory. There might have been a lot of joking, but Zahir still had his eyes on the prize. The two teams were also neck and neck.

'Right, it's the sack race next and I'm not in this one, but Danni and Esther are.' He'd gathered them all around for a team talk. 'From what I've seen, the first two lanes are on the part of the course with the least divots, which will give you the best chance of winning. So at least one of you needs to be in those lanes. No offence Esther, but Danni's got far longer legs and so if comes down to it, you might have to give up your spot for her.'

'No offence taken and I'd rather the pressure was on you than me.' Esther grinned and nudged her friend. Danni was in the early stages of pregnancy, but most people still didn't know about it, and if Isla hadn't already been told there was no way she would have guessed by looking at her. Danni clearly wasn't worried about the prospect of falling over either, but when you'd worked in A&E for any length of time you knew people had a lot of silly ideas about how risky things like that were so early on. The chances of any harm coming to the baby if she did end up tripping over her own feet during the sack race were almost non-existent. But as Esther pointed out, she might get some flak if she let down the team and Isla was very glad she wasn't taking part in one of the crucial races. 'The honour of A&E is resting on your shoulders.'

'More like it's resting on her ability not to fall on her arse.' Aidan winked. 'But remember the consequences if you're caught cheating.'

Gwen's threat had been enough to stop anyone breaking the rules too overtly, but there'd been some pretty sharp elbows during the space hopper race.

'Just make sure you shake your sack out.' Zahir looked deadly serious, but as Isla caught Aidan's eye, she couldn't help laughing. 'I'm not joking, having a wrinkle-free sack could be the key to a smooth race.'

'I'm sorry, but Gwen would never forgive me if I let a comment about a wrinkle-free sack go past.' Aidan was laughing too, and Zahir rolled his eyes. Ignoring the interruption, he turned to Danni and Esther.

'Focus on the finish line and don't look down at your feet. If we can beat The Sycamore Centre by a good margin, we should take the whole thing, even if they come first in the relay.'

'We'll do our best, and if sibling rivalry doesn't get me over that line first, nothing will.' Danni shot a look over to where her brother was also getting ready for the race.

'Let's do it!' Zahir high-fived them both, before Esther and Danni headed off to the start line.

'You don't still fancy him after that, do you?' Aidan whispered conspiratorially in Isla's ear, as Zahir walked off towards the midpoint of the track, where he'd positioned himself for every race he wasn't in, so he could shout out advice to the other A&E team members.

'I'd already decided that getting involved with someone at work wasn't a good idea.'

'Can you imagine how bad his competitive dad syndrome is going to be when he has kids?'

'Awful! He'll be the sort who tips over the Monopoly board if someone else gets to buy Park Lane or Mayfair.' Isla smiled at the thought, because it was all too easy to picture it. 'What about you and Jase, are you going to be the sort of parents who scream at the opposing team, when you're watching an under-sevens football match?'

'No, I'm a lover not a fighter. Although there's a chance Jase will challenge the parents from the other team to play Scrabble to the death, if one of them shouts at our kid. He's the mildest mannered guy you could ever meet, but he's a protector too.' Aidan looked serious for a moment. 'I know you've met him a couple of times, but the two of you should get to know one another better, if we're going to do this.'

'I'd like that, and I definitely want to do it, if you do?'

'I really do, and we couldn't be more grateful.' Aidan reached out to take her hand, just as Gwen's voice echoed over the sound system.

'Right, we're just about to start the penultimate race. So get ready folks, and get down to the track to shout for your team in the sack race. One minute to the off.'

As Aidan and Isla moved past the start line, all of the competitors seemed to have decided to give their sacks a vigorous shake before stepping into them, and a cloud of dust rose into the air, catching in Isla's throat, making her cough, and she only just caught what Aidan said.

'Zahir's going to be pleased that Esther and Danni have got themselves into the first two lanes. Are you okay?' He waited as she tried and failed to stop coughing. 'Let's go and get you a drink.'

'I'm fine, it's—' The rest of her words were stolen by a cacophony of sound that could almost have passed for a small explosion, if Isla hadn't witnessed Christine, the head of catering, giving an almighty sneeze. Everyone at the hospital knew Christine. Her ready laugh and willingness to provide a plate of toast and a cup of tea, to calm any crisis, even when the kitchen was officially closed, made her hugely popular among the staff, although Isla had known her long before she'd joined St Piran's. Christine was a friend of Isla's grandparents, and they all belonged to the Port Agnes Quicksteppers, where Gwen now headed up the over-sixties dance team. The sneeze might have been enough to make everyone jump, but Christine's reaction afterwards was even louder, as she screamed and clutched her back.

'Aargh! Oh my God, it's agony, I think I've popped something!' Christine's face was twisted in pain, as Aidan and Isla broke into a run, heading towards her, with Danni and Esther already focusing their attention on her too.

'Someone else is going to have to take my spot in the race. I don't think I can move.' Christine grimaced again.

'That's the last thing you need to worry about. You might have done yourself a serious injury.' Danni's tone was insistent, but gentle. 'Have you had back pain before?'

'In my job? You're joking, aren't you?' Christine managed a rueful smile. 'Sciatica is my old pal, but if I avoid doing stupid stuff like trying to lift sacks of potatoes, or leaning over the sink for too long, I can usually keep it at bay. But this feels worse than all the other times. Ow! For God's sake, how can I have done myself an injury from sneezing?'

'You'd be amazed what the force of a sneeze can do.' Aidan gave her a sympathetic look. 'I've had patients who've suffered whiplash from sneezing.'

'Can't your eyes pop out if you try to sneeze with them open?'

One of the other staff, who Isla recognised from the hospital restaurant, but whose name she didn't know, raised her eyebrows. But Danni shook her head.

'That's an urban myth. But you do need to get checked out, Christine. Do you feel as if you can bend forward or twist at the waist?'

'Ow, oh no, no, no!' Even the slightest movement of her body seemed to be agonising.

'Is she going to be able to walk again?' Christine's colleague from the restaurant widened her eyes in horror at the prospect of it being so serious.

'I bloody hope so, Janice, because Gwen's going to kill me if I can't. I'm supposed to be in her team for the dance competition in Redruth next month.'

'Don't worry about that now, Christine. We'll see if we can get you a bit more comfortable.' Isla positioned herself next to the older woman. 'Try putting your arm around my shoulder and using me like a sort of crutch, and see whether that eases the pain at all.'

'It does a bit, but I feel as though, if I could lie down, it might help even more.' Her body was stooped forward and the pinched look on her face seemed to have eased a little bit.

'Do you think it could be a vertebral compression fracture?' Isla had seen this once before, with a patient who'd desperately tried to hold in a series of sneezes during the delivery of a eulogy at a funeral service. When she looked at Danni, she was nodding again.

'It could be.'

'That sounds serious. That's a break in the spine, isn't it?' All the colour had drained from Christine's face, and she swayed against Isla.

'It sounds a lot worse than it is.' Danni's tone was reassuring.

'You're going to need a scan to make sure. But if it is a vertebral compression fracture, it'll probably heal without any intervention. You'll be given painkillers, but the most important thing will be to keep weight off the injury as much as possible, because sitting and standing will make the pain worse until it starts to get better.'

'How long for?' Christine still looked very pale.

'At least six weeks, but we're not even certain that's what it is yet. Let's just take it a step at a time.' Danni turned towards Esther. 'I'm sure Gwen said there's a first aid tent next to the practice green outside the clubhouse. We need to see if they've got anything that might be useful, until we can get Christine to the hospital.'

'I'm on it.' Esther was already heading in the direction of the clubhouse, and other people had begun to move over towards the starting line.

'Let's get Christine somewhere she can try lying down and have a bit more privacy. Behind the gazebo over by the tombola stall is probably the closest place.' As Danni spoke, Aidan moved to Christine's other side.

'So are you lot forfeiting the race then?' Rory, one of the physios, might have been smiling when he asked the question, but Isla had a strong suspicion he wasn't joking.

'Not on your life.' Zahir was already grabbing the sack out of Danni's hand, and he turned back towards where he'd been standing. 'Gary, you need to get over here to sub for Esther, or Amy can. Then we just need to get someone to take Christine's place.'

'Yep, there's definitely no danger of me wanting to start a relationship with Zahir.' Isla kept her voice low, as she and Aidan began to help Christine towards the tombola stand, and even their patient giggled, before she winced in pain again.

'You've got to stop making me laugh, it's bloody agony.' Behind them the sports day seemed to be getting back on track as quickly as it had been interrupted, but Isla was glad to be helping Christine instead. This was all she'd ever wanted to do, for as long as she could remember. Every time she managed to make someone feel a little bit better, it felt as though her father was watching her, almost like they'd never really had to say goodbye at all.

\* \* \*

Christine's popularity meant there was no shortage of offers of help in the wake of her accident. Isla's grandparents had been among the first to arrive in what had turned out to be the not-so-private spot behind the tombola. They'd come armed with blankets from the car, and as many cups of tea in cardboard cups as they'd been able to carry from the refreshment stand.

'We thought Chrissy and her rescuers might be in need of a cuppa.' Isla's grandmother beamed in her direction. She'd always been incredibly proud of Isla's job, and she used every excuse she could to slip the fact that her granddaughter was a nurse into completely unrelated conversations.

'Joy by name, and Joy by nature.' Christine reached up a hand from her position on the ground. 'Although I might have to let it cool off a bit, or I'll probably tip it straight on to my face, lying down like this, and add third-degree burns to the list of things I've got wrong with me.'

Isla hadn't wanted to worry Christine more by telling her that there was a good chance she might have osteoporosis, if she'd fractured a vertebra just by sneezing. But even lying on the ground hadn't been a barrier to her googling why it might have happened, and it was clear she was scared of what the implications might be.

'You'll be up dancing before you know it.' Aidan was the sort of person who radiated optimism and he refused to let Christine get downcast. 'If you have got osteoporosis then you've got to use it to your advantage. Tell Robert there'll be no more fishing trips with his buddies; he's got to take you somewhere with plenty of sunshine, where you can get your fill of vitamin D.'

'Not to mention the calcium.' Isla smiled at the blank looks on their faces. 'There are plenty of cocktails containing cream, and a nice white Russian in the sunshine could be just what the doctor ordered.'

'Or at least the doctor will pretend she didn't hear that!' Danni laughed, but the smile had slid off Christine's face.

'Oh my God! Robert's on his way back from a fishing trip, but he won't he home until late this evening. And my daughter and son-in-law are away for their wedding anniversary. I've got the kids tonight, and I'm supposed to be picking Joel and Freddie up from their match at Jury Park in Padstow. I need to be there by five.'

'We could go and get them for you.' Isla's grandfather looked towards his wife, who nodded. 'It'll be a bit of a squeeze for them in the back of the Micra, but I'm sure they won't mind.'

'I said I'd give two of the other boys a lift home as well, and it's our turn to wash the kit.' Christine tried to sit up, forcing Isla to gently rest a hand on her shoulder.

'Sorry to butt in, but as luck would have it, yesterday we traded in Aidan's old car for a seven-seater.' Jase, who'd been standing on the edge of the group, crouched down beside her. 'I know Joel and Freddie from school, and probably the other boys too. I can pick them up and take them to our place, or stay with them at yours until Robert gets home.'

'That's great, but what about getting Christine to hospital?' Isla looked at Danni.

'Esther's just texted to say that the St John Ambulance team are going to take her. It'll be a lot more comfortable than a car, and much quicker than waiting for an ambulance, given that she won't be a priority.'

'It sounds like the perfect solution then, Christine, what do you think?' Jase was still looking down at her.

'I bet that's the last thing you want to do on your day off, spend it chauffeuring around the kids you have to put up with all week.'

'They're the ones who have to put up with me.' Jase smiled. 'And it'll be great to hear how they got on. From what I gather, the Three Ports under-tens are in with a good chance of finishing at the top of the league this year.'

'At least you stake a claim in one trophy this summer then, Christine, because judging by the shouts coming from the track, the A&E team are about to win the relay race too!' Aidan dropped a kiss on her forehead. 'But if you're a very good girl and follow the doctor's orders, we'll let you have a look at our trophy.'

'I told you not to make me laugh.' Christine couldn't seem to help it. 'I might have a ridiculous injury as my only souvenir of the day, but I'll never forget how kind you've all been either.'

* * *

By the time Gwen got up to announce the winners of the sports day competition, Christine was already on her way to hospital.

'You might all be wondering why I'm dressed like this.' Gwen made the fact she was wearing what appeared to be a giant cockroach costume sound matter-of-fact. 'Well, I promised you that there would be a forfeit for anyone caught cheating, or not making an effort with the dress code today. As no one deserved that punishment, I thought it was only right that I should be the one to wear the costume, but after today, I'll be donating it to the sexual health clinic as I promised.'

'I thought it was a cockroach, but do you think it's supposed to be—'

Isla cut Aidan off before he could finish his sentence. 'I don't even want to think about what it's supposed to be.'

'After a very eventful day, I've got some announcements.' Gwen paused as a murmur went around the crowd. 'First and foremost, I'm delighted to tell you that our lovely Christine is going to be absolutely fine, but I'm also thrilled to say that the winners of the inaugural sports day are the team from A&E!'

Even though they'd known they were going to win, the cheer that went up from the A&E team was deafening. Zahir, as self-elected captain, went up first to collect the trophy, with the rest of his team following on behind. He did a good job of hiding his disappointment at narrowly finishing in second place to Chooky, who was the individual winner overall. He'd been muttering earlier about raising a protest over how the results had been calculated, but he was probably too worried about ending up in the cockroach costume to say anything to Gwen. The A&E team had also had another victory, with Aidan taking the prize for worst-dressed participant.

'Now that we have our sports day winners, we're just waiting for the final players in the golf tournament to finish their rounds, and then we can announce the tournament champions too.' Gwen addressed the crowd again, when the A&E team finally finished their slightly over-the-top celebrations. 'I hope you'll join me in the clubhouse, where more refreshments are available, to come and hear the results. If not, thank you so much for your support today, and don't forget there are buckets by the gate for any last-minute donations you want to make to the Friends of St Piran's appeal fund. Every penny raised will go to making our local hospital the best it can possibly be.'

'Are you coming up to the clubhouse?' Aidan turned towards Isla. 'Zahir has promised to buy the first two rounds for being such a dictator, emphasis on the first syllable. And Gary and Amy have already challenged the physios to a shot-drinking contest, so I've got a feeling the competition is far from over. I said I'd wait for Jase to come and pick me up anyway, so I might as well make an evening of it.'

'Yes, I'll be up in a bit, I just want to have a word with my grandparents and see what they're planning to do.' Isla touched his arm briefly. 'I'll catch you up.'

'Great and I'll order you the most expensive drink they do, seeing as Zahir is paying.'

'See you in a minute.' Isla turned away from him and headed over to where her grandparents were chatting with Gwen, who was still acting as though wearing a cockroach costume was an everyday occurrence.

'Oh hello sweetheart. How are you?' Grandpa Bill planted a kiss on her cheek, before she even had the chance to answer.

'It's been great fun.' Isla smiled at Gwen. 'I knew it would be with you organising it.'

'And I knew the A&E department were going to win too.' Gwen gave her a knowing look. 'Although, from what I could make out, Zahir wasn't giving you a lot of choice.'

'I've never seen him like that, he's usually so mild-mannered and easy-going.' Isla laughed. 'His excuse was that he grew up with four sisters, who tried to beat him at every game ever invented, which made him develop a competitive streak. And now he can't turn it off. Better than winning, I'm just glad that Christine is going to be okay.'

'I was so proud watching you.' Isla's grandmother slipped an arm around her waist. 'I always try to imagine what you're like at work, but today I got to see you in action.'

'She certainly had a crack team around her.' Gwen nodded in agreement.

'Those two lads are lovely, Aidan and John, is it?' Isla's grandpa furrowed his brow.

'Aidan and Jase. And yes, they're really lovely.' Isla took a breath, ready to share what she'd been wanting to tell them for months, but the lull in the conversation never lasted long with them around, and her grandmother got in first.

'I loved it when Jase said how much he enjoys spending time with the children at his school, and how they have to put up with him, not the other way around.' Joy put a hand on her chest. 'It's wonderful to hear someone talking about children like that, instead of always complaining about how hard it is. We looked after Isla and Lexi a lot of the time, once Nicky got ill, and people used to ask me if I ever resented how often we had the girls, but it was always the thing that made me happiest. And it felt like a blessing, didn't it, Bill?'

'It still does.' He took his wife's hand. 'But I bet it's rare to hear a teacher talking about their pupils like that, with some of the things they must have to deal with.'

'I've always thought Aidan and Jase would make lovely parents.' Gwen's gaze met Isla's for a moment, and it was like she knew. Maybe she did; after all, Isla had made the offer to Aidan outside the hospital shop, and St Piran's had a notoriously efficient grapevine. 'And I gather it's something they're hoping for.'

'Well I really hope they get their wish.' Joy's tone was resolute, and if Isla didn't take the opportunity now, she never would.

'I'm really glad you think that, Nan, because I'm going to help them.' She couldn't take her eyes off her grandmother's face as she waited for her to respond.

'Do you mean carry their baby?' Joy furrowed her brow, the concern in her expression as obvious as it was in her voice.

'No, I don't think I could do that, but I'm going to donate my eggs and then they'll find a surrogate to carry the baby.' Isla inhaled deeply; she needed to get the rest of the words out without pausing for breath. Then at least she'd have told half of her family. 'I've been thinking about it for a long time. It was because of someone else's generosity that I got to grow up as Nick Marlowe's daughter, and your granddaughter. I couldn't have asked for better parents, or grandparents, and I want to give that to someone else. At first I was going to do it anonymously, but it feels like even more of a gift to be able to do it for someone who I know deserves this chance as much as Aidan and Jase do. I hope you'll be happy about it, and I'll respect how you feel if you aren't. But I've got to tell you that I'm going to be doing it anyway.'

'I didn't think I could be any prouder of you than I already am.' Isla's grandmother pulled her into a hug, and her grandpa wrapped his arms around both of them.

'Well done.' Gwen mouthed the word to Isla, as she locked eyes with the older woman again over her grandmother's shoulder. She'd never have imagined it could be so emotional to have a conversation like that, while a woman dressed as a cockroach was looking on, but if she'd had any doubt left that she was making the right decision, every trace of it was gone. Now all she had to do was get through the fertility clinic screenings and then tell her mum and sister what she was planning to do.

# 7

'So you really don't think it's going to be the challenge of your career finding a match for us?' Aidan felt as though he'd been holding his breath throughout the entire appointment at the fertility clinic, but neither the matching coordinator, nor the counsellor that he and Jase had been sitting with for the last hour, had seemed fazed by anything they had to say.

'If I'm honest, I think you'll be one of our easiest matches.' Annabel, who headed up the team matching surrogates with intended parents, shot Aidan an encouraging smile. 'Lots of our ladies are keen to help same-sex couples become parents, and you guys are a dream in terms of your backgrounds too. What child wouldn't flourish in a household where one parent is a medical professional, and the other a headteacher of a primary school? Not to mention the fact that you're great fun, and I'm sure you'll hit it off with any potential matches you're introduced to.'

'I just won't mention the fact that everyone in Jase's family had to have braces for what looked like their entire teens. Or that even the women on my side have monobrows like Neanderthals if they're left to their own devices.' Aidan had been determined not to make any stupid comments, but the exasperated look he'd just got from his husband was enough to tell him he'd failed. Luckily, Annabel seemed to find it funny.

'Well, thankfully, if those things are genetic, only one half of them can be inherited.' She looked down at the sheet in front of her for a moment. 'I know that last time we all met, you still weren't sure about which one of you would be the biological father. But I wondered if you'd had any more thoughts about that?'

'We don't have strong feelings either way, do we?' Jase looked towards Aidan, and he forced himself to nod. The truth was he had much stronger feelings about it than he'd been able to admit to his husband, and maybe even to himself.

'It's definitely something you need to make a decision about.' Tim, the counsellor, leant forward in his chair. 'We talked about this before, I know, and you'll both be parents in every meaningful sense of the word but deciding who will provide half of your child's DNA is still a big decision. Now that you've chosen your egg donor, and you clearly feel it's right for you to use a donor you know, this is the last big piece of the puzzle. Particularly as Annabel feels so confident about finding you a surrogate quite quickly. Some people opt to mix sperm from both fathers and leave it to chance. But if you don't want to do that, you need to be certain you're 100 per cent on board with whatever choice you make.'

'I know.' Aidan avoided looking in Jase's direction as he spoke. Over the years, his husband had learnt to read him far too well, and the challenges Jase faced with his hearing meant he seemed able to pick up on every little nuance of body language too. But he didn't want to be honest about what he really wanted – for the first time – in front of people who could call a halt to their plans to have a baby, just by putting a simple cross in a box next to their names. This was a conversation they needed to have on their own. 'I think, like you say, we've just been so fixed on us both being the baby's parents, in a completely equal sense, that figuring out the mechanics didn't really seem important. But you're right, we do need to make a decision.'

'You really do. Then we can set up a meeting with...' Tim hesitated for a moment, flicking back a page on the notes he'd been taking. 'Isla. Just to make sure you really are all coming from the same place, in terms of any relationship she might have with the child in the future. But we can't do that until you two have made your decision.'

'We'll get it done in the next couple of days, and then we can go ahead and set up the meeting with Isla.' Jase made it all sound so easy, but Aidan had no idea how he was going to take the news when he told him that there was only one person he could imagine the biological father of their child being.

* * *

Jase looked at Aidan as they pulled into the driveway. 'You definitely want to do this, then? You don't think it's bad luck to start telling people before there's anything to tell?'

'There's everything to tell.' Aidan reached across and clasped his husband's hand. The feeling had been bubbling up inside him ever since Isla had offered to be their egg donor. When they'd first talked about becoming parents, the barriers had seemed insurmountable, but that had changed with those seven little words: *I'd love to do it for you.* From that moment the prospect was immediately more real, almost as if Aidan could feel the weight of the baby in his arms. For a long time he hadn't dared believe it would happen, and there'd been so many questions he wanted to ask, but nobody he could ask them of, not even at the infertility support group. So few people were in the situation he and Jase were, and it was why he wanted to create a record of their journey that might help someone else. 'Even if we aren't lucky enough to become parents this way, although I really think we will be, I want people to know it's an option, and that you don't have to be hugely wealthy to use a surrogate. There must be other people out there like us, who are desperate to become parents, and who'd love an honest account of the highs and lows of it all. I did find a couple of blogs, but there's scope for so much more, and I really want to share our journey with anyone who's looking for the kind of answers we couldn't find. But I won't do it unless you're happy with it, and I'm certainly not going to do it until we've broken the news to your family.'

'Of course I'm happy for you to do it if it helps someone else. But what about your family?' Jase reached up, putting a hand on his cheek, and Aidan swallowed against the lump that formed in his throat every time he thought about his family.

'I'll tell Mammy, and she'll tell the rest of them no doubt. But you know what my father's like. He barely acknowledges our existence, so I can't see him breaking open the champagne at the news we're trying for a baby.'

'Oh sweetheart, I wish he could see what an amazing son he's got.'

'And I wish he could see how happy you've made me.' Aidan closed the gap between them, pressing his lips against Jase's, before pulling away again. 'He doesn't want to see that, because then he'd have to admit that there's nothing wrong with me having a husband. But it's more than that, being married to you is the best thing that could ever have happened to me.'

'You know I feel the same about you, don't you?' Jase's eyes didn't leave his face, as Aidan nodded. 'But right now I need you to be strong, because when we break the news to my mother that her second grandchild might finally be arriving, after a wait of more than twenty-seven years, we're going to get the kind of hugs that could fracture a rib.'

'It's a good job you're married to a nurse, then.'

'I got all the good fortune I could ever have hoped for when I married you.' Jase took hold of Aidan's hand again. 'And whatever happens with the baby, I'll never forget just how lucky that makes me.'

Family dinner night was a must-attend event at Jase's parents' house every Wednesday evening. If Aidan was on lates, or working nights, Lin, Jase's mum, would package up the meal with every little detail the same as if he'd been there. On the last dinner he hadn't been able to get to, she'd put a little jug of apple sauce alongside the roast pork dinner, a pot of cream to go with the crumble, and even two after-dinner mints, so he didn't have to miss out on those either.

Lin, and Jase's father, Ray, had welcomed Aidan into their family as if he'd always been there. It was the same with Jase's sister, Natasha – who everyone called Tash. They were just the sort of family who used shortened names as a sign of affection and acceptance. They were also the only people who called Aidan, Aid. But what made him smile the most, was their insistence on calling Tash's husband Tone, even though Aidan was sure everyone else called him Anthony. His wife and stepson certainly did. He was a really nice guy, but quite serious and strait-laced, which made Anthony feel like a better fit. Not with the Taylors, though. Everyone got a diminutive form of their name, and their only grandson Reuben was always called Rube by his grandparents.

Reuben had already been in his late teens by the time Aidan met him, which would have been a difficult enough age to introduce a new family member. But that same year, Reuben had lost his father, Ricky, as a result of liver cirrhosis. It could have made Reuben bitter, and less than welcoming of his uncle's new boyfriend, but instead it had bonded him to both of them, and it had helped Aidan and Jase's relationship progress faster than it might have done otherwise, too. They'd done their best to be there for Reuben, and Aidan didn't carry any baggage about the man who'd left Tash to raise a baby by herself when she was just twenty-one. Ricky had come good in the end and his relationship with Reuben had really started to develop in the months before his death. But it had taken him the best part of five years to get involved in his son's life in any way at all, and for more than ten years after that he'd been unreliable and often absent. All of that had understandably coloured the way Lin and Ray viewed him. When Reuben had started to put him on a pedestal after his death, and hold him up like some kind of paragon of perfection, it had caused some tension. Aidan and Jase had been able to help defuse it. They'd been there for Reuben when he'd wanted to talk about how great his father was, without feeling the need to offer a counter argument, or even hint at one. Now, almost ten years later, Reuben had grown into an incredible young man, with a far more balanced view of his late father, and the world as a whole. He was a huge part of the reason why Aidan and Jase wanted to become parents.

'Here they are, my handsome boys!' Lin hadn't even heard their news, but the hug she enveloped them in, the moment they came into the house, was already almost as powerful as the Heimlich manoeuvre. In her go-to style, Lin was wearing a sequin encrusted top, and a cloud of Opium perfume that had apparently been her signature scent since the 1980s. Even though he choked on it every time, after ten years, it smelt like home to Aidan now.

'Give them some space to breathe, woman.' Ray's chastisement of his wife was always playful, and she poked her tongue out at him in response.

'You just want me out of the way, so you can take them down and show them the new addition to your shed.'

'It's not a shed, it's a man cave.' Ray raised his eyes to the ceiling. 'Women, eh? Can't live with them, can't live without them. Although, in your case, you got it spot-on and got yourself a fella who understands exactly where you're coming from.'

'That shed's just a place for you to hide out when I want a hand with the washing up.' Lin's attempts to berate her husband were ruined by the fact that she couldn't keep the smile off her face. The two of them bickered all the time, but it was always in a playful way, and Aidan had never once doubted his in-laws' love for one another, or for anyone else lucky enough to be a part of their family.

'We'll have a look at the new addition to your sh... *man cave*, later, Dad.' Jase clapped his father on the shoulder. 'But we've got something we want to tell you first.'

'Oh God, you're not ill are you? Or Aid?' Lin turned towards them, an anxious expression replacing her smile.

'No, it's nothing like that, it's good news.' Jase reached out and touched Aidan's hand, an understanding passing between them that even the chance of becoming parents was something to be celebrated. 'Is Tash here yet?'

'Yes, she's in the conservatory with Tone, and even Rube was on time for once. I keep telling him he's working too hard, but will he listen to a word I say? Of course not!' Lin was fussing like an old mother hen, but she was never happier than when her family were around her. When Aidan was Reuben's age, he'd probably been dreaming of winning the lottery. But at thirty-eight, this was his dream now. He wanted to fuss around his own children one day, when they came home for family dinner night, to welcome them through the door as if nothing could bring him greater joy than seeing them. He even wanted to worry, the way Lin did, about all the things that might go wrong, because having a family who were safe and well meant more than anything else ever could.

'It's the uncs!' Reuben shot up from his chair as soon as he spotted them, giving them each a hug in turn. 'You've got to save me from Mum and Anthony trying to press-gang me into joining them on a canal boat holiday.'

'But you always loved *Rosie and Jim* when you were little.' Reuben's mother made it sound as if commemorating his favourite childhood TV show, by going on a canal boat holiday in his twenties, was the most natural thing in the world. But her son was pulling a face that articulated exactly what he thought of the idea.

'I love you both, honestly, but I might not by the end of a week confined with you in a tiny wooden boat. In fact, there's a good chance I might have been arrested for drowning at least one of you.'

'Your mother's just worried that if you don't come away with us, you won't take a holiday again this year.' Anthony had a gentle lilt to his voice, which made the request sound all the more reasonable. 'We're very proud of how hard you've been working to grow the business, but you need to have a proper break every now and then.'

'I'll go on holiday with the uncs instead.' Reuben gave Aidan a beseeching look. 'You'll take me somewhere, won't you? Anywhere, as long as it doesn't include confined spaces, or sharing a bathroom Stuart Little would find a bit on the snug side.'

'If we decide to go away, you're more than welcome to come with us, but our holiday plans are on hold for a bit.' Aidan turned towards Jase. 'And we wanted to tell you all why.'

'We're trying for a baby.' Jase had barely got the words out before Lin shrieked with excitement, and a flurry of questions seemed to come from every corner of the room. Even Anthony, who'd always said how grateful he was to have become Reuben's stepfather when he was ten years old, rather than ten months, seemed thrilled about the prospect of getting a niece or nephew.

'I couldn't be more pleased for you.' Tash clapped her hands together when they'd finished outlining the process, and the progress they'd made so far. 'I just wish you'd done it ten years earlier, then Mum could have stopped nagging me for another grandchild before I started the perimenopause, and she finally had to accept that ship had sailed. I was never going to have another one after Rube came out sideways. Anthony wouldn't have coped with all of that anyway.'

'Babies are too fragile and all that responsibility is scary.' Anthony suddenly seemed to realise there was a chance he might be putting them off, not least because his words had earned him an elbow in the ribs from Lin. 'But you two are going to be brilliant at it. A teacher and a nurse? I'm not sure there could be a better pedigree for parenthood.'

'And I can't wait for all that baby stuff again. Having Tash and Rube here when he was tiny was one of the happiest times of my life.' A sigh of contentment escaped from Lin's lips, but then she frowned. 'The trouble was, I was still working full time then, and so was Ray. This time round we can be hands-on and help out as much as you need us to.'

'I'll have to get working on a high chair.' Ray tapped the side of his head. 'I think I've got some wood that would be perfect for the seat.'

'More excuses to disappear into your shed!' Lin was beaming, despite her words. 'I know you said we need to try and keep our excitement reined in until we know for sure that it's going to happen, but I already know it is. I can feel it in my waters.'

'That's what Aidan said, well not the waters bit, just that he knows for certain we'll get there.' Jase leant his head against Aidan's shoulder. 'And I'm starting to think you're both right.'

'Mothers are always right.' Aidan blew his mother-in-law a kiss, and a twinge of regret twisted in his gut. His mother might be excited if she heard the news, but he couldn't be certain about it. One thing he did know was that she wouldn't show it the way Lin had. She'd be too worried about what his father's reaction would be.

Aidan and Jase's news had dominated the whole evening, and it felt as though they'd covered every related topic – from baby names to the best way to induce labour – by the time they headed towards the door to leave. It had been the perfect evening, and the enthusiasm from Jase's family had made it even easier to believe that the arrival of a new addition was just a matter of time. But then Anthony caught hold of Aidan's elbow, just as they got to the end of the hallway.

'Sorry, I didn't want to say this in front of anyone else. In case it was a bit, you know... awkward.' Anthony shuffled from one foot to the other as he spoke, and a feeling of dread rose up inside Aidan. It was coming; the bucket of cold water that someone was bound to throw over their plans. He just hadn't expected it to come from Jase's family. 'It's just I know these things – IVF and surrogacy – can be very expensive, and I wanted to say that if money is ever an obstacle, don't let it be. I've never wanted children, but I can't think of two people who deserve them more, and if I can help financially, it would be an absolute honour to do so.'

That was when the tears Aidan had been fighting all evening, turned into a sob he just couldn't keep in. This was family, and it didn't matter that neither he nor Anthony had been born into it. The Taylors were their found family, and any baby who found themselves a part of that too, would be the luckiest child alive.

**8**

---

'I've had sixteen texts from Mum this morning. *Sixteen*. Asking me more questions about the process of Isla's eggs being collected, and when we might hear about being matched to a surrogate.' Jase shook his head, but he was smiling. 'Can you imagine what she's going to be like once there's a baby on the way? The surrogate is going to be lucky Mum won't have a direct line of communication with her.'

'Do you realise the one question she hasn't asked?' Aidan pulled himself into a sitting position in the bed, leaning his back against the headboard, so that he was side by side with Jase.

'I'm struggling to think of anything Mum hasn't asked!'

'She didn't ask whose sperm we're going to be using. None of your family did.'

'That's because they don't care. It won't matter to them whose baby it is biologically. The poor kid's going to be sucked right into the centre of the family either way, and I've got a feeling Mum's whole world is going to revolve around being a grandmother again.'

'I know what it feels like to be sucked into your family.' Aidan put his hand on top of his husband's, knitting their fingers together. 'And it's the best family I could ever imagine a child having. If my family accept the idea at all, it'll be because they think I'm adding to the Kennedy gene pool, and you can bet the first question out of my mother's mouth is who the father is going to be. They just won't understand that we both will be. That's why there's no question who the biological father should be. It should be you.'

'But that doesn't make any sense. If your family are more likely to accept the idea because they've got a genetic link with the child, then let's go down that route.' Jase stroked his thumb over the back of Aidan's hand. 'I want my child to have your eyes.'

'And I want the baby to have your crazy curls. But what I don't want is for our child to have a link with my family that relies on them sharing DNA. If they don't want to be a part of this, then that's on them. And it'll be no loss to us, or the baby, if that's what they decide.'

'Shouldn't you at least talk to them first before you assume this is how they'll react? I don't want you making this decision until you know the full picture.'

'It won't make any difference. I want our baby to have Taylor DNA; I love every single member of your family and, as much as I wish it wasn't true, I can't say the same for mine.' Aidan sighed, an invisible knife twisting in his chest, as he pictured what his father's reaction would be. He could never forget the look on his face, when Aidan had told him about his plans to marry Jase: the curl of the lip, and the distaste in his eyes that had said so much more than his words. *It's your life.* It could have been taken as benign acceptance, but what it had told Aidan, was that Sean Kennedy thought his son was ruining his life.

'I really think you should talk to them.' Jase's voice was gentle but insistent, his thumb still caressing the back of Aidan's hand.

'If I promise to talk to them, can I tell the clinic we've made a decision about who the biological father is going to be?'

'Okay, but if you change your mind, you know that's okay with me, don't you?'

'I do and it's just one more reason why I love you.'

'I love you too.' As Jase replied, Aidan rested his head on his husband's shoulder, knowing without any doubt that he'd love their child with a fierceness that went beyond anything biology could explain. The thought of telling his family their plans filled him with nothing but dread, but if that was what it took to persuade Jase, then he might as well get it over and done with.

\* \* \*

Isla shifted in her seat as the counsellor looked down at the notes in front of her. She hadn't felt this nervous since her interview for the job at St Piran's, which she'd been desperate to get, because it had meant working much closer to home. Most people in their mid-twenties could only dream of owning their own place, the way property prices had gone up. It was even harder to get a foot on the ladder in Port Kara, with its sweeping sandy beaches, the main one of which stretched over a mile along the Cornish Atlantic Coast. Then there were the beautiful coves, which according to local legend had been the haunt of pirates and smugglers for hundreds of years. It was part of what had turned it into something of a celebrity hot spot too, with second homes making it even harder for locals to stay in the village where they'd grown up. But Nick Marlowe had made sure his daughters had the option of staying in Port Kara if that was what they wanted, and he'd worked all hours before the Huntington's disease had forced him to give up. He'd managed to save the deposits for two apartments in a converted chapel, perched at the top of the hill on the road that led towards Port Tremellien.

He'd rented the flats out, and the girls hadn't had any idea that they'd each be gifted an apartment on their twenty-first birthday. Lexi was almost four years older than Isla, and Nick had been able to give her the key himself. The disease had already robbed him of so much by that stage. It had been ten years since the first symptoms had started to show, and he was having more and more difficulty finding the words he wanted, and his speech was laboured and difficult to understand. But he'd been able to tell Lexi he loved her, that he hoped having the apartment would give her the freedom to live wherever she wanted to, and that she shouldn't feel like she needed to stay in Port Kara when he was gone. His prediction that she might choose to leave had been right, and Lexi no longer owned the apartment that she'd continued to rent out until their father died, but the proceeds of the sale had helped her and Josh buy their first home together in Florida. When Isla had turned twenty-one, her father had already been gone six months. She'd known that the gift was coming, but had felt robbed of the conversation she should have been able to have with her father, and the opportunity to thank him. Instead, it had been her mother who'd handed her the key.

'You were always your father's shadow, from the moment you could walk.' Clare had hugged her daughter tightly, before she'd pressed an envelope into her hand. 'He was a Cornish lad through and through, and the call of the sea would always have drawn him back here. I knew better than to ever try and make him leave, and I can see that in you too. You're like your dad in so many ways, sometimes it's almost impossible to believe you don't have the same DNA.'

'I love the fact I'm like him.' Tears had fallen all too readily back then, at the mere thought of her father, and she hadn't even tried to hold them back.

'Dad knew there was a chance he might not be here to give you the key, and it broke his heart that you wouldn't get to have the same moment he had with Lexi. So he wrote you a letter, just in case.' Her mother had given a shuddering sigh.

'Thank you. Do you mind if I read it on my own?' Her mother had nodded, and it had been the closest thing Isla could get to having a final conversation with her father. Isla had re-read it so many times since then, and she could remember it word for word, even now.

*My darling Isla,*

*I hope you know how proud I am of you. By now, you'll be training as a nurse and any patient you care for is going to be so lucky.*

*I've got a feeling that Lexi will never live in her apartment, and that's okay. From the first moment we took her to visit your mother's family in America, it was like she'd found the place she was meant to be. But not you. You always wanted to come back to Cornwall and, every time we came home, you'd tell me you never wanted to leave Port Kara again. Mum and I would laugh about it, but deep down, I had a feeling you might end up meaning every word.*

*Maybe I'm wrong and you've discovered a wanderlust that will take you around the world. But even if that's true, your love for where you came from will always occupy a huge space in your heart. That space is where I'll be, even when I'm gone, and you can find me there, any time you need me.*

*Meeting your mum and having you and Lexi made me the luckiest man on earth. I just wish I could have stayed. I love you so much, and I hope, whatever you decide about the*

*apartment, that your life is filled with the kind of joy you
gave me.*

   *All my love now and always, Dad xxx*

Her father had been right in his second prediction too. Isla
had never once thought about selling the apartment, and she'd
commuted from there to her first nursing job in Truro. But
getting a post at St Piran's had made it feel as if she was even
closer to her father. She could picture him on the beach in Port
Kara or walking up the high street, before the muscle contrac-
tions and balance problems had resulted in him needing to use a
wheelchair to go any kind of distance. She could imagine him
swimming in the sea, and having a pint in his favourite pub. It
was something else he'd understood perfectly, when he'd written
her that letter. When Isla was in Port Kara, it was as if her father
had never really left, because every corner of the village held
memories of him, and she couldn't imagine ever wanting to live
anywhere else.

   'I'm sorry you had to go through the general health questionnaire twice.' The counsellor's voice jolted her back to the present.
'But changing clinics meant we needed to go through our own
questionnaire.'

   'It wasn't a problem.' Isla smiled at the woman, who'd said her
name was Roseanne. The truth was, the questionnaire had been
the easy bit; giving her medical history had been a breeze
compared to the counselling session she'd just undertaken. The
only difficult part of the health assessment had been knowing how
to answer the question about the medical history of her family. The
information her parents had been given when they'd chosen a
sperm donor had been sparse, and all the donor had been required
to do was to declare that he didn't have any known genetic condi-

tions. Changing clinics to the one Aidan and Jase has signed up with had meant beginning the process again, and the stakes seemed much higher this time around. All of which meant Isla was terrified of saying or doing something that might derail their plans, and it was making her feel like a rabbit caught in the headlights.

'It's a wonderful thing you're doing for Aidan and Jase. Being an anonymous donor probably wouldn't have been an option for you through this clinic, and I was wondering if that was part of the motivation for choosing to donate to friends?' Roseanne had an intense way of looking at her when she asked a question, and Isla found herself blinking even more than usual as a result. God knows if she'd read something into that, but Isla couldn't seem to help herself. The more she tried not to blink, the faster her eyelids flickered.

'No, they didn't even tell me at the first clinic that the gaps in my medical history might be a barrier.' It had been a shock to discover, in her first call with the new clinic, that potential donors usually needed to be able to provide a full medical history of their family, in order to be able to donate eggs. But the rules could be applied more flexibly with a known donor, because Jase and Aidan would be aware of any risks arising from not having a full family history and could factor that into their decision. All Isla needed to do was to pass the health screening that would come after the counselling. 'Like I said earlier, I've been thinking about donating for a long time, because of my dad. But when I discovered that Aidan and Jase needed a donor, I couldn't think of anyone better.'

'And how do your family feel about it?' Roseanne had the intense look back on her face again, and Isla's eyelids were flickering so much she was sure she must be creating a breeze.

'My grandparents are very supportive, but I haven't had the

chance to speak to my mother and sister about it yet. They live in America.'

'Hmmm.' Without even speaking, Roseanne had managed to convey that she didn't believe a word Isla had just said, and the excuse had sounded every bit as lame as it was. 'Well that's something I'd very much recommend you do before we proceed to the next step.'

'Okay, I was planning to do it this week anyway.' It wasn't exactly a lie, but even thinking about breaking the news during her weekly FaceTime call with her mum and sister made her feel a little bit sick.

'That's very good.' Roseanne nodded. 'And I expect Jase and Aidan might have told you that my colleague, Tim, has recommended the three of you have a joint counselling session to talk about boundaries and expectations. With known donors or surrogates, this is not just useful, it's essential.'

'Yes, Aidan told me about that and it sounds like a great idea.'

'Excellent, in that case, I think I can go ahead and recommend that you start the screening process while we complete the remainder of the counselling sessions, as I haven't heard anything that would suggest we need to put things on hold.'

'Really?' Isla was going to have to change her name to Blinky McBlink-Face at this rate.

'Absolutely.' Roseanne finally lost the intense look she'd been wearing and gave Isla a warm smile, which matched the tone of her voice. 'But I really do recommend you have that conversation with your mum and sister as soon as possible.'

'Oh I will, I promise.' Isla fought the urge to cross her fingers over one another. She had to do this, and making a promise meant she couldn't back out. From the moment she'd decided to become an egg donor, she'd had a really strong sense that her father would have been proud of her. But she was every bit as certain he'd have wanted her to tell her mother first, and one thing she never wanted to do was let her father down.

\* \* \*

Aidan took a deep breath as he watched Lucas Newman, one of the trauma surgeons, marching off down the corridor.

'God I hate that man.' He hadn't meant to say the words out loud, but Isla looked up from the computer.

'We all do and not just because of what he did to Esther and Danni.' She wrinkled her nose and Aidan couldn't help smiling. Isla hadn't even been working at the hospital when Lucas had become the number-one nemesis of the A&E team, but it was another indicator of just how tightly knit they were. Esther's former fiancé had tried to come between her and her best friend, by relentlessly pursuing Danni and attempting to convince her that their tricky childhoods meant they were soulmates. Aidan had a difficult time growing up too, but that didn't make the idea of tripping off into the sunset with Lucas any more appealing than it had been for Danni in the end. Aidan would rather wax his undercarriage with duct tape than spend a single second in Lucas's company outside of work and he was certain Danni felt the same.

'Well I dislike him even more now, because he's saying the patient in cubicle three doesn't need surgery and we can stitch him up ourselves.' Aidan shuddered. 'I hate the injuries where you can see the tendons almost as much as I hate Lucas Newman.'

'Do you ever wonder if you're in the wrong job?' Isla laughed.

'Listen, I can handle fingers hanging by a thread, and head injuries where I could put my finger inside the patient's skull and have a feel around if I wanted to. But there's just something about the tendons in the arm and watching them move when they aren't covered by the skin.' Aidan shuddered again. 'French windows need to be banned, given the amount of patients I've had who've tried to walk straight through one.'

'If you can't get them banned, people could hire out their kids to put sticky finger marks on the glass. No one would ever mistake it for an open door then.'

'Now there's an idea. Would it be a dealbreaker if you knew Jase and I were going to do that with our child, to try and make a bit of pocket money?' Aidan was rarely serious, and he definitely wasn't on this occasion, but he'd spent a lot of time worrying lately about what might be a dealbreaker for Isla.

'No. But if you don't make me that cup of tea you promised me before our shift is over, we could be looking at a dealbreaker then.'

'If I throw in one of Gwen's brownies, could I persuade you to do the stitching up in cubicle three?'

'I thought they'd all sold out this morning; I went to get one on my first break, as soon as I heard she had them, but she said they were gone by ten.'

'I saw the potential of an early investment and bought four of them.' Aidan shrugged. 'One of them could have your name on it if you save me from having to look at those flexor tendons, and I might even be persuaded to bring you in a packet of Crunch Creams tomorrow.'

'Even though you know that Crunch Creams are the love of my life, we can forget the biscuits. But if you're willing to do two brownies, we've got a deal. I'm going to see my grandparents after work, and Nan is always raving about Gwen's baking.'

'You drive a hard bargain Miss Marlowe, but we've got a deal. Given the gift you're giving me and Jase, I could hardly say no, even if you'd wanted all four.' Aidan dropped a kiss on the top of her head. 'And when we go to our counselling appointment, we can tell Tim we're already skilled at negotiating an agreement between us.'

'Do you think we should save one of the brownies for him, in case he needs bribing?'

'As soon as he meets you, he's going to see how amazing you are. It'll be obvious you're doing this for all the right reasons, which is why I love you enough to have given you 50 per cent of my brownies.' Aidan grinned. 'Even if you weren't stitching up the arm of the guy in cubicle three.'

'Why do I get the feeling I'm the one who's been stitched up?' Isla laughed as she looked up at him, and that same feeling he'd had when he was with his in-laws washed over him. It was the sensation of knowing he was loved and accepted for who he was. Aidan couldn't allow himself to think about how much it hurt to have never had that from his own family. The prospect of facing up to that reality was even less appealing than an exposed flexor tendon, and every bit as painful.

# 9

Working shifts sometimes made it hard to see friends who weren't in the same job and who didn't understand that planning something on the weekend didn't automatically mean everyone would be able to make it. Isla had a group of friends from secondary school who she was still close to. They met up at least once a month, and she tried to ensure she made the get-togethers, even if she ended up having to try and swap a shift. This time around, they were in a country pub about six miles inland from Port Kara, and Isla really wanted to talk to her friends about her plans to donate her eggs. It wasn't that she was doubting her choice, but telling five of her friends would be a good rehearsal for talking to her mum and Lexi. There was no doubting they'd have questions, just as her mother and sister would, and it would be a good opportunity to work through her response to any concerns they might have. The trouble was, Cleo had been holding court for the last thirty minutes about her plans to join an environmental protest group, and stating categorically that the best thing women of their generation could do was to refuse to continue over-populating the planet, and remain childless. It hardly provided the perfect segue for Isla to open up about her plans.

'You're very quiet tonight, is everything okay?' Phoebe had been Isla's best friend at school, from the day in Year Nine when she'd deliberately fallen over to deflect from the fact that Isla had come out of the loos with her skirt tucked into the back of her tights. She'd even managed the impressive trick of yanking Isla's skirt downwards, before hitting the ground, to cover the granny-sized knickers her friend had been wearing. Phoebe had been prepared to be laughed at for supposedly tripping over her own feet, just to save Isla embarrassment. So, if there was anyone she could tell about her plans, it was the girl who'd earned herself the nickname Phoebe Faceplant.

'Just a lot on my mind.' Isla tucked a strand of hair behind her ear, as they stood side by side in the pub toilets, facing the mirrors.

'It must have been tough having your dad's big birthday.'

'Thanks for remembering, but it's not that.' Phoebe had been at university in Brighton when Isla's father had died, but she'd come back as soon as she'd heard the news and had stayed on until after the funeral to support her friend. It had meant a lot to Isla, who'd stayed close to home to study at the Truro School of Nursing, because of her father's failing health. She hadn't had the kind of carefree university experience of most people her age and she knew it must have been hard for Phoebe to come away from that and be there for her grief-stricken friend, but it was something she'd never forget.

'Are you going to tell me what it is then?' Phoebe was still watching her in the mirror, and Isla breathed out.

'I haven't even told Mum and Lexi about this yet, but I've decided to become an egg donor.' Turning to look at Phoebe, she scanned her face for the inevitable *are-you-mad?* look that she fully expected to see. But she was smiling.

'That's amazing, your dad would be so proud of you.' Phoebe hugged her. She was one of the few people Isla had told about her parents' decision to use a sperm donor. It meant she really understood the significance of what Isla was planning, and she was still smiling as they pulled away from one another. 'Oh my God, will you get to find out if a baby has been born as a result? How awesome will it be to know you've done that!'

'It would be amazing and I'm pretty sure they tell you if anyone's treatment has been a success, as a result of your donation, because the child can access your details when they're older, if they want to. But it's going to be different for me, anyway. I'm donating the eggs to my friend Aidan from work, and his husband, Jase.'

'Oh Isla, that's incredible.'

'You don't think I'm mad, and opening up my life to a world of complications I don't need?' She'd expected her friends to ask whether she'd really thought about the possible long-term consequences, and she was pretty sure her mother and sister would challenge her on that, but Phoebe was shaking her head.

'Life is full of complications, and I know you'd never have done this without being certain your friend and his husband will make great parents.'

'They'll be the best.'

'That's all that matters then.' Phoebe linked an arm through hers. 'But if you need to feel as if you're getting the third degree, we could always tell Cleo. I'm sure she'll be willing to lecture you about how you're single-handedly responsible for climate change. She certainly made me feel that way when I drove her over here. The only thing that shut her up, was me telling her I could always drop her off at the bus stop if she felt that strongly about me owning a car.'

'Tempting as a lecture from Cleo is, I think I'll keep it to myself for now.' Isla pulled a face. 'But I'm really glad I told you, and I just hope Mum and Lexi are half as positive about it when I break the news to them.'

'If they aren't, it'll only be because they're worried about you.' Phoebe hugged her again, and she felt some of the tension drain out of her body. Not everyone was going to react to her decision as positively as Phoebe had, but she was more certain about it now than ever. And she couldn't imagine anything stopping her from going through with it.

* * *

Isla was jigging up and down on the spot, as if she was desperate for a wee, while she waited for the FaceTime call to connect. But the only thing she was desperate for, was to get the next ten minutes over and done with.

'Hello, Mum? Are you there?' All Isla could make out was a black screen and some muffled voices.

'Sorry, I dropped the phone; your sister nearly wiped us both out by turning too quickly with her giant baby bump.' Isla's mum was grinning when she finally appeared on screen, but Lexi, who was sitting next to her, looked far less amused.

'You try squeezing into a tight space on a sofa with two babies and a paddling pool worth of water strapped to the front of you. I took out three trays of doughnuts in Walmart yesterday, just turning to reach for the trolley. I can't keep doing this for much longer.'

'How many weeks are you now?' Isla still couldn't believe her sister was going to become a mum while they were living so far apart, but it sounded like it couldn't come a moment too soon for Lexi.

'Twenty-eight and they want me to try and get to thirty-six, but it's already so uncomfortable and I'm hardly getting any sleep.'

'I hope you're not expecting that to change when they arrive.' Their mother laughed. 'Neither of you two slept all through the night until you were about three. Your dad always used to joke that you didn't get that from me, and that I could sleep standing up, given half the chance.'

It had been a running joke in the family that Clare didn't need a bed to get a good night's sleep. She hadn't even noticed when the airbed she and her husband had been sleeping on had deflated overnight and left them lying on the ground, when they'd all gone camping one summer. Isla's dad had teased her mum about losing count of the number of times he'd started a conversation, when they'd climbed into bed, only to realise she was already asleep by the time her head hit the pillow. It was an ability Isla had always been quite envious of, but she and Lexi had both suffered from bouts of insomnia since their teens, as well as being difficult to settle as children. Whether it was heredi-tary she had no idea, but any kind of traits they had, which weren't shared with their mum, might well have come from their biological father. He was never mentioned and, somewhere along the line, it was almost as though their parents had forgotten the sperm donor's role in their daughters' conception. Her mother had told Isla once how keen they'd been to make sure the girls had the same donor, to limit any differences there might be between them. Yet despite their shared DNA, Lexi and Isla had still ended up being very different people in many respects. And every time she spoke to her sister, Lexi seemed more and more at home in the US. Any hint of a Cornish accent she'd had was gone, and in its place Isla could already hear the beginnings of a slight Southern twang in her sister's tone.

'You don't look like you've been sleeping either.' Lexi peered at the screen. 'And you're doing that blinking thing you always do when you're worried about something.'

'Why do you always say that?' Isla tried to keep her tone breezy, but her sister knew her far too well.

'Because it started when my best top went missing, and you swore you hadn't seen it, but then you started blinking like crazy and I knew straight away you were lying.' Lexi narrowed her eyes. 'It happens every time you're trying to hide something. Just don't ever take up playing poker, because you'll be rubbish at it.'

For a moment, Isla considered telling Lexi that she was the one talking rubbish, but putting off the conversation any longer wasn't going to change what her mother and sister thought about it.

'There's nothing wrong is there, sweetheart?' Clare suddenly looked so worried, and Isla couldn't hold out any longer. Her mother had already been through so much, and the prospect of something bad happening to one of her daughters was her greatest fear. When they'd left home, she'd begged them to text when they got back to their own places after an evening out, no matter how late it was. And she still nagged them both to make doctor's appointments for the smallest complaints, because '*there's no telling where it could lead.*'

'Nothing's wrong, but I have got something to tell you.'

'You've met someone!' Lexi clapped her hands together and beamed into the camera, almost mirroring the statement their grandmother had made, the first time Isla had thought about sharing her plans. 'I knew there had to be a reason why you were so determined not to leave Cornwall.'

'I have met someone, but unfortunately he's already got a

husband.' Isla couldn't help smiling at the look that crossed her sister's face.

'I don't understand. So, you've met someone, but he's married to a man?' Her mother pushed her glasses up her nose. 'Please tell me it's not one of those weird polyamory set ups.'

'Aidan's just a friend, and he's very happily married to Jase, but they're desperate to have a baby and I've agreed to be their egg donor.' For a moment there was silence, and she held her breath, waiting for the reaction she knew would come. Only the furrowing of her mother's brow gave any indication that the screen hadn't frozen, and when her sister finally spoke, her tone was tight.

'Will you be having the baby for them, like my friend Misty?' Lexi's eyebrows shot up, but her whole face seemed to relax when Isla shook her head. 'Good, because being handed a baby as a reward for suffering through pregnancy-induced haemor-rhoids seems like a fair exchange. But having to go through all of that and having to hand the baby over to someone else at the end, sucks on all levels.'

'At this stage of my life, I think I'd rather have the haemor-rhoids.' Isla laughed, but then she looked at her mother, whose face was completely blank. 'I'll just be donating my eggs. Some other far more selfless woman will be carrying the baby for Aidan and Jase. I've wanted to do it for a long time, for Dad, and as a thank you for the opportunity that our donor gave us, of being raised by a wonderful man. My only worry was that the parents of any child that might be born could never live up to Dad's standards, but I think Aidan can. And the more I get to know Jase, the more I believe he can too. Dad would have loved them, they're great guys, and they really deserve to be parents.'

'What about what happened to Misty?' Clare looked from Isla to Lexi, and back again.

'It's not the same. I won't have any part in the pregnancy itself, and there's absolutely no chance of Aidan and Jase changing their minds anyway.' Isla watched her mother's face, as expressions seemed to flit across it, like images on a TV screen.

'How about the process itself? Are there any risks?'

'It's very safe and I'll be monitored really closely.'

'What about your fertility later on, if you use up lots of eggs?' Her mother frowned. Isla couldn't imagine being ready to follow in her sister's footsteps for a very long time, but it was something the clinic had covered in detail anyway.

'It won't affect my chances of having a baby.' Isla wished she could give her mother a hug, because it was obvious how worried this was making her. She'd expected Lexi to be the one to hit her with loads of questions, but her sister was just sitting quietly. Clare wasn't done yet, though.

'And what about if it's successful and they have a baby? Will you be involved? I told you before, they've changed the laws now.'

'I know, I've had counselling to discuss all of that, and we've got more sessions booked in together. I'll be making an agreement with Aidan and Jase about what our relationship will look like if they do have a baby, so we all know where we stand.' If Isla was making it sound simple, it was because that's exactly how it felt with Aidan and Jase. It was why she was so certain that it was something she was supposed to do, with them. 'And if it makes you feel any better, I'll be getting a whole series of health checks before I donate. I've also been trying to eat better, to be in the best possible condition when the treatment starts. So it's actually having loads of health benefits.'

'I'm not going to pretend I'm not worried, but I can't really remember a time when I haven't been. That's parenting for you.' Clare sighed. 'And I know my girls. Nothing I've ever been able to say to either of you has made any difference once you'd made up your minds.'

'I think Dad would have approved.' Lexi's words made Isla's head jolt up in surprise. She'd been almost certain her sister would tell her she was crazy, but there was no sign of that. 'And Isla's right, we wouldn't even be here, if someone hadn't been willing to do the same for us.'

'How can I argue with that?' Clare put her arm around Lexi, and blew a kiss to Isla with her other hand. 'But if you change your mind at any point, that's okay too.'

'I know.' Isla blew a kiss back towards the screen, and her whole body felt lighter than it had ten minutes earlier. The only thing she was worried about now, was whether the fertility treatment would be a success, because the last remaining obstacle to going ahead had just been removed. Or so she thought.

* * *

The moment Isla saw Sarah Vardy sitting in the waiting area of A&E, as she headed in to start her shift, her heart sank. Sarah looked exhausted, there were violet shadows under her eyes and her legs were bouncing up and down, as if she was finding it impossible to keep still. She was obviously distressed, and, in all likelihood, what was wrong with Sarah couldn't be fixed by a visit to A&E. What made it saddest of all, was that there might be no fix for it. And Isla could only imagine how torturous it must be for Sarah to live with such relentless levels of anxiety.

'How are you doing, Sarah?' She stopped in front of the older woman, who looked up, but seemed to take a moment to register that she needed to respond. When she finally spoke, her eyes were wild with fear.

'The cancer's everywhere now, I can feel it crawling through my body like ants.'

'That must be a horrible sensation, but you know from coming in before that your symptoms often have another explanation. Have you spoken to Dr Carter about it?' As Sarah's psychiatrist, Joe was the only person who stood any chance of helping her through this latest crisis, but she was vehemently shaking her head.

'I need to be admitted to the cancer centre, but they keep telling me I haven't got it. I know the previous scans were clear, but it's different this time and no one's listening. I can *feel* it inside me, and it's going to be too late for anyone to help me.' She was on the edge of hysteria now, her voice carrying across the waiting area. It was unusually quiet with only a handful of people waiting, but every one of them seemed to have their eyes on Sarah.

'I'm going to take you through to examine you, and we'll take it from there.' Isla had no idea whether she could do anything to calm Sarah down but getting her out of such a public area seemed like a good start. They'd have to call The Sycamore Centre and see whether Joe or one of his colleagues could attend, but in the meantime, Sarah was getting more and more distressed. It might not be a physical emergency, but she needed urgent treatment all the same.

Fifteen minutes later, Sarah was settled on a bed in a cubicle and Isla had just returned from putting the call in to The Sycamore Centre. It was still unnervingly quiet throughout the emergency department and Esther, who was nursing lead, had told Isla to take as long as she needed with Sarah.

'Are you feeling any more comfortable?' As she approached the bed, Isla was relieved to see that Sarah's fidgeting seemed to have stopped.

'Just having someone listen and take my symptoms seriously

helps more than you know.' Sometimes she could be incredibly candid, and seemed able to grasp the idea that her carcinophobia was at the root of her problems, but she could flit straight back from that to being convinced she was dying of cancer, in an instant.

'I know you said you can feel the cancer, but are there any other symptoms?' Isla wasn't just humouring Sarah. Experience had taught her that there was always a chance something physical could be going on, even with a patient like her. If there was something else wrong, she didn't want it to get lost in the mental health crisis that had her patient in its grip.

'I'm exhausted all the time. It doesn't matter how much I sleep, when I wake up I'm still tired.' The circles under Sarah's eyes looked even darker under the harsh lights in the cubicle. 'I'm losing weight and the headaches I'm getting feel like the bones in my skull are too tight. They're all symptoms of the cancer, but nobody will listen.'

'What kind of cancer do you think you have?' Isla would have staked her salary for the next ten years on the fact that Sarah had googled her symptoms and come up with a diagnosis. She wasn't wrong, but it wasn't any of the cancers the patient had diagnosed herself with previously.

'It's leukaemia.' Sarah's response was as resolute as if she was reading the outcome of some test results. It was as black and white to her as those words would have been on a sheet of paper. Maybe that was what she needed, results that couldn't be misinterpreted in the same way that symptoms could. Isla knew Sarah had undergone a lot of testing in the past, but since her diagnosis of extreme health anxiety and carcinophobia, the treatment had been confined to her mental rather than physical health. Some reassurance that nothing had changed since her last results might help, even a little bit, and Isla couldn't see how it would hurt.

'When did you last have a blood test?'

'I don't know, maybe a year?' Sarah furrowed her brow. 'They keep saying it's all in my head, but I know my body, and I know something's wrong.'

'Let's get your bloods done and then we'll have some more information to take forward.' She gave Sarah's hand a quick squeeze, and the tension seemed to drain away from the other woman's face. Sometimes being heard was all a patient needed, and Isla just hoped that by the time the results came in, the team from The Sycamore Centre would have a plan that could help Sarah through her latest crisis, because no matter what anyone said, to her, the cancer felt terrifyingly real.

\* \* \*

'I still can't believe how quiet that shift was.' Amy tipped a packet of Maltesers onto the table outside the hospital shop, as she spoke. 'It means I've got absolutely no excuse to scoff any chocolate, but I'm going to do it anyway.'

'What excuse have we ever needed to eat chocolate?' Isla reached out to grab a Malteser and popped it into her mouth.

'I wouldn't mind, but I swear you eat way more of it than I do, and you never seem to put on any weight. Whereas I've tried every diet known to woman and my uniform is still straining at the seams.'

'I've just got a good metabolism. Lexi's the same and she'll be one of those annoying people who can fit into their jeans a fortnight after giving birth. I don't know why, and don't kill me, but I've lost half a stone in the last couple of months without even trying.'

'I bloody hate you.' Amy took three Maltesers and rammed them into her mouth, not letting that stop her talking. 'I might as well give up. I'm just glad I'm not competing with your skinny arse on the apps, as well as with every other woman who's got a profile picture like a supermodel's.'

'Just tell yourself they're all catfish.' Isla laughed. 'Most of them probably are and you're gorgeous anyway. Inside and out.'

'What I don't get is why men can't at least make the same effort as the women seem to. Most of their profile pictures are taken from underneath their chins, with the kind of camera quality you'd have got from a Nokia in 2001, although sadly it's still clear enough to make out all the hairs up their noses. It's either that, or they're posing with a giant fish they've just caught. I don't know why I bother with restricting my chocolate intake for the potential benefit of any of those toads.'

'You shouldn't lose weight to please anyone but yourself.' Gwen had suddenly emerged from the shop and taken the words right out of Isla's mouth. 'You're a beautiful girl, Amy, and you don't need any man to tell you that for it to be true. But if you want my opinion, you should get off the apps and see what the real world has to offer.'

'God I wish it was that simple, Gwen. But it's not like when you got together with Barry, people just don't meet like that any more.' Amy picked up another handful of Maltesers. 'It's really depressing.'

'Getting out into the real world doesn't just have to be about meeting someone. Widening your horizons is good for the soul, and if you get a bit of action as a result, then great. But if not, you'll still have had fun.' Gwen's delivery was completely dead-pan, but Isla couldn't stop herself from laughing. There was something joyous about hearing a woman in her seventies talk about getting a bit of action, and Gwen frequently made it clear she was no slouch on that front. If that didn't give Amy hope that all was not lost on the dating front, when she was barely thirty, then nothing would. But Gwen was right about something else too, there was a hell of a lot more to life than dating.

'I think I'd be too bloody knackered for any action, even if I got offered some.' Amy grinned. 'This job is exhausting, especially when you're on a change of shift.'

'You don't have to tell me, I was a midwife for more than forty-five years, but I always found that trying something I'd never done before could reinvigorate me. That's how I've ended up doing half the stuff I have, and volunteering here has given me a whole new lease of life.'

'I suppose widening my horizons wouldn't do me any harm.' Amy looked at Isla. 'Are you up for trying out something new?'

'I am, as long as it's not too high adrenaline until after I've finished my treatment at the fertility clinic. The number of injections I'm going to need, and the way I bruise every time I get one, makes me suspect I'm going to be black and blue until after it's all over.'

'What you're doing for Aidan is such a gift.' Gwen squeezed Isla's shoulder. A week earlier, she'd have wanted Gwen to keep her voice down. But the hospital grapevine being what it was, it hadn't taken long for the news to get out. And now that her family were aware of her plans too, she didn't care who else knew. 'I'd have offered to be the surrogate myself, if I was twenty years younger.'

'You'd have wanted to be a surrogate at fifty?' Amy screwed up her face. 'Although to be fair, even at seventy, you're probably fitter than I am. Not that I'd be volunteering to be a surrogate, the thought of giving birth is terrifying. Seeing Danni's scan pictures today did make me a little bit broody, though.'

'And did you see Aidan trying not to cry when Esther said

that could be him and Jase soon?' Isla smiled at the thought of it; she'd never seen someone more ready to be a parent.

'Does it make you feel even a tiny bit weird, that the baby will be a part of you?' Amy was down to her last Malteser, and she picked it up as she spoke.

'No, it's just something I don't need and won't use, which could change Aidan and Jase's life. And unlike you, seeing Danni's pictures didn't make me feel remotely broody.'

'Really? I still get that broody feeling now and then, and I went through the menopause at forty-five!' Gwen shook her head. 'Danni told me she thought she was never going to get the chance to be a mother, but she and Charlie are the perfect example that you never know who or what might be out there, until you put down your phone and give real life a try.'

'Yes, ma'am.' Amy gave her a fake salute. 'And if you can promise me a Charlie of my very own, I'd pretty much be prepared to do anything. I suppose I am lagging behind both of you in doing my bit for others, so maybe that's where I should start. Although if there's some kind of volunteering I could do while I'm lying down, that would be great.'

'I can think of something you could do, but it might not be legal.' Gwen had that deadpan look on her face again, but then her mouth began to twitch at the corners and they all started to laugh. It was a relief to Isla to hear that Amy was every bit as exhausted by the job as she was, because just lately she hadn't been up to much more than curling up on the sofa when she got home. It was the nature of shift work, but Amy seemed to have renewed energy as she turned towards Isla.

'Maybe I could start with speed dating; that's in the real world, isn't it? I know you don't want to date right now, but you could just come and be my wing woman, and get in a bit of practice for the future.'

'I did say no adrenaline sports, and I think going speed dating with you could be very high stress.' Isla laughed again. 'But I will come, as long as you promise to come with me if I need anyone to hold my hand during my treatment.'

'There's no one I'd rather watch have eggs sucked out of their ovaries than you.'

Isla nearly choked on the mouthful of coffee she'd just taken, and she was still spluttering as she spoke. 'You might want to work on your chat if that offer is anything to go by, but we've got ourselves a deal.'

Isla suspected she needed a change of scene, and to try something new, every bit as much as Amy did. And Gwen was probably right about it being the best way to combat exhaustion. Although the very last thing she wanted was to meet someone and have to explain her decision to be an egg donor. That was the story she was telling herself for now, but the truth was she'd been frightened of the idea of meeting someone special for a long time and she wasn't sure if she'd ever find someone capable of making her want to take that risk.

**10**

---

As Jase closed the door of the counsellor's office behind him, Isla had to fight the urge to cheer. And she could tell by the look on his and Aidan's faces that they felt exactly the same way.

'I can't believe we're all signed off and they think they might be able to find you a surrogate within the next couple of months.' Isla whispered the words, almost afraid that, if she said them too loud, someone would come and tap them on the shoulder and say they'd changed their minds.

'Me neither. It feels like we've been chugging along at ten miles an hour, and now we're flying at full speed.' Jase took hold of Aidan's hand. 'He seemed to think we've got good reasons for deciding which one of us will have a biological connection to the baby.'

'That's because we have.' Aidan stopped and looked directly at his husband. 'When we have a child, I couldn't think of anything better than seeing a likeness of you in them somewhere, or of them having some of your traits. I fell in love with you for a thousand reasons, and if I can see just a handful of those in our kid, I'm going to love them all the more because of it.'

'I don't know how I got so lucky.' Jase shook his head. 'Although I've got a horrible feeling we're going to put Isla off her celebratory lunch, before we even get to the restaurant, if we don't shut up soon.'

'I am feeling a bit queasy.' She smiled as Aidan turned to look at her in mock horror.

'We could bump this down from lunch on the Sisters of Agnes Island, to a drive-through at McDonalds you know.'

'Do you know what, I could actually go for a big juicy burger right now and I never normally fancy things like that. Maybe all this talk of making babies is giving me cravings.' Isla pulled a face. 'God knows what I'll be like when I start the treatment.'

'If you need a burger at 2 a.m., all you have to do is call.' Jase linked an arm through hers. 'In fact, if you need anything at all, at any time, we'll be only too willing to help from now until forever. We owe you more than we can ever hope to repay.'

'Unless it involves DIY, in which case we'll pay to get someone in, because the Chuckle Brothers look like a crack team of builders compared to us.' Aidan linked his arm through hers on the other side, and they set off like they were reenacting the *Wizard of Oz*. But Isla didn't share the longing Dorothy had had to go home to Kansas, because right there, in the clinic corridor, sandwiched between Aidan and Jase, she had more of a sense of home than she'd had since her mother had left for America.

\* \* \*

As the aroma of garlic and herbs she couldn't have hoped to identify, drifted across the restaurant, Isla was very glad she hadn't persuaded Aidan and Jase to take her to the drive-through. She might not have any idea how to pronounce the name of some of the dishes on the menu, but whatever it was the chefs were cooking up, it was making her stomach rumble.

The restaurant in the hotel on the Sisters of Agnes Island, which was cut off from the mainland in Port Agnes at high tide, was rated as one of the best in Cornwall. It was booked up for months in advance and Isla had no idea how Aidan and Jase had managed to get a table. From what she'd read, the restaurant was a favourite with the celebrities and other wealthy incomers who had second homes in the area. One glance at the prices on the menu had made her swallow hard, and it didn't really matter that she didn't recognise the name of most of the dishes, or know what they tasted like, because she'd be going for the cheapest option. Aidan and Jase had already insisted this was their treat, but she wasn't going to let them blow a small fortune on her. They'd said they'd been given a gift voucher for the hotel at Christmas, which they needed to use, but Isla couldn't help worrying that they felt they owed her in some way. When the truth was, they were the ones giving her a gift by allowing her to honour her dad in this way.

'So, what's it going to be, Isla?' Jase lowered his menu to look at her.

'The Caeser salad looks lovely, and I'll just have some water I think.'

'Nope, no salad leaves, not today. Anyway, calories don't count when you're celebrating. Everyone knows that, and I fully intend to have a day off from my diet.' Aidan raised his eyebrows. 'And if anything, you need feeding up.'

'Now you sound like my nan.' Isla couldn't help smiling. Her grandmother had been known to turn up at the hospital with a

Tupperware box of sandwiches, if she'd thought her grand-daughter was looking too thin. It wasn't something Isla felt was justified, but the love behind her grandmother's gesture nourished her soul in a way that even the best sandwich in the world couldn't compete with.

'Not only that, but the minimum spend per table is two hundred pounds, so a salad and a glass of water just isn't going to cut it.' Jase smiled and she wondered for a moment if he'd worked out the real reason for her choosing a salad. But it didn't matter, because he and Aidan were clearly determined to push the boat out.

In the end, she'd decided on the three courses Aidan had suggested she went for, because they sounded delicious: roasted red pepper and Cornish cheddar crostini, chilli, garlic and lobster bucatini, and warm pecan pie with clotted cream. Two courses in, and the food had exceeded even her highest expectations.

'Well it's going to be hard to go back to stir-in pasta sauce after this.' Aidan pushed his plate away and sighed. 'I didn't know it was possible for something as simple as pasta to taste like it had been woven by angels. I knew it was going to be good when Gwen said the food here was almost better than sex, but I'm definitely going to have to drop the almost.'

'Me too.' Jase laughed at the look that had appeared on his husband's face. 'Hey, you said it first, which means you're not allowed to be offended.'

'You should know me better than that.' Aidan was still feigning a look of mock outrage, but the twinkle in his eyes completely gave him away.

'Well look who finally decided to take my advice.' A strikingly good-looking man, who Isla guessed was probably in his late twenties, had suddenly appeared at their table. He had dark blond hair, green eyes, and the easy golden tan of someone who looked as though he spent a lot of his time outdoors. He wasn't dressed like the other waiting staff, and he was hugging Jase in a way that suggested their relationship was a close one.

'You were right, Rube, we should have splashed out ages ago, but we might never have done it without your very generous gift.' Aidan held out his arms toward the younger man, earning him a hug too.

'It's nothing less than my two favourite uncles deserve.' His words were muffled as Aidan held him close, releasing him just in time to regain the look of mock outrage.

'We're your only uncles!'

'That doesn't make it any less true.' Aidan's nephew shrugged, his eyes framed by long, dark lashes, and Jase suddenly clapped his hand over his mouth, as he looked at Isla.

'Oh God, sorry, I'd forgotten you two don't know each other. This is my sister, Tash's, son, Reuben, but we all call him Rube.' Jase turned towards him. 'And this is Isla, who you've heard so much about.'

'I certainly have. It's so nice to finally meet you.' Reuben held out his hand and, when she took it, the last thing she'd expected was for her body to react the way it did. It had been so long since she'd been attracted to anyone, for a moment she appeared to forget how to speak. When she finally regained the ability, she blurted out something she had no idea whether Aidan and Jase would rather have kept to themselves.

'I've heard a lot about you too, especially in counselling today.'

'Oh God, is it that tough having me as a nephew?' Reuben grinned, matching dimples appearing on either side of his mouth.

'It's a bloody nightmare.' Aidan's smile mirrored his nephew's, and Isla's shoulders relaxed. It didn't look like she'd given away any family secrets after all. 'But as you well know, you're also a big part of the reason why we're desperate to become parents, and today the counsellor gave the three of us the go-ahead. So if the meeting with the surrogate goes well, this could just be the first thing of many that we have to celebrate.'

'That's amazing.' Reuben didn't look as if he could have been any happier if the good news had been his own. 'I've got to go and meet with Francesco about next week's order, but I'm going to start dropping off a fruit and veg box to you every week, and you can sort out the best bits for Isla. After all, you're all going to need to be in tip-top shape to make sure I finally get a little cousin. Surely this is all about me, after all!' Reuben laughed again and dropped the perfect wink. 'It's great to meet you Isla, and hopefully I'll get to see you again some time. Nan keeps telling these two to bring you over for a family dinner. And that's what you'll be, soon – part of the family. Although, on second thoughts, that might be why they haven't brought you, in case you do a runner.'

'That's exactly why we haven't subjected Isla to family dinner night.' Jase rolled his eyes.

'You two just don't appreciate it, because you were born into it. But, believe me, you're lucky to have a family dinner night.' For a moment, Aidan's tone was more sombre than Isla had ever known it, but then he smiled again. 'Even if you are all as mad as a box of frogs.'

'We might be as crazy as Aidan claims, but I can at least promise good quality food. I run an organic greengrocers and deli, and I keep telling these two they need to ditch all the processed stuff they eat whenever Nan's not cooking.' Reuben's dimples put in a reappearance. 'I tried dropping off produce boxes before, but they never got through them. Left to their own devices, I swear they'd live off chicken nuggets and takeaways. This is my chance to get them to embrace the good stuff for a change. Nan always uses stuff from the deli when she cooks for us, and they never turn that down.'

'It's just the prep that always seems to stand in our way.' Aidan pulled a face. 'But you're right, we must do better and my mother-in-law is a fantastic cook.'

'So what do you reckon, Isla, are you up for a family dinner night?' Reuben looked at her and she found herself nodding.

'It sounds great.' There was a note of wistfulness she just couldn't keep out of her voice. It had been so long since she'd had a family dinner, where all of the people she loved most were in the same room together, without the aid of FaceTime. Aidan was right, Jase had no idea how lucky he was.

'I'm looking forward to it already. I'll let Nan know; she'll be thrilled. I'll deliver the first fruit and veg box tomorrow, so don't let these two keep all the best stuff for themselves. They'll eat the strawberries and grapes straight out of the box like donkeys, and leave you with all the stuff that's supposedly hard to prepare.' Reuben grinned again, and gave a wave of his hand, disappearing towards the kitchen, before his uncles could even respond.

'We'd love to have you come to dinner, but don't feel pressurised by Rube. I think he's got his own agenda.' Jase exchanged a look with Aidan, and she decided not to even ask what they meant. She already knew that a child raised by Aidan and Jase would be surrounded with love, and meeting their extended family would just enable her to picture that more clearly. It had nothing to do with Reuben's slow smile, or wanting to hear that easy laugh of his again. She didn't do romance and, even if she had done, she'd have steered clear of Reuben. The only way to keep your heart safe was to keep it to yourself, and she had a horrible feeling he might find it all too easy to make her drop her guard. She wouldn't have taken the risk, even if there hadn't been the added complication of him being Aidan and Jase's nephew. He was off limits and, given how attracted she'd felt to him, it was probably just as well.

* * *

'If you suddenly discovered your dad wasn't your biological father, or there'd been a mix-up at the hospital and neither of your parents were genetically related to you, would you want to find your biological family?' It was a question Aidan had asked himself so many times since he and Jase had decided to become parents, but he still didn't know what the answer was, even as the woman seated across the table from him waited for a response. It was difficult to think about it from a general point of view when it was impossible for him to be objective, because the parents in question would be *his* parents.

Discovering that Sean and Anne weren't related to him might have been a relief. It would mean he didn't have to keep striving for their love and approval, or steadfastly avoiding a visit to their home just to discover he was no closer to the holy grail of being accepted for who he truly was. They could part ways, without the ties that bound, and all the platitudes about only having one mother and father and learning to cherish them whatever their faults. His dad wouldn't have to sit nursing a pint, and occasionally glancing up at his son, po-faced, hoping that his dress sense would suddenly have changed, and that he'd finally have learnt to be 'less obvious about all that gay stuff', as his father had urged him to be so many times before. They could walk away from one another without any need for a backward glance, and let go of all the expectations that he'd find a way to fit in eventually. It was only when he realised that Chooky was still staring at him, that he remembered he hadn't answered the question.

'It's a bit different for me than for most people.' Aidan looked down at his hands, and twisted his wedding ring around his finger, the way he always did when he was anxious about something. He hadn't minded any of the questions the clinic had asked him, but he'd dodged opening up too much about his relationship with his family. Now he had no choice, and he'd asked for this. Chooky, whose real name was Angela, was a good friend of Esther's partner, Joe. She'd just joined The Sycamore Centre to work alongside him, as a children's mental health specialist. They'd met when he'd been living out in Australia, where she'd apparently gained her nickname of Chooky, when she was still just a baby, because she'd had big eyes and a mop of hair that had made her look like a chicken. It was a name that had evidently stuck, and almost no one call her Angela. Aidan and Jase had first met her at a party, which Esther and Joe had hosted, and she'd felt like someone they could open up to from the start. So, when Aidan had discovered that she worked in children's mental health, he'd asked if she'd be willing to meet with him and Jase, on their own, to talk about how a child might feel, when they discovered they'd been born as the result of egg donation. Now he was trying to avoid answering her questions with complete honesty, but Chooky wasn't easily put off her stride.

'What do you mean it's different for you?'

'I don't have the greatest of relationships with my parents. So, I guess I would be interested in discovering if that might be different with someone else.' Aidan finally looked up at her. 'But I've got my father's eyes and my mother's nose, so I know there was no mix-up at the hospital. And, in a way, I guess that helps, because it proves that a genetic connection isn't always important. I feel much closer to Jase's family than I do to my own. If I'd grown up in a family like his, I really don't think I'd be interested in becoming part of another one, just because I discovered I had a genetic link with them. Maybe I'd be a bit curious, but there certainly wouldn't be any sort of gap I needed to fill.'

It was exactly what Isla had said about why she'd never wanted to register with one of those DNA testing sites. As far as she was concerned, Nick had been her father in every meaningful sense of the word, and no one else could fill the gap he'd left behind. It was obvious how much losing her father had hurt Isla, which made Aidan feel all the more awful for envying the relationship she'd had with her dad. But he couldn't help it. No one had ever loved him in the kind of unconditional way that Isla and Jase had experienced. But he didn't want to allow that to affect him any more, a child would be his opportunity to experience that same kind of unconditional love, and to make sure that their baby would never feel they had a gap to fill either.

Jase took hold of his hand. 'I think Aidan's right and that it wouldn't go beyond curiosity for me. My parents are the people who raised me and loved me, and that's what we want to replicate.'

'That's the single most important thing you can do to support a child's mental wellbeing.' Chooky had a gentle reassuring tone, and it was easy to imagine young patients finding her easy to talk to, as a result. 'Having at least one stable adult in their lives, who loves them and protects them, makes an unimaginable amount of difference. I've seen it in with the children I work with, who've been through a lot of trauma. If they've lost parents in a devastating way, but have a grandparent, or an aunt or uncle, who steps up to be there for them, the impact of that loss on their mental health is far less damaging. Other children can seem, on the surface, to have gone through something far less traumatic, but if they don't have that loving, stable adult around them, the impact can be catastrophic. It's a terrible cliché to say that all you need is love, but when it comes to children, it's a rule I wish the world would live by.'

'Do you think we should tell them, from the start, how they were born?' Aidan was fully aware that he was talking about a child that didn't even exist yet, but he was so determined to get this right that he wanted to have every step straight in his head before they even began.

'I'd say to be open and honest from the outset, in a way that's age appropriate for the child to understand.' Chooky picked up her phone. 'There are some great children's books on surrogacy and egg donation, and I can send you some links now if you like?'

'That would be great, thanks.' Aidan smiled. 'I probably sound over-prepared, but I just want things to be perfect.'

'I know you do, but they never are, not for anyone.' Chooky's voice was still just as gentle, but there was a firmness in her tone that left no room for argument. 'You need to let go of the idea that it can be, because that will mess you up and put pressure on your child too. I don't know how much counselling you've had as part of this process, but resolving the way you feel about the relationship with your own parents might be an important part of the process for you. I can't foresee any problems with the two of you showing a child the love they need, but you really need to be okay too.'

'I've been thinking for a while that it might be time we took a trip over to Ireland.' Jase squeezed Aidan's hand. 'We can tell them face to face about our plans to start a family, and hopefully that will give us all a chance to start this next phase of our lives in a good place.'

'You've got to have hope, haven't you?' Aidan painted on a smile, doing his best to give a casual shrug, but it felt as though someone had placed a slab of concrete on his chest. He knew exactly how his parents would react to the news, and the thought of looking at their faces when they did filled him with dread. But if it was a process they had to go through, in order to be ready to welcome a baby into their lives, then he was willing to face the pain he knew it would bring.

**11**

---

Jase had suggested waiting until the next half term to visit Aidan's parents, so that they could spend a few days in the small town where he'd grown up. But instead, Aidan had paid way over the odds for flights from Newquay to Knock, leaving on the Friday evening and arriving home in Cornwall on the Sunday. He'd also vetoed the idea of them staying in the family home, despite his mother's apparent delight at the prospect, and Jase reminding him that they were supposed to be saving as much money as possible for the IVF treatment. It might be a valid argument, but that didn't stop it feeling like the walls were closing in, whenever he pictured spending time in the house where he'd been born. He also knew his father would be far from delighted at the idea of Aidan staying there with his husband. *Homosexuality is an abomination.* Unbelievably they were words that had actually left his father's lips, and they weren't something Aidan would ever forget.

There were fewer than two thousand people in Ballaghaderreen, where Aidan had grown up, and it always felt as though his father knew every single one of them. It couldn't have been true, but Aidan still hadn't been able to do or say anything when he'd lived there without it getting back to Sean. Given that his father had rarely approved of whatever it was that Aidan had been saying or doing, it had made life in the small town feel claustrophobic at the best of times. Forty-eight hours back home would be more than enough.

By the time they'd driven to their guest house on the Friday night, both of them had been ready to crash out after a busy week at work. When Aidan had woken up just after eight the next morning, there'd been five missed calls from his mother and a voicemail telling him that a table was booked for lunch for the whole family at their favourite local pub. It was where Aidan and all his siblings had been taken when they'd passed their Leaving Certificates at the end of school. His mother had been so proud every time, but the grades Aidan had got had been the highest of all her children, and she'd told anyone who'd listen that it had given him the pick of universities to choose from as a result. She'd never wanted him to follow his dream of going to art school, so it must have been a great relief to her when he'd been rejected. Even his father had shaken his hand, and bought him a beer on the day he'd got his Leaving Certificate. It was one of only a handful of times that Aidan could remember his parents being proud of anything he'd done, and it hadn't happened again since then.

'It's lovely that they want to make a big thing of you coming home.' Jase pulled Aidan into his arms, after he'd relayed the message from his mother, and he wished he could feel even a frisson of excitement about a lunch with his family.

'Uh huh. She said they wanted to make up for the fact that not everyone got over for the wedding.' It was quite possibly the understatement of the year, given that his mother had been the only one there. But his three sisters had always been daddy's girls, and his brother was cut from exactly the same cloth as their father, they even worked together: *Kennedy and Son*. Every time Aidan saw one of their signs around Roscommon, or looked at the van parked on the driveway, it was like the words were taunting him. The slogan might be factually correct when it came to the business, but son in the singular was probably how Sean viewed his whole life, because Aidan had never lived up to any of his hopes in that respect.

'That's really nice.' Jase was beaming at the prospect of a family lunch, but then he'd never really understand. There was no way he could, when all he'd ever had was unconditional love and support. 'What time do we need to be there?'

'Not until twelve.'

'Are we going to see your family beforehand, or just meet there?' Jase was still brimming with enthusiasm, but if he was ever going to have a hope of understanding how hard it was for Aidan to come back here, or to stop believing in the fairy tale that his family would truly accept them, there was something he needed to see.

'There's something I want to show you before we go for lunch. It's a little church in a village about ten miles from here.' Aidan fought to keep his tone level, as his head filled with images from a past he'd tried so desperately to leave behind. He should have told Jase about this years ago, but he hadn't been ready then.

'If you've arranged for a vow renewal, I'm going to need to upgrade my outfit.' Jase circled his arms around Aidan's waist, and all he could do was shake his head. They weren't going to the church as a place of celebration, they were going to mourn the loss of someone who should have been there for every major milestone in Aidan's life, but who hadn't even made it to his twenty-first birthday party.

\* \* \*

Every time Aidan had been back to visit the church where his best friend had been laid to rest, the sun was shining. In some ways it felt right, because Cian had a smile that could light up any room. Even the teachers couldn't be angry with him, when he was getting into trouble for playing the class clown, the way he'd seemed to do most days. Yet it seemed wrong, too, for Aidan to feel the warmth of the sun on his back, when Cian had been lying beneath the cold, wet ground for almost twenty years.

They should never have become best friends. Aidan was serious and studious back when they'd first met, at the age of twelve. Cian was far more flamboyant, and he'd spend hours on art projects and designing his own clothes in his spare time, but was never more than a comedian during school hours. Aidan's father had said on more than one occasion after Cian's death, that the two boys had only ever been friends because of their 'inclinations'. He'd also insisted, from the time they'd first met, that Cian was a bad influence on his son and had tried to stop them spending time together. It was an odd thing to do given that Cian's father was a close friend of Sean's, and neither statement could have been further from the truth. What the two boys had shared had been a deep friendship, that had never crossed the line into anything that might have spoilt it, despite Aidan questioning whether they were the only gay teenagers in the whole of Roscommon. At times it had certainly felt like it. Cian was the best influence Aidan could possibly have had, and he'd encouraged him to be honest about his sexuality, not just with others, but more importantly with himself.

Cian had never hidden who he was and had been the most authentic person Aidan had ever known, and he'd worn his heart on his sleeve. Yet he'd been hiding a secret of his own, a battle with depression that had been exacerbated by the rejection he'd experienced from some of his closest family. Cian had kept the pain of that to himself, and for years after his suicide, Aidan had blamed himself for his best friend's death, for leaving to try and have a new start in England, and for not seeing the signs of just how unhappy Cian was. It had taken the journey from the guest-house to the church, and two laps of the graveyard, for Aidan to tell Jase the full story of his friendship with Cian, whose parents had kicked him out, when they'd discovered he had a boyfriend at his university in Dublin.

Cian hadn't seen them in the two years after that, which had led up to his death. That hadn't stopped them playing the role of broken-hearted parents at his funeral, and Aidan had wanted to stand up in the church and scream that everything that John and Eileen were doing was just an act. Those people had turned their backs on their son, and it had killed him every bit as much as if they'd been the ones to administer the overdose he'd taken. They should have loved him unconditionally, exactly the way Chooky had said every child deserved to be loved. But they hadn't, and the truth was Aidan was almost certain he'd never had that kind of love either. Being gay shouldn't have been a reason for his or Cian's parents to withhold love from their children, but they had, and it had cost Cian his life. It had also made Aidan feel less at home in the place he'd been born than he did anywhere else on earth. He hadn't had things nearly as bad as Cian, because his mother had at least tried to accept his sexuality, while his father pretended his coming out hadn't happened at all. But there'd been no safe space for him to return to; nowhere he felt he could go when life was at its toughest. And that was something else he was desperate to provide for his own child.

'Oh sweetheart that must have been so hard.' Jase put his arms around him, and Aidan breathed out. This was home now –

it wasn't a place, it was a person – and he could get through whatever the weekend back home brought, as long as he had his husband by his side.

'I'm sorry I never told you any of this before. I try not to think about it too much, because it breaks my heart that I didn't know Cian needed help. But I wanted you to understand why I find it so hard to be around my father.' Aidan blinked away the tears that had filled his eyes, despite his best efforts to hold them back. 'He saw what happened when Cian's parents rejected him, and yet he still barely more than tolerates me. If Cian's death wasn't enough to make him realise that none of the things he thinks are important really matter, then nothing ever will be, not even our baby. And that kills me too.'

'However your parents react, this baby is going to be the luckiest kid in the world, because it's going to have you as its dad.' Jase held his gaze and Aidan knew his husband meant every single word.

'I love you so much.'

'I love you too.' Jase rested his forehead against Aidan's, and for a moment they stood in the churchyard, in the shadow of the building where Cian's far-too-short life had been remembered, without any mention of the person he'd really been. But Aidan wasn't going to let his best friend be forgotten, and he was more determined than ever to live his life every bit as authentically as Cian had. If that wasn't something his parents could live with, that would be their choice, but there was no room in Aidan's life for compromise when it came to them accepting he and Jase would be starting a family of their own. If it came to a choice, Jase and the baby would win every single time.

\* \* \*

The lunch had gone better than Aidan had expected. It had been noisy, his siblings and their families laughing and bickering, and treating not just him, but Jase, like a part of the family, giving every indication that they'd missed seeing the two of them. His sister May had apologised again for missing the wedding, telling him how hard it was to organise a trip like that, with three under-fives, especially when money was tight, but had said how much she wished she'd been there. His other siblings had echoed her sentiment, and it was easy to believe they meant what they said. It had been on the tip of his tongue to say he might soon have a far better understanding of what life with a young child was like, but he'd decided to wait until the lunch was over. His nieces and nephews were all having so much fun, and he hadn't spent nearly as much time with them over the years as he should have done, so the last thing he wanted to do was to spoil the meal and create a drama in front of the children, if his father reacted badly to the news. Sean had worn an enigmatic expression throughout the lunch, like someone who'd been asked to smile for a photo, but who couldn't quite persuade his face to comply.

'This has been such a lovely day, darlin', hasn't it?' Aidan's mother leant into him as she spoke, the two of them watching Jase showing some of the children how to play noughts and crosses, with the aid of a grid he'd drawn on a serviette.

'It has, Mammy.' He hadn't imagined there'd be a time during the lunch when he'd want to freeze a moment to preserve forever. But seeing how brilliant Jase was with his nieces and nephews, and sitting so close to his mother that even their breathing was in synch, he felt as if it really could be a new start for them all. But it wouldn't happen unless he was honest, and he knew how they really felt about their plans to become parents. 'Jase is great with the kids, isn't he?'

'He really is. You're both of you made for a big family and I couldn't be happier that you're here.' Aidan's mother clutched his arm, and even though his father had wandered off somewhere, it was now or never.

'Actually, we're trying to have a baby of our own. A friend is going to donate her eggs and we're being matched with a surrogate.' He couldn't take his eyes off his mother's face as he watched her processing the information. He didn't know what he was expecting her reaction to be, but he knew what he wanted: an expression of delight that she'd be getting another grandchild. It might be too much to ask, but he was watching her face so intently his eyes stung and the silence hanging in the air between them seemed to last forever.

'Well, I can't say I'm not happy for you. The pair of you'll be grand.' His mother was still clutching his arm. But he didn't miss the way her eyes had darted to one side. She was looking for his father, both of them knowing what Sean's reaction was likely to be. He couldn't hold that against her, though, and she was saying the right things. Expecting a Hallmark moment was only asking to be hurt, and all he could do was take what she'd said at face value. His mother was trying, even if her thoughts were at least partly occupied by what her husband's reaction was going to be. 'Have you decided which one of you is gonna be the father?'

'We both are.' He'd anticipated the question, certain that his response would have a big impact on the way his mother took the news, and he held her gaze until she nodded, making him catch his breath. He'd felt sure she'd push to know about genetics, but if it bothered her as much as he'd thought it would, she was doing a good job of hiding it. All the adrenaline that had built up, as he'd waited to tell her, flooded out of his body, washing over him in a wave of relief. But his mother had always been the more accepting, and he wished he didn't have to ask her what he was about to. 'What do you think Da will make of it?'

'He's an eejit if he can't see what good parents you'll make.' She was smiling, but there was a hint of something else in her eyes that looked a lot like fear. Aidan knew only too well just how capable his father could be of ignoring the obvious, if it didn't suit his agenda, and his mother knew it too. 'You can ask him yourself when he comes back; he's just at the bar.'

'I will, I'll be back in a minute.' Excusing himself, Aidan hoped his mother would make the assumption that he needed the loo. That way she wouldn't try to stop him leaving. The truth was, he wanted to speak to his father outside the confines of the function room at the back of the pub, which his mother had reserved for their family lunch. When he told Sean about his plans to start a family, he didn't want it to be under his mother's watchful eye. No doubt she'd warned her husband not to do or say anything that might upset Aidan, but he wanted honesty more than anything else. If his father couldn't be happy for him and Jase, Aidan would rather know the truth.

'Do you want one?' Sean gestured to a half-drunk pint in front of him, as Aidan joined him at the bar.

'No, thanks. Are you coming back in?' It was blatantly obvious his father was more comfortable out in the bar than back in the function room, and that should have told Aidan all he needed to know.

'I said I'd have a drink with Jimmy. He'll be back in a minute.' Even as his father spoke, his best friend of more than fifty years, Jimmy Doyle, opened the door of the gents' toilets and crossed the bar towards them.

'Well there, and aren't you a sight for sore eyes?' Jimmy gave Aidan a rough hug, thumping him on the back in what probably passed for a show of affection in his world. 'And to what do we owe the honour of your visit home?'

'I thought it was about time Jase and I came over.' Aidan smiled, but it melted away as his father's face clouded over.

'Jase?' Jimmy raised a questioning eyebrow, and it was clear his father's best friend had no idea who Aidan's husband was.

'He's Aidan's housemate, and he's not had a chance to see much of Ireland before. So he wanted to come over, isn't that right, son?' His father was giving him a beseeching look, but Aidan had promised he'd be authentic. He'd sworn it to himself and to Cian in the churchyard just hours before.

'No, it's not right.' He turned towards Jimmy, ignoring the fact that his father's mouth was opening and closing like a fish out of water. 'Jase is my husband of over two years, but we've been together for more than ten. We came over here to tell the family that we're trying for a baby, with the aid of a surrogate and an egg donor. But since my father clearly can't even face up to telling anyone that his son married another man, even though Jase has given me the kind of happiness I never thought I'd have, I think this visit is over.'

Tears were burning at the back of Aidan's eyes, but he wasn't going to give a bully like Sean Kennedy the satisfaction of making him cry. He'd done it so many times in the past, and breaking down now would just play into all the stereotypes someone like his father pedalled. He'd called Aidan a nancy almost as often as he'd used his name in the last year he'd lived at home. And a man expressing difficult emotions, whatever their sexuality, had always been something his father had ridiculed. Instead, as the pain and anger that Aidan had tried so hard to bury welled up inside him, he clenched his jaw, determined not to allow either emotion to overwhelm him. Not even stopping to listen to what Jimmy was saying in response, he turned on his heel and headed back to the function room.

'What's wrong?' His mother held out a hand as he stalked

past her, but he couldn't bring himself to reach out to her. A part of him felt guilty that he was leaving, when she'd clearly relished every moment she'd spent with him, but she'd choose his father every time. Just like he'd pick Jase. 'Da just told Jimmy that Jase was my housemate. It's enough that I've put my husband through hiding in the shadows for more than a decade when it comes to my family, but there's no way I'm doing that to our child. You can come and see us whenever you want, Mammy, but I swear to God this is the last time I'll ever come back here.'

'Aidan, don't, please.' His mother was already crying, but he shook his head.

'Don't let the kids see.' He held her gaze again, until she finally nodded, and he walked towards where the rest of the family were now engaged in a noisy game of twenty questions, confident that none of them had overheard what he'd said to his mother. 'I'm really sorry, it's been grand to see you all, but something's come up – an emergency at the hospital has left them really short-staffed – and we're going to have to go.'

'You can't leave already.' His eldest sister, Siobhan, looked close to tears, and it was hard not to follow suit.

'I'll give you a call, and we'd love to see you all whenever you can make it over, wouldn't we?' Aidan turned towards Jase, who was looking shell-shocked, but who hadn't questioned the announcement that they needed to leave. He'd know the reasons Aidan had given were utter nonsense, but he was clearly prepared to go with it, if that was what his husband wanted. Jase had his back, 100 per cent of the time. And, if it was possible, Aidan loved him even more in that moment than he ever had before.

There was a round of heartfelt goodbyes with his siblings and their children, and promises of visits from all of them. His mother's body was rigid when they embraced, and he knew that holding in her emotions was every bit as hard for her as it was for him.

'I'll see you both soon.' It was only when she said those words, that the tears finally began spilling out of her eyes, but she wiped them away vigorously with the aid of her napkin.

'You're welcome any time, for however long you want to stay, don't forget.' He hugged her one more time and then headed for the door, knowing that he'd allow himself to cry only after he'd told Jase exactly what had happened. He had his safe space, and his home, in the man he'd built his life with. He just wished he could be certain that his mother had the same thing.

## 12

It was almost 5 p.m. in Cornwall, but only lunchtime in Florida, and Isla had been expecting to see her mother's smiling face when the FaceTime call connected. But it was Lexi who answered, looking red-faced and clammy, and she was clearly out of breath as she uttered an unusual greeting.

'God, what a morning!'

'Are you okay, Lex? It's not the babies, is it?' The anxiety that plagued Isla when it came to the prospect of any of her family being ill, was already clawing at her throat.

'No, but Mum tripped coming down the stairs and she's badly broken her ankle. She's going to be fine, but she's in surgery now.'

'Oh my God! What have the doctors said? Are you sure she's going to be okay?' Isla's heart was thudding in her ears, and she suddenly felt a million miles away from where she needed to be.

'They said once they've aligned the break, it should all be straightforward and she should be in and out of surgery within an hour. I was just heading to Walmart to get some ice chips and some other bits for when she comes round. But it's so hot today, and lugging these two around with me is really starting to get old.' Lexi was weaving her way between cars in a huge car park, as she spoke.

'Oh Lex, I should be the one doing that; you've got so much on your plate already.' Relief had flooded through Isla's veins at the news that her mum's accident didn't sound serious, but guilt was stabbing at her all the same. Lexi had texted her a couple of days before to say that Josh had gone to Denver for work and that she was paranoid the babies would come while he was away, even though she still had over two months to go until her due date, but that at least she'd have their mum there if the worst happened. 'I could get a flight out tomorrow, if I can clear it with work.'

'No way!' Lexi fixed her with the big sister look she'd perfected over years of Isla asking to borrow her stuff and often being turned down flat. Lexi had almost always relented in the end, but she knew how to give a firm no when she wanted to. 'I need you to be able to come out when the babies are here, like we planned, not before. You'll never be able to come over for three weeks then, if you take time off now too. Even if you could afford two lots of flights. And besides, aren't you about to start the cycle for your egg collection?'

'I'm just waiting for the call from the clinic, once the results of the screening tests have been confirmed as all clear. Then we can get started with the medication.' Ten minutes ago, it had seemed like the most important thing in the world for Isla to get the go-ahead to help Aidan and Jase, but now the pull to be there for her own family was almost overwhelming. 'But another month or two won't be the end of the world; they haven't even been matched with a surrogate yet, so any embryos we manage to make would have to be frozen anyway.'

'I said no.' This time Lexi clearly had no intention of backing down, and Isla couldn't help noticing the definite shift in the accent her sister had developed since moving to Florida. She sounded more American than British now, and the thought made the distance between them feel all the greater, as it so often did lately. Lexi hadn't switched to calling their mother Mom, just yet though. 'Mum feels guilty enough about this happening when she wanted to be able to help prepare everything for the twins, but she'll be devastated if you put the egg donation on hold because of it.'

'I didn't think she was that keen on the idea.'

'She just worries; you know Mum. Ever since Dad died, she's wanted to protect us from anything bad happening, but she's really proud of you.' Lexi furrowed her brow. 'A couple of days after you told us what you were planning, I found her crying. When I asked her why, she said it was because she knew how thrilled Dad would have been that you were doing this for someone else, because a donor like you had made all their dreams come true. It's an amazing thing you're doing, and if you dare let Mum's ankle get in the way of that, it'll break her heart. And I need you to make sure Nan and Grandpa Bill get over here after the twins are born. I want all my family together to celebrate. So you promise, right now, that you'll stay put. Don't make me break out the Lexi flick.'

Isla laughed at the look on her sister's face and the mention of Lexi's signature move, which she'd deployed whenever her little sister had annoyed her just a bit too much. She'd flick the side of Isla's forehead, in what she'd claimed was an attempt to wake up her brain, because she clearly wasn't thinking straight. It must have been more than a decade since Lexi had retired that move, and the two sisters had got even closer since their father's death, but Isla still wasn't going to risk it. 'I promise I won't come over, unless anything changes. Will you call me as soon as Mum is out of surgery? And promise to let me know if you decide you do need me after all.'

'I promise. But right now, I need to get into my air-conditioned car, and drive to Walmart to stand in the refrigerated section until I don't feel as if I'm being cooked from the inside out.' Lexi sighed, as she finally reached her car. 'I love you and I really am desperate to see you, but if you turn up here before you've donated those eggs, there'll be hell to pay.'

'Yes, ma'am.' Isla grinned. 'I love you too, and that nephew and niece of mine. So make sure you take good care of all three of you, and let me know if you need anything.'

'I will, I promise, and I'll call you again as soon as Mum's awake.' Lexi blew her a kiss and ended the FaceTime call. She trusted what her sister had said about their mother being okay, and that she was coping for now too. But that wasn't going to stop Isla letting work know what was going on, and making sure she'd be able to take some emergency leave if anything changed. She knew Aidan and Jase would understand if she had to do that, but for now she'd keep her promise to Lexi and assume things would be going ahead as planned. She was just about to text Esther, when her phone started ringing again. Her heart racing, she looked at the number, terrified it might be Lexi again with unexpected bad news, but it was the fertility clinic.

'Hello.'

'Is that Isla?'

'Speaking.'

'Hi, it's Sandy from the Forever Family clinic, I'm ringing about the results of your screening tests.' There was a note of something that sounded like hesitation in Sandy's voice, and Isla shivered, despite the sunlight streaming through the window behind her.

'Are we all good to get started with the treatment?' Isla was vaguely aware that by saying the words out loud, she was willing them to somehow be true, but Sandy was already sighing.

'I'm afraid not. One of the blood tests has indicated something that needs further investigation and it's really important that you see your doctor as soon as possible, so that further tests can be arranged.'

'Tests for what?' Goose pimples were prickling on Isla's arms. Her own health had never been something she thought about much, because she spent so much time worrying about the rest of her family. But Sandy's response wasn't the most reassuring.

'The screening tests have shown up an abnormality with the white cells and platelets in your blood.'

'Leukaemia?' Isla almost dropped the phone. It couldn't be true, she felt fine. Maybe a little bit tired, but in her job that was to be expected. And, yes, she'd lost some weight, but that could be explained from rushing around all day too.

'Not necessarily, but it's one of the things that will need investigating. You gave the clinic consent to contact your GP when you underwent the tests, and we've already been in touch with your surgery. My understanding is they'll be calling you about a referral to the hospital for further tests and to meet with a haematologist.' Sandy's voice sounded falsely bright, as she carried on. 'I'm so sorry Isla, and I know this must be really worrying, but try to keep in mind that there could be a lot of potential explanations. Have you got someone there you can talk to, or someone you can be with? It will really help if you have some support while you wait for the next set of results.'

'I'm going over to my grandparents' for dinner, so I can talk to them.' As the words came out of her mouth, Isla crossed the fingers on her left hand. She wasn't going to tell her grandparents about this. She wasn't going to tell anyone until she knew what it was they were dealing with.

'That's good, but, if you need to, you can always access the counselling service here too. I really hope the further tests show that the initial results are nothing serious.' Sandy might be hopeful, but she sounded anything but convinced, and Isla suddenly realised she was shaking.

'Thank you.' It was all she could manage before she ended the call and, as she turned to put down her phone, she caught sight of herself in the mirror above the mantelpiece. She didn't look any different than she had a few moments before, and it was still almost impossible to believe that something could be happening inside of her that had the potential to be life-threatening. Almost, but not quite. And even the tiny possibility made Isla go cold.

Aidan had been wanting to have the first beach barbecue of the summer almost since Easter, but he'd finally persuaded Jase that tonight was the night. He'd been on an early shift, and Jase had managed to finish work on time for once. So they were down at the Taylor family beach hut, at the north end of Port Kara beach, just after half past five. The beach hut had been in Jase's family for over forty years, and he'd recounted numerous tales of the fun he'd had with Tash, and their friends, when they'd been growing up. It was just one more Taylor tradition that Aidan couldn't wait to follow when he and Jase finally had a child of their own. He'd been driving himself mad over the last couple of weeks, jumping every time the phone rang, in the hope that the clinic had found them a potential surrogate, so going down to the beach and just enjoying some time with his husband, was a desperately needed break from it all.

It had been a tough time since the trip to Ireland. Jase had been stunned by their sudden departure, but he hadn't questioned it when Aidan had insisted they needed to leave straight away. Later on, they'd talked about what had happened, and Jase had held him, when he'd eventually cried the tears he'd been determined not to shed in front of his father. His mother and sisters had all been in touch, begging him to come back for another visit soon, and promising him it would be different next time. He'd told them again that they were welcome to come to Port Kara, but he wouldn't be going 'home' any more. It had been years since Ballaghaderreen had felt that way. The revelation that had hit him, that home was wherever Jase was, hadn't changed. And Aidan now had the kind of unconditional support and love his husband had been lucky enough to grow up with. He'd never find that in a place where Sean Kennedy's opinions seemed to overshadow everything else. He'd never allow their child to be exposed to that either. And if the rest of his family wanted a relationship with Aidan, it had to be on his terms.

'Do you think four sausages each is too much?' Aidan turned to look at Jase, who was taking a bottle of wine out of the cool box.

'Given that we're having king prawns and chicken too, I'd have to say probably.'

'Yeah, but all this talk of trying for a baby seems to have convinced my body that I need to eat for two!'

'I thought we'd agreed not to mention the B word tonight.'

'We did, but—' Aidan's response was cut off as his phone started to ring and, when he looked at the display, he realised it was the call they'd been waiting for. 'Oh my God, it's Forever Family.'

'Don't build your hopes up, until you know what it's about.' Jase reached out and touched Aidan's arm, but it was obvious from the look on his face that he was excited about what this might mean too. Either way, Aidan couldn't wait another second to find out.

'Hello, Aidan Kennedy speaking.'

'Oh, hi Aidan, it's Fraser, one of the matching coordinators from the clinic. I work with Annabel, who you spoke with before.'

'Hi Fraser, how are you?' He was itching to just blurt out: *have you found someone?* But he was trying to follow Jase's advice and keep some of the hope damped down, so that it didn't crush him if it wasn't the news they'd been praying for.

'I'm fine, thank you, and I hope you guys are going to be even better than that, when I tell you I think we've found you a match.'

After that, most of what Fraser said was a blur and thank God he'd told Aidan that he'd follow everything up in an email, with guidance on how to proceed in setting up a meeting with their potential surrogate, whose name was Ellen. As soon as the call was over, he and Jase were both whooping and hugging, and neither of them had been able to hold back the tears.

'I can't believe it's true, can you?' Aidan was shaking his head as he spoke, and Jase was laughing and crying at the same time.

'No, I can't. I think I spent so long trying not to get too excited and convincing myself that it could take ages if it ever did happen, that I almost stopped believing it would.'

'Me too.' Aidan suddenly stopped and put a hand on the side of his husband's face. 'But you would tell me if you had any doubts, wouldn't you? It's not too late to stop this, if it isn't 100 per cent what you want.'

'I've never wanted anything more, apart from marrying you.' Jase put his hand over Aidan's. 'What about you?'

'I can't wait to see what you'll be like as a dad.' The smile that had spread over his face felt as though it reached right down inside him. 'And to have a mini you running around the place.'

'I've been thinking about that, and which one of us should donate the sperm.'

'We agreed. It's got to be you.' Aidan swallowed hard. 'If the trip to my family didn't prove that a genetic connection is no guarantee of a close relationship, then I don't know what does. I'll love this baby like it's my own, because it will be, and I'll love it even more because it's a part of you.'

'That's exactly how I feel, though, and we've already got Reuben, who I've got a feeling is going to be no slouch when it comes to passing on the Taylor genes. The baby is going to be loved so much by my family, and there'll be a link there that nothing can break. I know what it's like to have that kind of bond to people you share a biological connection with, and I want you to have that experience too. Not to mention that the idea of us having a kid that's even a tiny bit like you fills my heart up. That's why it's got to be you.' Jase held Aidan's gaze for a moment and then smiled. 'At least with the first baby, we'll talk about the second one, when the times comes.'

'Are you sure?' Aidan was blinking back tears again, as Jase nodded, pulling him into his arms. He'd have been fully on board with Jase being the biological father, but in that moment he realised his husband might be right; maybe this was some-thing he needed to experience to come full circle with his past. And one thing it proved for certain, was that his husband loved him more than he'd dared to believe anyone ever would.

'I'm 100 per cent sure, and I'm just as certain that everything's going to work out okay. I know we haven't even met the surrogate yet, but it's my turn to have the feeling that nothing is going to stand in our way.' Jase sounded so confident that Aidan couldn't envisage any other outcome either. There'd been times along the way when he'd had to fake it until they made it, with his belief that it would happen. He'd wanted Jase to see his confidence, and for that to give them both the hope they needed. But finding a woman who wanted to be their surrogate had been a huge hurdle he hadn't ever really been sure they'd overcome. Surely nothing could stop them now.

# 13

Isla had done all she could to try and follow Sandy's advice and not panic too much about the results of her screening, but she had enough medical knowledge to know what the implications could be. The prospect of cancer was terrifying, but what worried her even more was the thought of having to break the news to her mother, not to mention the rest of her family. She'd witnessed her mum being pushed to the limit when her father was dying, almost killing her too. She'd said afterwards that she wasn't sure how she'd survived it and, if anyone ever asked whether she might ever want another relationship, she was always resolute in her response that she wasn't prepared to risk the heartbreak again. It was a sentiment that had rubbed off on Isla, and she couldn't bear the thought of putting her mother through so much pain, when she had sacrificed the chance to fall in love again, in order to protect herself.

'I know you're worried about your mum, my love, but I wish you'd eat a bit more of your dinner.' Her grandmother put an arm on Isla's shoulder as she moved to stand behind her. 'She's going to be okay you know. Lexi said in her text that the operation went fine, and she'll call as soon as your mum is back in the land of the living.'

'I know, I just wish I was there.' Isla managed a half smile, as she turned to look at Joy. She was concerned about her mother, but that wasn't the reason she'd been pushing the food around her plate for the last half an hour. Although it suited her to let her grandmother believe it was. At least for now.

It had taken all her resolve, when she'd first walked into the house and had been folded into Grandpa Bill's arms, before being on the receiving end of one of her grandmother's warm hugs, not to tell them everything. Tears had filled her eyes when Joy had remarked, as she almost always did, that Isla looked like she could do with a long rest and a good meal. Normally Isla would have brushed it off, knowing it was just another way in which her grandmother showed how much she cared, but the truth was she had been feeling more tired than usual, and she had lost weight without trying to. Both of those things had been down to her job, or so she'd thought, but suddenly there was a far more sinister alternative whispering its name in every quiet moment.

'We'll all be going over there to visit before you know it, after those babies arrive. I just can't wait!' Bill was smiling from ear to ear at the prospect, and he held a hand out to his wife, pulling her towards him. 'When we lost Nicky, I was worried we'd never get this kind of happiness again, but having great-grandchildren is going to be incredible.'

'One of each, too.' Joy let go of a long breath, a look of contentment spreading across her face. 'I love having granddaughters more than you girls will ever know, but holding a little boy in my arms again is going to be so special.'

'The babies will be really lucky to have you in their lives, just like me and Lexi have been.' Isla blinked back the tears that were stinging her eyes again. Any thought she'd had of telling her grandparents about the results of the screening was buried for good now. There was nothing to tell yet anyway and even if there had been, she wouldn't burden them with it unless it got to a point where she couldn't hide it. Just like her mother, they'd been through far too much heartbreak already. So, whatever the next round of tests revealed, she'd just have to try and be strong enough to deal with it by herself.

'Aargh!' Isla dropped her handbag on the steps outside her flat and clutched her chest, as the figure who'd been lurking in the shadows lurched into view. 'Bloody hell, Reuben, you scared the life out of me.'

'I'm really sorry, are you okay?' He scrambled to pick her bag up, a genuine look of remorse on his face. 'I thought you were out.'

'I was, but now I'm back. Obviously.' Isla knew she was being curt, but she was in no mood for small talk. She and Reuben had been chatting on a WhatsApp group that Aidan had set up, which he'd titled *Encouraging healthy eating for the chicken nugget kings.* It had been a joke after Reuben's claims that his uncles barely bothered with anything more adventurous than frozen food when they were left to their own devices. Aidan's first message in the group had been a plea for easy recipes that took less time to prepare than it took Just Eat to deliver. The chat had soon ventured off topic and the four of them had exchanged messages about a wide range of topics. Aidan and Jase would tease their nephew, and Reuben would respond in kind. It had been a lovely window into their relationship and had offered Isla even more reassurance about the wonderful family Aidan and Jase's child would be born into. Sometimes she'd make a joke too, or send a meme that summed up the direction the chat was going in.

When she's been quieter on the group for a bit longer than usual, because work had been hectic, Reuben had messaged her separately to check she was okay and that nothing any of them had been joking about had upset her. She'd reassured him that it hadn't, and they'd carried on exchanging messages both inside and outside the group. She'd found herself checking her phone far more often than normal, and always hoping that there'd be a message from Reuben. It was strange how much easier it was to open up to someone when you weren't face to face with them, and how a virtual stranger could so quickly come to feel like a trusted friend as a result. There was only one thing she couldn't be honest about, but the results of her screening were something she hadn't told anyone else about either. None of the closeness they'd built up made it any less terrifying to find someone creeping around in the shadows outside her house. She suddenly felt embarrassed, too, at just how candid she'd been with Reuben about her feelings, and it was making her lash out at him in a way she knew was unreasonable, but that she couldn't control. 'The fact that you were lurking around here in the dark, because you thought I was out, makes it sound even more dodgy. Why are you here?'

She'd left her grandparents' place twenty minutes after they'd finally had a video call from Lexi, and a very woozy Clare. Isla had been relieved to see her mother smiling, despite the events of the day, and her grandparents had wanted her to stay over, so that she could have a drink to celebrate the good news. But she wasn't in the mood for celebrations, so she'd blamed an early shift the next morning for leaving just after 9 p.m. The last thing she'd expected was to find Reuben standing outside the entrance to her flat, which had its own front door, where the side entrance to the chapel had originally been. She couldn't think what possible reason there could be for him being there, but then he gestured towards the bottom of the door.

'I brought you these. Aidan gave me your address when I told him I wanted to drop them off.'

'Flowers? What an earth for?' If Reuben was labouring under the illusion that she was interested in him, *like that,* then she was more than happy to put him straight. She'd always known that love would have to find her, if she was ever going to experience it. Actively seeking it out would mean deliberately taking the risk of getting hurt, and admitting her attraction to Reuben would have been doing just that. So she wouldn't have given him any indication that she liked him, even if she hadn't had a terrifying call from the clinic.

'I've started stocking some flowers from a wholesaler in Camborne, and I had a couple of bunches left over when I closed the shop. So I thought I'd drop them off with a fruit and veg box, in case my uncles aren't sharing all the good stuff with you the way they should be.' Reuben was smiling and he had such an easy manner that made it much harder to maintain a barrier between them now they were face to face, and for a moment she had an almost overpowering urge to tell him about the phone call from the clinic. She had to get rid of Reuben before she made a stupid mistake and opened up to him even more than she had already.

'Thank you.' The words might have been appropriate, but her tone wasn't. She couldn't afford to let her guard down or it was all going to come tumbling out. Telling Reuben could wreck all of Aidan and Jase's plans, and she didn't want to make them worry unnecessarily when she didn't even have any of the facts yet. She was already worrying enough for all of them.

'Are you okay?' Reuben narrowed his eyes as he looked at her, and she bit her lip, trying to steady her voice before she answered.

'I'm fine.' Her voice broke on the second word.

'No, you're not.' Reuben's tone was gentle. 'And you can tell me to sod off and mind my own business, if you like, but I don't think I can walk away and leave you like this. If you don't want to talk to me, is there someone I can call for you?'

'Have you got time to come in?' The words were out of Isla's mouth before she even realised how much she wanted him to say yes. Maybe it was because it seemed easier to talk to someone she barely knew outside the messages they'd exchanged, and who might be able to see the implications of the call from the clinic more objectively than the people who loved her most. But, whatever the reason, she couldn't deny the urge to confide in Reuben, despite her fears about where that might lead.

'I've got as much time as you need.'

Ten minutes later, Isla had made them both a coffee, opened two different types of biscuits, but she still hadn't told him about the call from the clinic.

'As much as I like a chocolate HobNob, and Fox's Crunch Creams, I feel like I should ask you again if you want to talk about what's bothering you, because something clearly is. You haven't stood still from the moment we got in.' Reuben had such an open face, his green eyes filling with concern when he looked at her, that it would have been impossible for her to lie to him, even if she was capable of it. And he was right, she hadn't been able to stand still, because her physical movements seemed intent on mirroring the whirring of her brain. She might as well just tell him.

'I had a call from the clinic today, about the results of my screening tests. They're worried about something that's shown up in my blood. I've been referred for more tests, but if I had to guess, I'd say they strongly suspect it's leukaemia.' The word felt so alien as she said it out loud, as if she was trying to pronounce something she'd never heard of before. Her teeth were chattering and, as she reached for her coffee, her hands were shaking too, fear making itself plain. The shock on Reuben's face was just as obvious.

'I'm so sorry, Isla. I can't even imagine what it was like to get a call like that. What have your family said?'

'Nothing, because I haven't told them.' If it was possible, he looked even more shocked at that revelation. No one would understand unless they'd been through the things her family had experienced, but Reuben clearly wanted to try.

'Why not?'

'Because they'll worry themselves to death about it, after what happened to my dad, and I don't want them to have to deal with it, unless they really have to.'

'Aidan told me about your dad and I'm really sorry about what happened to him, but I'm almost certain your family would want to know, so they can support you with this.'

'They would, but this is my choice.' For the first time, something stronger than fear was firing inside of Isla and her tone was sharp. If Reuben even thought about finding a way to go behind her back and speak to her family, she wouldn't be the only one facing a terrifyingly uncertain future.

'Okay, but you need to let someone be there for you, and I know my uncles will want to support you.' Reuben curled his fingers around hers, and the strangest thing about it was that it wasn't uncomfortable, or odd, it felt right. 'And I'd like to be there for you too, in any way I can. I'm hoping to God that it's nothing to worry about, but if you need anything, I want you to know I'm here.'

She'd barely registered what he was offering to do for someone he hardly knew, because her mind was whirring again. All she could think about was how devasted Aidan and Jase would be if all the plans they'd made to start a family came crashing down. She couldn't do that to them, she wouldn't, and she had to make Reuben understand why. 'I can't tell Aidan and Jase either. Not when all their hopes for a baby are resting on me being able to donate my eggs.'

'They'll never forgive themselves, or me, if you go through the next round of tests without their support, and I don't think I could live with that either.' Reuben still had hold of her hand and he seemed every bit as determined to make his point. 'Like I said before, when you agreed to donate your eggs, you became a part of this family. Like it or not.'

'You're not going to give me any choice, are you?' Isla knew what Reuben's response was going to be, even before he shook his head. She could have carried on fighting it, and trying to convince him that telling his uncles was a mistake, but she didn't have the energy. More than that, deep down, a part of her had to admit she must have wanted this, or she'd never have changed her mind about telling him. As much as she hated the thought of burdening Aidan and Jase, relief was flooding her body too, because she was no longer carrying this weight completely on her own. There was still a chance that there was nothing to worry about, but Isla knew too much to pin her hopes on being given the all-clear. If she had to sit in a room and hear the words confirming she had leukaemia, she wasn't sure she could face that on her own.

'Okay then.' Her words were barely audible, but she knew Reuben had heard her because he was squeezing her hand. A few hours before she wouldn't have been able to imagine this scenario in her wildest dreams, but the call from the clinic had sent her whole world spinning off its axis. And suddenly Reuben felt like the only solid thing she had left to cling on to.

# 14

When Reuben had called Aidan to say he was at Isla's flat, and that she'd had some bad news, he'd been certain it was going to be about her mother or sister. Isla had opened up about how much she missed them, and how her father's health had made her fear losing another member of her family. Most people were able to push those kinds of thoughts to the back of their minds, but when you'd watched someone slowly die as Isla had, it was much harder to believe that the people you loved were always going to be okay. He'd really felt for her, but he hadn't really been able to put himself in her place. If his own father were to die, the tragedy was that Aidan didn't think it would affect his life at all. At least not in a day-to-day way. There were no regular visits or phone calls to miss, no turning to his father for advice or support, and no in-jokes that only the two of them shared. All that would be left behind was regret.

Discovering that Isla's bad news was about the results of her screening tests had taken Aidan's breath away, but what had surprised him even more was that his first thought hadn't been about how that might affect the egg donation. He'd heard the fear in her voice, when Reuben had put her on the phone, and all he'd wanted was to get to her, and to promise her that it was all going to be okay, even though he had no idea if it would be. Her mother was in hospital thousands of miles away, and Isla had sobbed when she'd told him why she couldn't tell her grandparents that she might be facing a leukaemia diagnosis. But Isla needed family around her more than ever, and Aidan and Jase were going to fill that void. He didn't even stop to question whether his husband would be prepared to drop everything and rush over to Isla's flat, because he'd known Jase wouldn't have been able to imagine doing anything else.

By the time they'd got there, Isla had been apologetic and clearly wishing she hadn't said anything until she knew for certain that there was something to say.

'I'm giving you all this worry now, but it could be nothing, couldn't it?' There hadn't been much conviction in Isla's statement, but Aidan had nodded all the same.

'It could easily be nothing but, either way, the last thing we want you to worry about is the egg donation. That's nothing in the big scheme of things.' He'd caught Jase's eye for a moment, and an unreadable expression had crossed his husband's face, but there was no way they could discuss it further in front of Isla. Instead, they'd rallied around her, talking about all the other things her blood test results could mean, and that, even if it was leukaemia, the chances of successful treatment were really high. Isla had sat close to Reuben all night, and the irony of the situation hadn't been lost on Aidan. The spark between them the first time they'd met, had been obvious, and he'd been certain there was a connection in the messages they'd exchanged in the WhatsApp group. Being the old romantic he was, he hadn't been able to stop himself from secretly hoping that they might end up together. After all, there'd be no better way of making Isla a part of their family than that. But this wasn't the kind of closeness he'd wanted them to develop. Isla had admitted that the only reason she'd confided in Reuben was because he wasn't someone who'd be devastated by the idea that she might have cancer. But Aidan could see on his nephew's face and hear it in Reuben's voice that he already cared about Isla. None of them wanted her to have to face something like this, and it had shocked him, when they'd discussed it afterwards, that Jase didn't seem to think it automatically meant their plans should go on hold.

Two days after they'd been to Isla's flat, Jase had bounded in, fizzing with excitement about arranging a phone call with their potential surrogate. 'I've set up the call with Ellen, and I said we'd ring at eleven, so make sure you're ready to be your sparkling best, and you've got the list of questions you wanted to ask.'

'Do you think we should be calling her now? When we don't know what's happening with Isla?' There was no way they could commit to the next phase of the process with all of this going on, but Jase was looking at him with a quizzical expression on his face.

'I'm as worried about Isla as you are, but you do remember what they said to us at the clinic, don't you? Finding a surrogate is the biggest key to us having a baby. There are a lot more options for egg donation.'

'I can't believe you're saying that. Is that what Isla is to you? An expendable part of our plan?' The words caught in Aidan's throat as he turned to look at his husband, not wanting to believe that the man he loved could even think like that, but Jase was already shaking his head.

'Of course it isn't. I'm really fond of Isla, and I know she's come to mean a lot to you too, but she wouldn't want us to give up the chance of finding a surrogate. She said so herself, and none of that will stop us being able to support her with whatever she might need.' Everything Jase was saying was perfectly reasonable, and it was true too, which meant Aidan couldn't explain the way it made him feel. But he had to try.

'The thing is, she doesn't feel she can talk to any of her family about this, and I understand what that's like. I know how lonely it can be facing something potentially life changing, when you've got no one to lean on. You've always had people you can turn to. But if Isla needs me, I want to be there for her.' Aidan had a feeling he wasn't making any sense, because Jase was right. In theory, there was nothing stopping them from doing both things. Except when Isla had told him there was no one in her family she could confide in, something had clicked inside Aidan's head. If she was diagnosed with leukaemia, she needed to be someone's *number-one* priority, and he wanted that someone to be him. Until he'd met Jase, he'd spent most of his life feeling like he was no one's priority, and he didn't want Isla to feel that way for a single moment.

'This is not going to stop you being there for Isla, I promise. *Please*, let's just talk to Ellen on the phone and see how it goes.'

'Okay, but I'm not just going to go elsewhere for egg donation and act like what Isla offered to do for us was nothing.' Aidan had a sharp edge to his voice, but Jase reached for his hand.

'I'd never do that either, and I hope you know that, deep down.' As Jase's eyes searched his face, Aidan found himself nodding. His husband was the kindest man he'd ever known, and the last thing he'd want was to do anything to hurt Isla. But there was something Aidan hadn't told Jase, the doubt that had begun creeping in about starting a family, after their last conversation, when he'd insisted Aidan should be the biological father. If genes played a stronger part than either of them thought, then Aidan could prove just as inadequate as his own father in forming a bond of unconditional love with their child. It was something that had been playing on his mind more and more since his last visit to Ireland. Isla's health scare might be the main reason why they needed to consider putting their fertility treatment on hold, but it wasn't the only one.

\* \* \*

'Do you think we should get some of these for when Danni comes back from her appointment?' Amy gestured towards the balloons in the hospital shop, in pink and blue, with the words *it's a girl*, and *it's a boy*, emblazoned across the front. 'We could get one of each, to cover all bases.'

'Danni's not the kind of person who needs a metallic balloon to tell the world the baby's sex. All she'll care about is that everything's okay.' Aidan had barely been able to crack a smile all morning, and he knew he sounded as miserable as he felt. Poor Amy was probably wishing she hadn't asked him to come for a coffee at the hospital shop, during their break. Danni had been sent for extra scans after experiencing some bleeding, which had now thankfully settled down. But she'd booked a private scan at sixteen weeks, just to help reassure her and Charlie that everything was still okay and because it had felt like too long to wait until the twenty-week scan. They'd been told they could find out the baby's sex if they wanted to, and the rest of the team seemed every bit as excited as the expectant parents. It was just Aidan putting a dampener on things, and he needed to snap out of it. 'It's a lovely thought, though, Ames. But maybe we should just get a couple of boxes of doughnuts delivered, so we can celebrate with her at the end of the shift. She's developed some scarily intense cravings for sweet stuff.'

'Me too, but the tragic part is I'm not pregnant. I can barely even remember the last time I went on a date.' Amy grinned, but suddenly her expression changed. 'Are you okay? You don't seem yourself lately. I haven't upset you banging on about Danni's scan results, have I? It must be really hard with what you're going through.'

'Of course you haven't upset me. I'm just turning into a miserable old sod before my time.'

'Not that much before your time!' Amy grinned again, and for the first time that shift, Aidan laughed. Isla was currently elsewhere in the hospital, having some tests, and he'd offered to go with her when she got the results. She'd seemed much calmer since that first night, and she'd even tried to make him promise that he wouldn't put off trying for a baby if she wasn't able to donate her eggs. In the end he'd agreed, without actually saying the words '*I promise*', because he still wasn't sure it was something he'd be able to do.

The phone call with Ellen had gone as well as it possibly could. She was bubbly and upbeat, but even more importantly she was an experienced surrogate, with a track record of following through on the promises she'd made to the intended parents. Jase had been bouncing around with excitement at the end of the call, and a date had already been made for them to meet Ellen in person. It suddenly felt like a train that was hurtling down the tracks, and Aidan had a feeling he'd be powerless to stop it, even if he wanted to. But the fear that had crept in about his ability to bond with their child, seemed to be getting more powerful. Isla was such a sweet girl, who'd been devoted to her father and had a close and loving bond with her whole family, so the baby having half of her genes had to give it a good chance of being loving and loveable as a result. But without Isla's influence, there'd be nothing to counter whatever it was in Aidan that made him so unlovable to his own father. Deep down, he knew it was an irrational fear, and that genetics didn't determine family relationships, but since the trip to Ireland, he couldn't shake it, and no amount of telling himself he was being ridiculous made any difference. The worst part of all of it, was that Jase had no idea how he felt.

'I read your latest post on your journey to parenthood page.' Amy was smiling again, and he managed to nod. He'd only put it up there because Jase had asked him why he'd stopped updating the page, and he'd had some messages from followers asking what was going on. It would have been the perfect opportunity to admit to Jase that he was having doubts, but he hadn't been able to do it.

'Me too.' Gwen had suddenly appeared from behind the counter in the shop. 'It must be so exciting now you've been matched with a surrogate. I told Amy before, that if I was a few decades younger, I'd seriously think about doing it. But these days it's strictly a one-way street down there.'

'I think mine must be a dead end with a big road-closed sign.' Amy pulled a face. 'Because every man I meet seems to turn around and go in the opposite direction.'

'Maybe you just need to give the entrance a bit more kerb appeal, if you know what I mean.' Gwen and Amy both started laughing, and Aidan couldn't help joining in.

'What are you suggesting? A couple of hanging baskets, and a welcome sign?' Amy raised her eyebrows as she looked at Gwen, and Aidan shook his head.

'I can't take the mental images; you two have got to stop!'

'It's just nice to see you smile.' Amy gave him a gentle nudge, just as a group of people came into the shop. One of whom was Isla.

'Everything okay?' He mouthed the words, but before she could even respond, there was a loud crash as the woman to the right of her, went down, taking a shelf filled with magazines with her. The woman's body was jerking violently, and it was immediately obvious she was having a seizure.

'It's okay, we're going to look after you.' Isla had already moved to crouch beside her, checking the woman's airway, as Gwen ushered the other customers out of the shop. The woman's limbs were still jerking, her eyes had rolled back and for a moment Aidan didn't recognise who she was, but Isla did.

'It's Sarah Vardy.' Isla loosened the silky neck scarf that was looped tightly around Sarah's neck. 'Do you know if she's epileptic?'

'I don't think so.' Aidan looked around for something to put under Sarah's head as her body continued to jerk. 'Is there anything we can use as a pillow, Gwen?'

'Take this.' She took a fleece off the row of hooks behind the counter and passed it to him to place under Sarah's head. Once she'd stopped convulsing, they could move her into the recovery position, but for now all they could do was try and stop her from hurting herself during the seizure.

'I'll go back to A&E to let them know we're bringing her in.' Amy rushed out of the shop and Aidan checked his watch, silently praying that the seizure would be over quickly. The longer it lasted, the more serious the cause and aftereffects were likely to be.

'She's breathing okay.' Aidan pressed the back of his palm against Sarah's forehead. 'And it doesn't feel as though she's got a temperature. We just need to ride this out before we can move her. I'm going to try and time how long the seizure lasts.' As far as he could recall, she didn't have any ongoing medical issues, apart from the health anxiety over having cancer that seemed to rule her life, but having a seizure like this, out of nowhere, needed to be investigated.

By the time the seizure finally ended, almost four minutes

after it had started, Amy was back at the hospital shop, with a wheelchair. Aidan and Isla had moved Sarah into the recovery position as soon as the jerking in her limbs had stopped, and she had regained consciousness. As far as Aidan could tell, she seemed okay, apart from some confusion.

'Do you remember what happened, Sarah?' He took her hand, as she stared at him for a moment, and then she blinked.

'I just went in to get a *Take a Break*, and the next minute I was on the floor.' The magazine Sarah had been reaching for had ended up underneath her, like most of the others on the shelf that had come down with her.

'Did you hurt yourself when you fell?' Isla's voice was gentle and reassuring.

'I banged my elbow, and my head feels like I've been drinking.' Sarah attempted to get up, but Aidan kept hold of her hand.

'We'll help you up into the wheelchair, and take you to get checked over, so we can find out what's caused this. Is it the first time you've had a seizure, Sarah?' Even as she nodded in response to Aidan's question, he could see in her eyes that she was hiding something. A seizure like this could have a number of causes, some far more serious than others. For someone like Sarah, it seemed unusual that her mind wasn't immediately going there, which made Aidan suspect she already had some idea what was behind it. She looked different too, like she'd started making an effort with her appearance again. Something she'd evidently stopped doing after her mother's death.

'Let's get you moved then, and I'll treat you to the magazine, so you don't get yourself into any more trouble.' Aidan smiled, and a single tear slid out of Sarah's eye, into her hair, as she clutched his hand. Whatever the reason behind the seizure, Sarah had clearly decided to keep it to herself for the moment, and all he could do for now was to be there to hold her hand, until she was ready to talk.

* * *

'Are you sure you want to hang around?' Aidan had asked Isla the question at least three times before she'd finally managed to persuade him that she had nowhere to rush off to. She'd been off work because of her further tests, but when Sarah had collapsed, she'd accompanied her and Aidan back to A&E. It was an even busier than usual shift, and a big, county-wide inter-school football tournament, in Port Tremellien, had resulted in a steady stream of patients needing stitches and X-rays. Aidan had people asking for his help every five minutes, but it was obvious he'd been struggling with the idea of leaving Sarah on her own while she waited to be sent for a scan.

'I don't think this is the first seizure she's had.' Aidan had lowered his voice to a whisper when they were outside Sarah's cubicle. 'There's a chance this could be something serious, but she's not reacting the way she normally does and it's worrying me, but we're short-staffed as it is, and I can't just sit with her.'

'I can.' Isla's response had been resolute, but Aidan had still shaken his head.

'You've got enough on your plate, and the last thing you need is to have to hang around here when you're not at work.'

'I'm fine.' She'd widened her eyes, to try and convince him that she meant it. 'All I can do now is wait for my results, and if I'm sitting at home that time isn't going to pass any more quickly. Anyway, I want to be here when Danni comes and tells us about the scan. It's no problem for me to sit with Sarah until then. I think half the reason her health anxiety is so bad, is because she's got no one in her life she can talk to about what's worrying her.

I'm really grateful I've been able to tell you about everything, especially after the latest with Mum. But I think I'd have gone mad if I hadn't been able to talk to anyone about what's going on in my head.'

For a moment Aidan had looked as if he was going to say something, but then he'd just given her a hug. Lexi had called the morning after Isla had broken down in front of Reuben and had told her that their mother had deep vein thrombosis as a result of the break to her ankle. Thankfully, it had been spotted by one of the nurses before it caused any complications, and was being treated with blood thinners, but it was another thing to worry about and it also meant flying was off the cards for Clare for the foreseeable future. There was even less chance of Isla telling Lexi or her mother that she was going through tests for leukaemia now. It would kill Clare not to be able to get on a plane to come straight over. Having Aidan, Jase and Reuben to confide in was enough, until she knew more. She was still carrying the guilt of burdening them with the worry about how it might affect their attempts to have a baby, but any time she even tried to mention that, Aidan told her not to be ridiculous and that none of that mattered as long as she was okay.

Being part of the A&E team in St Piran's had always felt like finding a second family, but never more so than in the past week. That feeling of closeness also explained why they were all waiting with such anticipation for Danni's scan results. The baby she and Charlie were expecting was important to the whole team, but Isla couldn't help wondering how it made Aidan feel to see his friend getting closer and closer to becoming a parent. If he held any bitterness about it at all, he was doing a very good job of hiding it.

Dr Moorhouse, one of the A&E consultants, had been liaising with the neurology team, and Sarah had been given a bed in the

Clinical Decisions Unit until they knew a bit more, but Isla was almost certain that Aidan was right about this not being her first seizure. Something was going on, but instead of questioning every little symptom the way she usually did, Sarah seemed to be in denial. Maybe it shouldn't have surprised Isla as much as it had. After all, she was doing more or less the same thing herself. With Sarah awaiting her own results in the CDU, Isla was now in the hospital restaurant with her colleagues, grateful for the distraction that Danni's news would provide.

'I decided to get four boxes of doughnuts delivered in the end.' Aidan peered over the top of the stack he was holding. 'Seeing as so many of us are here for the news.'

'Has she told you what sex it is?' Gary, one of the other nurses, looked at Esther as she came into the restaurant. Almost all the A&E staff who'd just finished their shift were there too, plus some of the staff from other departments who were particularly friendly with Danni. They included Gwen, and Gary's girlfriend, Wendy, who'd recently been promoted to head of housekeeping. Danni had been through a lot before meeting Charlie, and anyone who knew her story wanted to celebrate her good news with her.

'She texted to confirm that everything is okay with the baby, but I promise I'm none the wiser about anything else, which I'm secretly a little bit miffed about. Especially as I know Charlie promised to ring Joe straight after the scan. Just because he's away at a conference, I don't see why he gets to find out first.' Esther smiled despite her words, and Isla knew that all that really mattered to her was that her best friend's baby was okay.

'I just wish my ex-husband would have been as upfront about his baby news. That way, our daughter wouldn't have needed to find out from another student that her art teacher was having her dad's baby. Apparently it wasn't enough that he got caught having sex with one of our neighbours in a garden shed, at a barbecue she and her husband were hosting. As soon as they split up, he started dating a woman thirty years younger than him and within a few months he'd got her pregnant.' Wendy pulled a doughnut out of one of the boxes that Aidan had set down on the table. 'Sorry, but after the week I've had, I need one of these to stop me from punching a wall, or running down my ex in the car he claims he needs more than me. Even now, he's not man enough to talk to our girls about his new baby and he expects me to pick up the pieces.'

Aidan exchanged a look with Isla, as Wendy shoved almost the whole doughnut into her mouth.

'Keeping secrets from people who deserve to hear the truth has a way of coming back to bite you in the bum, and I'm sure your ex won't escape that. In the meantime, you can have my doughnut; I think your need is greater.' Gwen handed Wendy another doughnut, and Isla caught Aidan's eye again, but he looked away even more quickly than she could. She was keeping a huge secret and, even though she was certain she was doing it for the right reasons, it still had the potential to hurt the people she loved when it came out. Aidan must have been thinking the same thing and his mouth was turned down at the corners.

'Here she is, the woman in question!' Esther ran towards Danni as she came into the restaurant; the baby bump that had been invisible just a week or so before was now becoming more obvious. When Isla looked towards Aidan again, she'd expected him to look even more downcast, being confronted by something that he longed for so much, but he was smiling.

'You can't keep us in suspense for a moment longer. There are four boxes of Krispy Kremes we're waiting to crack open here.' He looked at Wendy, who'd already broken her second doughnut in half. 'Wendy just agreed to do a taste test for us, but no one else is allowed to have one until you've spilled the beans.'

'I can't believe you've all stayed on after your shift, just to hear my news.' Danni was close to tears as she looked around at everyone, and she didn't quite make it to the end of her next sentence before she started to cry. 'But it looks like I'm getting myself another little Charlie!'

There was a chorus of congratulations after that, and within minutes it looked like a swarm of locusts had been set loose on the Krispy Kremes. Everyone was smiling and there was such an upbeat mood in the room that, for a few moments, Isla completely forgot about the fact that in less than forty-eight hours' time she'd be meeting the haematologist to discuss the result of her tests. Then she spotted Aidan again and this time there was no mistaking the pensive look on his face. So much hung on the outcome of her tests, and it wasn't only her life that was on hold until she found out what she was facing.

# 15

The very last person Aidan had expected to see on his doorstep was his sister. When the doorbell had rung, he'd assumed it was another of the million or so things Jase seemed to have ordered online over the last few months. They had more supplements to help improve their fertility and general wellbeing than a health food shop, and enough books about parenthood to fill a whole section of Port Kara's tiny library. Except this wasn't just another delivery, this was May, who should have been back home in Ireland, juggling life with three kids and a busy job as the office manager of a transport firm. She didn't have time to hop over to Cornwall on a whim and Aidan's heart dropped down to his boots at the sight of her. Something terrible must have happened.

'What is it? Is it Mammy? Or Da?' As hard as things had been between Aidan and his father, the thought that the conversation they'd had in the pub might be the last thing they ever said to one another made his chest ache. He'd carried a tiny grain of hope in his heart for most of his life, that one day something would happen to make Sean change, and finally accept his son for who he was. If that hope was extinguished for good, he was going to grieve for all the things he'd dreamt their relationship might one day be. And if he'd lost his mother, it would break him in a different way. When he'd walked out of the pub, she'd called his mobile, begging him to come back and try to find it in his heart to understand the things that drove his father's behaviour. But he'd had enough of making excuses for a bigot. Just because Sean had been brought up to believe something, it didn't mean he couldn't question it. He could see for himself how much joy Jase brought into his youngest son's life, and yet he'd reduced the man Aidan loved to nothing more than a housemate. This time, it wasn't about Aidan, it was about Jase, and that's why his resolve to walk away hadn't wavered, even as his mother had sobbed and told him how much she loved him. He didn't want that to be their last conversation either, because that would mean he'd lost her, but at least he'd told his mother that he loved her too. He'd never exchanged those words with his father and, regardless of the news May was bringing, he was almost certain now that he never would.

'It's not about either of them. It's you, it's me, and it's all the things I should have said and done over the years.' There were tears streaming down May's face, as she held her arms out towards him. He still didn't understand why she was there, but he pulled her towards him all the same. He hugged her in the doorway of his house until her tears finally subsided, and she managed to speak again.

'I'm sorry, I had this big speech all planned, but when I saw you. I just couldn't get the words out.'

'Will you come inside, or we'll be giving the neighbours far too much to talk about.' Aidan smiled, despite the lump that was lodged in his throat. The air felt as though it was charged with emotion and he still didn't really understand why she was there.

'I was starting to wonder if you were ever going to ask.' May gave him a gentle nudge in his side, as she must have done hundreds of times before. They had always been the closest as kids. Play fighting and pushing one another into the dyke that had run along the back of their garden, whenever they could catch each other off guard, had all been part of that. But that closeness had drifted away after Aidan had left home, and he'd felt as abandoned by May as he had the rest of his family. He'd buried the hurt of that, because he wasn't sure he could have carried on functioning if he'd given those feelings air and allowed them to be as raw as they'd been in those first few years.

Aidan put the kettle on, after he'd shown May into the sitting room, which was filled with photographs of Jase's side of the family. While he was waiting for the kettle to boil, he fired off a quick text to his husband.

> You're never going to believe it, but May has turned up at the house. I'm not sure what's going on, but she keeps apologising. I'll be on my way in for the night shift by the time you're home from work, but I don't know if she's got anywhere to stay. Is it okay with you if she stays here, if she needs to? I know it might be awkward, since you hardly know each other, but I can't just send her away. Love you xxxx

More often than not, Jase seemed to spend his entire working day in meetings, so Aidan had no idea when he'd pick up the message, but by the time he dropped two teabags into mugs, his phone was pinging with a response.

Of course she should stay with us. Oh my God, I
can't believe she's actually here! I love you so
much and whatever she's come to say, I want
you to remember that. Call me when you
can xxxx

Sending a single love heart in response, Aidan set down the
phone and breathed out. Whatever the reason for May's visit, and
however difficult it might be to hear what she had to say, it would
be okay because Jase would be his rock, the way he always was.

In the end, it took half an hour for his sister to tell him all the
reasons she was there. May had talked almost non-stop, all the
guilt she felt tumbling out as tears streamed down her face and
she refused to let him comfort her. She talked about how she
should have supported Aidan when he came out, and stood up to
their father when he'd spouted his venom about the life Aidan
was living, and most of all her regret at not being there when he
married Jase. He'd told her that it didn't matter, but she'd picked
up a photograph from the day, of Aidan and Jase, with Tash sandwiched between them, as they each planted a kiss on her cheeks.

'This is Jase's sister, isn't it?' May's eyes were glassy as she
looked up at him and he nodded. 'I should have been there, and
no excuse I try to make about being busy with the kids will ever
allow me to forgive myself for missing the most important day of
your life.'

'Like I said, it doesn't matter, we've got a chance now to forget
that and move forward.' He reached out for her hand, but she
shook her head.

'It does matter! That was the biggest moment of my little brother's life, and I couldn't make the effort to be there for you, because I
was so bloody worried about disappointing Da.' May balled her
hands into fists. 'I hate that I can't undo it, but my God, things are

going to change from here on out, I promise you that. And it's not just me. I've never seen Mammy as angry as she was the day you left the pub. She was inconsolable, shouting at Da and telling him she'd leave too if he didn't stop driving a wedge between you and the family. He expected me to take his side, but I told him I was done being the daughter he wants me to be and that I wish I'd never tried, because there's nothing I regret more than losing the closeness you and I always had. Niall stood up for you too, asking Da if he wanted what happened to Cian to happen to you. I thought Da was going to hit him, but then he just stormed out.'

'It means a lot that you all tried so hard, but nothing's going to change him, May.' Aidan moved to take her hand again, and this time she let him. He wasn't sure he'd ever felt such a mix of emotions in his life. The idea of two of his siblings and his mother, standing up to a man whose word had always been law in their house, filled him with the kind of warmth he hadn't felt towards his family in years. Yet there was still an aching void, in the place his father's love and acceptance should have occupied and it was the kind of emptiness that nothing else could ever really fill.

'Maybe not, but there's no way I'm going back to how things were before I spoke my mind, and I don't think there is for any of the rest of the family either. He's in danger of losing us all if he carries on, and there's something else I need to say.' As May held his gaze, the feeling of dread he'd experienced when she'd arrived on his doorstep rose up inside him again. 'Mammy told me about you and Jase wanting to start a family, and I found your journey to parenthood page online, where you were talking about looking for a surrogate. I want to do it for you, carry the embryo that the two of you create. I know I'm not as young as I was, but I can still carry a baby. I've done loads of research, and even grandmothers have carried their grandchildren, when their daughters couldn't for some reason.'

'May.' Leaning forward, he kissed his sister on the cheek, wanting to laugh and cry at the same time. It was too complicated and not an offer he and Jase would ever want to take up, because of the potential for things to go wrong. But an overwhelming rush of affection for May washed over him all the same; she'd clearly meant every word. He didn't want to burden her with the worry that he and Jase were shouldering since Isla's screening results, and, she didn't need to know there might be a good chance that they were back to square one. All they were focusing on for now was making sure their friend had the support she needed, but he could at least help May to understand why they could never take up her offer. 'Have you talked to Jack about this? And how it's going to affect him and the kids? Not to mention what Da would say.'

'I don't give a shite what Da says, and Jack and the kids will understand. I need to do this for you, to make up for letting you down so badly before.'

'No you don't, but I love you so much for offering. We've thought about what we want, and we need the surrogate to be someone who's done this before and knows what they're getting themselves in to, emotionally and physically. I couldn't risk putting you through that, I just want you to be the best auntie you can be.'

'Just try stopping me!' May pulled her hand away and threw her arms around him. The tears she was crying this time were almost certainly the happy kind, and she wasn't the only one. Aidan wanted to hold on to the moment forever, and he wasn't going to let his father spoil it. Sean would never give him the acceptance he craved, no matter how hard the rest of the family tried to convince him that his behaviour was wrong. But Aidan had already been given the moon, so it would have been greedy to ask for the stars too, and he'd got really good over the years at being grateful for all the things he did have. He had no intention of reaching for the stars, or reaching out to his father, ever again. He'd been hurt once too often, and he was finally ready to let go of the last grain of hope that his father would ever accept him for who he was.

* * *

'I can't believe she was in Cornwall for three hours!' Jase sounded every bit as incredulous as Aidan had, when May had explained she was flying back to Ireland that evening.

'I know, and when I asked her what she would have done if I hadn't been on nights and I'd already been at work when she arrived, she admitted she hadn't even thought about it.' Aidan laughed, still barely able to believe that his sister had got on a plane, having booked another one back to Ireland, just hours later, because she had to be home for a concert at her son's nursery school the next day. Seeing her off had been such a rush and Aidan had been forced to wait until his break at work to call Jase, and explain everything May had told him. 'She said she just needed to talk to me face to face.'

'I can understand that, and I'm really glad she did. I'm just sorry I missed her.'

'Oh, don't worry, she's already said she's coming back with Jack and the kids in the school holidays. Now she's seen the house, she knows we've got three spare rooms!'

'Two spare rooms and a nursery.' Aidan could hear the longing in Jase's voice.

'Two spare rooms and a nursery.' He repeated the words, as if putting them out into the universe somehow made it more real.

With everything that was going on with Isla, it felt more uncertain than ever in some ways, but they had to keep believing. 'I wish I could come home now.'

'Me too, but, as we're both off tomorrow, I'll take you out for breakfast in the morning. That's if you can stay awake.' It was Jase's turn to laugh. 'I know you find the transition from nights much harder now that you're knocking on a bit, and I'm starting to realise that a fry up is the best way to combat those mood swings.'

'Have you forgotten you're older than me? You're just lucky I can't resist the offer of a free breakfast, otherwise we might never have ended up together!' Aidan could imagine the smile on his husband's face, matching his own; the yearning to be with Jase was every bit as strong as it had been in the early days of their relationship.

'I'll see you for breakfast then, I love you.'

'I love you too.' As Aidan reluctantly ended the call, the same warm feeling that May's offer had brought enveloped him again. He was loved for exactly who he was, by the person who meant the most in the world to him, and that made him the luckiest person he knew.

# 16

Two days after Isla's extra blood tests, instead of getting her expected results, she'd been asked to go for a lumbar puncture and Aidan had gone with her. Thankfully it hadn't been painful, but the drip, drip, drip of fear that all these tests could only lead to one outcome meant she was incredibly grateful that someone was there with her. At first it had seemed impossible that something of that magnitude could be going on inside her body without her knowing it. The tiredness and weight loss had seemed such minor symptoms, a side effect of everyday life, and it wasn't like things had been plain sailing lately. The switch between night shifts and days had definitely become harder, but there was a lot going on with the news about her mother's DVT, and the shock that Sarah Vardy had been diagnosed with a brain tumour after a recent visit to A&E, before her seizures had started. She'd been referred for an MRI, as much to placate her as anything else, and the brain tumour had been discovered then, two weeks before she'd collapsed in the hospital shop. Despite witnessing Sarah's seizure, it had still seemed impossible to Isla that her patient would ever be diagnosed with cancer,

when Sarah had falsely suspected it so many times, but now she
had the thing she feared the most. All of that made it far easier
for Isla to believe she had cancer too, but the results of the
lumbar puncture would confirm it.

'You're not going for the results on your own.' Aidan hadn't
given Isla any opportunity to protest, even when she'd pointed
out that he was due to be on shift.

'I've already swapped with Amy.' He'd folded his arms across
his chest at that point and she'd known there was no point in
arguing with him, and the truth was she didn't want to. Aidan felt
like the big brother she'd never had, and she'd seen time and
again how caring he was with patients, so it wasn't that much of a
surprise that he'd turned out to be as protective of her as he was.
What had shocked her more, was how much support Reuben
seemed to want to offer her too. In the week since she'd told him
about the screening results, there were fresh flowers every day,
which he'd claimed were more leftovers from his new venture,
lots of fruit, and other lovely things from his shop, which had
tempted her to eat, even on the days she hadn't felt like it. He'd
sent her silly cracker-style jokes too, which had made her laugh,
even when she hadn't felt like that either. *What do frogs wear on
their feet? Open toad sandals.* That had been one of her favourites,
and if her laughter was teetering on the hysterical the night
before she was due to get the result of her lumbar puncture, at
least she'd been laughing.

* * *

Aidan had picked Isla up from home and driven them both to the
hospital, a place so familiar it was like a second home to them.
Only this time she'd felt nervous as she'd walked through the
doors, and turned in the opposite direction to A&E. It wasn't a

routine day at work, no matter how much she tried to convince herself that it was.

Handing her letter over at the desk, the administrator pulled a face. 'I'm afraid Dr Yang's clinic is running over an hour late at the moment, so you're going to have a bit of a wait.'

'Maybe I should just make another appointment?' Isla had been counting on going straight in and getting the news over and done with as soon as possible. Having to wait around had never factored into her plans and fight or flight was already kicking in. But Aidan had put his hand on her arm before she could even try to turn away from the desk.

'No chance. We're seeing her today and then we can make a plan. Worrying ourselves sick about this until you can get another appointment isn't going to help.' Maybe it should have been odd, the way he was talking about 'us' and 'we', but it wasn't. It helped to know he was concerned about the outcome too, and she was certain it wasn't just because of the egg donation. She could see in his eyes that he really cared, and she was more convinced than ever that Aidan was going to make a great dad.

Isla scanned the faces of the other people waiting. There were four clinics running from the same waiting area, so not everyone had an appointment with Dr Yang. She'd been relieved to be referred to a consultant haematologist, rather than an oncologist in The Thornhill Centre, but a quick bit of googling had revealed that didn't mean it wasn't cancer. It meant she'd already known that leukaemia was still a possibility, even before she'd seen patients who were clearly in the midst of chemotherapy. Almost unconsciously, she reached up to touch her hair, unable to stop herself from wondering if she was going to lose it. The idea shouldn't have bothered her as much as it did, as long as she could be treated, but she couldn't stop her thoughts from going there. Aidan was right, she needed to know what she was facing, but time seemed to be passing unbearably slowly. An hour after her original appointment was supposed to have started, she wasn't the only one constantly glancing at her watch. Aidan's phone had pinged three times in the last five minutes too.

'If you need to be somewhere, I'll be okay on my own. I promise.' Isla dropped her left hand down by the side of the chair, so he wouldn't be able to see that she'd crossed her fingers.

'The only somewhere I need to be is here. Got it?' Aidan held her gaze until she nodded. 'And I'm putting this bloody phone on silent.'

'Isla Marlowe?' The woman who'd called her name wasn't Dr Yang, but Isla still caught her breath as she stood up. This was it, she was about to find out whether she had leukaemia, and suddenly it felt as if she'd forgotten how to walk.

'It's going to be okay.' Aidan linked his arm through hers and propelled her forward, following the woman who'd called her name into one of the consulting rooms.

'Hi there, good to see you again, Isla.' Dr Yang smiled broadly as they entered the room, and gestured towards the woman who'd showed them in. 'This is Vanessa, one of the nurses from The Thornberry Centre, and I see you've brought someone with you today.'

'Aidan's my friend.' Even to her own ears Isla's words sounded like the statement of a five-year-old, but it was all she could manage as her heart hammered against her rib cage. A nurse from the oncology centre had come along to the appointment, and even a five-year-old could have worked that one out.

'Nice to meet you, Aidan, I'm Dr Yang. I'm sure I recognise you from somewhere?'

'I work in A&E with Isla and, once seen, this face is never forgotten.' Aidan's words were light-hearted, but he took hold of

Isla's hand as they sat down. She was more grateful than ever that he'd come with her, and that she had something solid to hold onto.

'It can be really useful to have someone with you when you get your results, as I often find patients don't take much in after they hear a diagnosis. It can be a lot to process.' Dr Yang was still smiling, which surely had to mean that the news she was about to impart wasn't so bad after all. 'As I think we all expected, the lumbar puncture confirmed that you do have leukaemia.'

Isla had heard patients talk about having out-of-body experiences before, but she'd never really believed they were real, until the word leukaemia had reached her ears. Dr Yang kept talking after that, but Isla found herself watching the other woman's mouth moving, without really being able to take in the words. For a long time, no one seemed to notice that Isla wasn't really in the room any more, but then Vanessa leant forward in her seat.

'Do you understand what that means, Isla? The tyrosine kinase inhibitor therapy will target and block the enzyme that's causing your stem cells to develop more white blood cells than your body needs. It's the first line of treatment for chronic myeloid leukaemia, and it's been found to be very effective in many patients.'

'But it doesn't always work?' Isla had probably read up enough about the different types of leukaemia and their treatments, to be able to brief a patient herself if she had to, but she needed to hear it from the experts.

'If it comes to that, there are other options, including chemotherapy.' Dr Yang made it sound so easy, but there was something else Isla knew about her type of leukaemia that was making the news more difficult to deal with than she'd expected. Especially when a diagnosis of acute myeloid leukaemia was the thing she'd really been dreading. She should have been reassured to discover it was the chronic kind, but none of that relief seemed to be forthcoming.

'CML's not curable, though, is it? This is something I'm going to have hanging over me for the rest of my life.' Even as she said the words, Isla could picture her dad's face. He'd lived with the knowledge that a deadly condition was going to kill him sooner or later, and he'd sacrificed so much to make sure his children never had to go through something like that. Except now here she was.

'For most people it's not considered curable, although in rare instances that is possible with a stem cell transplant.' Dr Yang looked directly at Isla. 'However, with the right treatment, many patients can expect a normal life span and a good quality of life.'

'But I'll be having treatment for the rest of my life?'

'The targeted therapy is aimed at stopping the CML from progressing to the accelerated phase, which can become life-threatening. So, yes, you'll be having treatment for the rest of your life, but that's no different from other chronic conditions, like diabetes.' Dr Yang clicked the keyboard in front of her. 'We'll also be running some tests to see whether you have the Philadelphia chromosome, an abnormal fusion of genes in your DNA, which 95 per cent of patients with CML have.'

'Does that mean any children I have will be affected?' Isla glanced at Aidan as she spoke, and he squeezed her hand again.

'No.' Dr Yang shook her head. 'It's not something you've inherited. It's a genetic change that happens during a person's lifetime, so there's no risk of passing it on either.'

'Well that's something.' The doctor's words had planted a tiny seed of hope inside Isla that was already growing. She might not have to let Aidan and Jase down after all but going through with the fertility treatment wouldn't be entirely selfless. It would give her a reason to keep looking forward, and she had a feeling she was really going to need that. Until now, starting a family of her own hadn't been anywhere near the forefront of her mind. There were plenty of people who parented alone and made a brilliant job of it, but she'd always imagined a different set up – a family like her mum and dad had built, and Aidan and Jase were trying to create, with two parents sharing the highs and lows together. But it had never felt like a priority, especially when she was so scared of losing someone she loved that she didn't let people in. Except suddenly, she knew for certain she wanted to be a mother at some point and, if she could help Aidan and Jase, it had to mean there was a good chance of her having children of her own one day too. She had to believe she had a future, and to try and push down the nagging fear that she might not live long enough to do all the things she'd planned to do 'one day'. Anything that helped her focus on a life beyond her diagnosis was a positive, and being able to fulfil the offer she'd made Aidan and Jase was a huge part of that.

'This provides a lot of information you might want and the answers to some frequently asked questions.' Vanessa handed Isla a booklet. 'There's a sticker on the front with my contact details, in case you have any other questions, and you can find the details of support groups and drop-in sessions on The Thornhill Centre's website. There's a counselling service too.'

'Thank you.' There were a million questions whizzing through Isla's mind already, but she needed some time to think before she asked any of them. If there was a chance she might need chemo, if the targeted therapy didn't work, then freezing her eggs now could be a sensible option. That might mean reducing the number she could offer to Aidan and Jase, but now she had no idea if they'd even want to use her eggs. Dr Yang had said there was no genetic link with CML, but would they really want a woman with cancer and a potential gene mutation to be the biological mother of their child? A tiny part of her also wondered whether she should be maximising her own chances of becoming a parent, by keeping any eggs that were frozen as insurance against the possibility of future infertility. And yet she still couldn't imagine not going through with the plan, if they wanted her to.

'We'll be in contact in the next few days about an appointment for the first stage of your treatment.'

'Thank you.' It was Aidan who responded this time, because the questions that were still racing around, faster and faster, in Isla's brain, seemed to be preventing her from even being able to form two simple words, let alone making sense of the plans she'd had for fertility treatment. Her thoughts were so mixed up and confused, as if someone had put them in a blender and turned it up to max speed.

'I know this is a stupid thing to ask, but are you okay?' Aidan put an arm around her shoulder as they walked away from the consulting room.

'I honestly don't know.' Isla wanted to be able to tell him that she was, to convince herself as much as anything, but she wasn't sure how she felt. 'The news could have been far worse, but there's something about this not being curable that feels so...'

'Triggering? Like what your dad went through.'

'Exactly.' She couldn't believe Aidan had understood without her having to explain, and he didn't seem to think she was being ridiculous, even though part of her thought she was. 'I know this is nothing like Huntington's, and I probably sound over dramatic, but I saw the shadow it cast over not just Dad's life, but all of ours. And as crazy as it sounds, having something potentially less serious, but incurable, almost feels worse than having a more serious form of leukaemia that could be cured completely.'

'It doesn't sound crazy to me.' Aidan stopped and turned her to face him. 'You can't expect to make sense of any of this straight away, and I want you to know I'm here for you. If you need to talk, or to go out and do something, anything, to avoid having to even think about all of this for a little while, I'm here. For any of it.'

'I can't expect you to do that. You've got your own life, and I know there was somewhere else you needed to be when the appointment ran late. So I feel guilty enough as it is.'

'I told you, this is the only place I need to be.' Aidan smiled for the first time. 'Well obviously not in St Piran's, because that feels far too much like being at work when we've got a day off. But I know just the place we can go.'

Over the last seven days, Isla had eaten more produce from Reuben's greengrocers and deli than any other kind of food, but this was the first time she'd actually been inside. Port Kara was a foodie's paradise, with not one, but two Michelin-star restaurants, lots of independent shops, and a high-end supermarket. Even with all that competition, his business stood out, and there was a queue out of the door when Aidan and Isla arrived. But as soon as Reuben spotted them, he ushered them in, and through to the little courtyard garden at the back of the deli, where a bistro table was perfectly positioned to catch the last of the afternoon sun.

'This is so lovely.' Isla took a seat at the table, instantly feeling as if some of the dark shadows were lifting as the sun warmed her face.

'Rube's hoping to be able to have a little café garden eventually, but for now this is exclusively for the use of his most VIP customers. I texted him when we were leaving the hospital, and he said he'd whip us something up.'

'Does he know? About the diagnosis?' Isla wasn't sure why she felt so awkward about the idea. After all, Reuben was the one she'd confided in first. But there was nothing attractive about being a cancer patient and, as hard as she wanted to deny it to herself, she didn't want Reuben to think of her as someone sick, or worst of all, needing his pity.

'That's your news to choose to share, not mine.' Aidan had barely got the words out of his mouth, when Reuben came through the back door of the deli and into the garden.

'Unc said you needed something that tasted as good as a Jack Daniels and Coke but was a bit on the healthier side. So what could be better than a double hit of chocolate: chocolate and walnut brownies, and a chocolate milkshake made with almond milk. It all tastes amazing, but the ingredients will actually do you some good too.'

'Rube you know better than to tell me that something's good for me before I eat it. Something just tells my tastebuds I don't like it otherwise.'

'It's not at the level of a beetroot and tomato salad, with a kale smoothie on the side, I promise. But it'll do you more good than harm.'

'As long as it's at least on the margins.' Aidan gave him a sceptical look and then took a bite of his brownie, unable to hold back the exclamations of delight. 'Oh my God, that's good!'

'Well, you'd better eat your fill, because Uncle Jase has texted me three times to ask if I know where you are, and I've got a feeling he'll be feeding your dinner to the dog by the time you get home.'

'We haven't even got a dog.'

'That's how much trouble you're in!' Reuben laughed, but Isla couldn't join in. She'd known there was somewhere Aidan needed to be, and now it looked as if he'd upset Jase. She should have insisted he left, but deep down she was still glad he hadn't.

'I'll go and give him a call now; it'll force me to pace myself with this brownie.' As Aidan got up to leave, Reuben slid into the seat he'd just vacated and looked at Isla.

'Are you not hungry? I can get you something else if you don't like brownies.'

'It's not that, it's just… today has been a lot to process.'

'Do you want to talk about it?'

'I don't want to bore you.' The weird thing was, now that she was sitting face to face with Reuben, she'd realised she did want to talk to him about her diagnosis. It was exactly like the first time she'd confided in him, when she'd told herself she wasn't going to, and the next minute the words had come rushing out. Whatever the reason, she was ready to open up to Reuben for a second time.

'You could never bore me.' His fingers traced the outline of the metal work on the table top, moving so close to her hand it was almost as if she could feel him touching her, and then another unexpected thought struck her – she wished he was.

'I've got a form of leukaemia. It's chronic, which means it's slow to progress and manageable with treatment, but they probably won't be able to cure it.' Isla didn't miss the look that had crossed Reuben's face. This was hard to hear, but even harder to say and she had to get it all out. 'That doesn't mean I'll die from it, any sooner than I might die from something else. The consultant said it's like diabetes in that way. But, if the inhibitors stop working, they'll have to move on to other treatments, like chemo, and it could be life-threatening if it gets to that stage. I know the news could have been a lot worse, but I'm struggling with the fact that this is something that's going to follow me around for the rest of my life. I saw what that did to Dad, but in some ways it was even harder watching Mum go through it. I thought for so long that I didn't want to meet someone, because I didn't want to risk loving them as much as she loved him, and feeling the way she did if I ever lost them. But now I know that if I do meet someone, they'll have to accept that possibility from the start, and that's going to be a lot to take on. The strangest thing is that it's made me realise I do want to find someone to make that kind of risk worth taking.'

Isla could hardly believe she was being so honest with him, and she'd had to drop her gaze when she'd come to the last part. It sounded as if she was talking about him and, if she was honest, she couldn't say for certain that she wasn't. It was too complicated to ever work, but denying the attraction between them would have meant lying to herself, as well as Reuben. She could keep her feelings hidden from him if she didn't look into his eyes, but she had a feeling they'd be painfully obvious if she did.

'I can't imagine what it must be like to love someone with the knowledge that you could lose them, or to be on the receiving end of that kind of love, the intensity of every day really counting, and a desire to make each moment matter. But doesn't everyone want to be loved like that?' Reuben's fingertip grazed the edge of her palm for just a second and every nerve ending in her body seemed to light up. 'I know that's what I want, and it's what I want to feel for someone else too. If love isn't everything to you, then surely it's nothing.'

'I suppose so.' Pulling her hand away, she dug her fingernails into her palm, trying to feel something other than an almost overpowering attraction to Reuben. Things were complicated enough as it was, and she had no idea whether her plans to help Aidan and Jase had been ruined by her diagnosis. But a fling with their nephew would just muddy the waters even further. And that's all it would have been, a fling. Someone like Reuben probably had his pick of anyone he wanted to date, and Isla had a horrible feeling she was mistaking sympathy for something else. All she could do was hope that the attraction she was feeling was just her brain's way of distracting her from her diagnosis, because she really didn't need such strong feelings for him, or anyone else for that matter. The trouble was, there wasn't 'anyone else' remotely like Reuben, and he was fast becoming the only person she could completely open up to. But crossing the line would almost certainly mess that up and she needed a friend more than ever right now.

'Thanks for the brownie, but I really don't think I can face eating anything.'

'I'll box it up for you.' Reuben's tone was gentle as he stood up, but none of the intensity had left his face. 'I know you've got loads of other friends, but if you need anything, anytime, you've got my number.'

'Thank you.' Isla repeated the words she'd said to the nurse from The Thornberry Centre, and they were every bit as hollow. She'd wanted to make it clear to Reuben that the last thing she needed right now was any kind of blurred lines between them, but describing himself as her friend had made it crystal clear how he felt too, and for some reason that hurt far more than it should have done.

**17**
_____

The house was eerily quiet when Aidan got in. He'd tried to ring Jase, but the call had gone straight to voicemail, and his husband hadn't replied to the string of texts he'd sent either. He could feel the atmosphere as soon as he walked in; there was a tension in the air that was undoubtedly down to him, and he probably deserved it. He'd missed the first meeting with their potential surrogate Ellen, and Jase's texts – while Aidan had been in the waiting room with Isla – had become more and more frantic. There was no way Aidan could have left Isla to face the appointment alone, but there was no excuse for him not texting Jase back at the time either. The thing was, he'd known that Jase wouldn't have put any pressure on him to get to the meeting with Ellen under the circumstances. He'd have explained the situation to her, and she'd no doubt have been happy to delay or reschedule. All of which meant Aidan couldn't really offer a justification for why he'd ignored all the messages, and if Jase was angry enough to do something drastic, he'd only have himself to blame.

'Hello?' The word echoed along the hallway as he called out, and he shivered in response. It was almost as if the entire house was empty, but there was no way Jase would have left and taken everything with him, just because Aidan hadn't replied to the texts. His car was on the driveway too, so the idea that he might have done something as drastic as walking out was ridiculous. Aidan was still telling himself that as he pushed open the door to the lounge, holding his breath in case the wing-backed armchair that Jase adored, which they'd picked up from an antique fair on a trip to France, was gone. Thank God it was still there, complete with their beloved cats, Babs and Ange, curled up on the seat, neither of whom bothered to open their eyes as Aidan came into the room. There was no sign of Jase, but at least he could breathe again, because he knew for certain his husband wouldn't have gone without the cats. Deep down he realised he was being ridiculous, even allowing the thought to cross his mind, but sometimes he couldn't help catastrophising. Having a parent who was incapable of loving Aidan for who he was had caused more damage than he wanted to admit, and given him a fear of abandonment that never fully went away.

Leaving the lounge, he headed out to the sunny kitchen, which they'd loved from the moment they'd bought the house. They'd both been able to picture family life in that room. There was space for a big dining table, where a family could eat together, or the children could do their homework while their dads cooked up a storm. The kitchen overlooked the back garden, which had plenty of room for a sandpit and a swing set, maybe even a treehouse. They'd found the home of their dreams, and from that moment their desire to build a family had grown stronger and stronger. But now Aidan was no longer sure if it was what he wanted, and he had no idea how to tell the man he loved about his doubts.

Jase wasn't in the kitchen either and Aidan had just taken out his phone to call him, when he spotted him out in the garden. He was digging and, even from thirty feet away, Aidan could tell that it was anger driving the spade into the ground every time it hit the soil. Physical activity was how Jase always coped with things when there was a lot on his mind. He'd trained for a marathon in the run-up to their wedding, when the reaction of Aidan's family to their upcoming nuptials had left them both feeling hurt. Aidan only wished his coping mechanisms were half as healthy, but the only solace he'd found was working as much overtime as he could, just so he was too tired to think. It was that or hitting the bottle, and that was one stereotype he'd always sworn he wouldn't perpetuate.

He had no idea if Jase heard him approaching, but either way his husband didn't look up. 'Do you want a drink? That looks like thirsty work.'

'What I want is a husband who keeps the promises he's made.' Jase drove the spade into the ground again, with enough force to send a sod of earth flying into the air, but he still didn't look in Aidan's direction.

'I was with Isla, at her consultant's appointment.' This time, Jase's head shot up in response, his eyes full of concern.

'What did they say? Is she okay?'

'It's leukaemia.'

'Oh my God, she's not on her own, is she? You should have brought her here.' The hostility that had been radiating from Jase had completely disappeared, but Aidan had only told him half the story and guilt at using Isla's diagnosis as a get-out-of-jail-free card was fizzing inside him.

'We went to the deli for a bit and sat in the garden; she just needed some time to process it all. But after that she looked done in, and she said she just wanted to sleep. I don't think she's been getting much lately.'

'That poor kid.' It was obvious Jase wasn't thinking about

himself in any of this, and another stab of guilt twisted Aidan's insides. 'What did they say about treatment? The thought of chemo must be terrifying.'

'The type of leukaemia she's got is chronic, rather than acute. It progresses more slowly and can often be managed in a way that could give her the same life expectancy as anyone else. It means the first-line treatments are far less aggressive than chemo, but they won't cure it. That will mean living with the illness, and the risk of it one day progressing, for the rest of her life. After what happened with her dad, that's understandably something she's struggling to get her head around.'

'I don't even know what to think about whether that counts as good news or not, so God knows how Isla is coping with it.' Jase ran a hand through his hair. 'I mean it's positive that it's not aggressive, but facing the fact that it will always be there must be overwhelming. I just wish you'd told me you were going with her. I'd never have kept messaging you, and I could have told Ellen that now wasn't the right time to meet.'

'Did you go on your own?' If someone had held a gun to Aidan's head and asked him what he wanted Jase's answer to be, he still wasn't sure he could have told them.

'Yes.'

'And have I blown it for us?'

'Do you want to have?' Jase held his gaze, and Aidan had no idea how to answer that question either, but he didn't need to and his husband's eyes had filled with tears. 'You don't want to do this any more, do you?'

'I don't know.' His uncertainty was the first thing he'd been sure of in days, but watching Jase wipe away tears with the back of his hand made Aidan feel like the worst person in the world.

'Is it because of Isla? Because you can't imagine doing this without her as our egg donor?' Tears were streaming down Jase's

face now, and it would have been so easy for Aidan to tell his
husband that was the reason. But using Isla like that would have
been even more unforgiveable, and he wouldn't have been able to
live with himself if he didn't tell Jase the truth.

'She still wants to be our donor, and according to the consultant there's no risk of passing anything on to the baby. But I told
her not to even think about that right now.' He was delaying,
playing for time, but he couldn't keep doing it. 'The truth is, I
don't know any more. What if I'm like my father?'

'You're nothing like him.' Jase made a move towards Aidan,
but he took a step back. He had to get the words out and say
everything that needed to be said.

'Even if I'm not, what if my relationship with him means I
don't know what a healthy relationship between a father and
child should look like? I don't want to ruin our baby's life and
make them feel the way I have.'

'Aidan Kennedy, I've heard you talk your fair share of utter
bollocks in my time, but this is something else.' Jase was too
quick for him this time, and he wrapped his arms around Aidan's
waist before he could get away. 'Rube adored you from the
moment you came into his life, because you knew how to listen
to him – *really* listen – when none of the rest of us did. You
understood when his feelings about his dad got conflicted, and
you were able to put yourself in his shoes precisely because of
what you've been through. All I'll be any good for with our kid, is
if life all goes swimmingly. Okay, I had the challenges with my
hearing and got a bit of bullying at school, but I've had such an
easy ride, being loved and supported by Mum and Dad like I was
the best thing since sliced bread. And then to top it all, I found
someone like you. No one is supposed to get that lucky in life,
and the chances are that our kid will one day come up against
stuff that's tougher than anything I've been through. They'll need

to talk to someone who's had to be resilient and still been able to care for others, even when I know there were times when it felt like no one really cared about you. That's something you can offer our child. You've done it for Isla today, even though you've obviously been wrestling with how to talk to me about this. But I bet if you asked Isla, she'd have had no idea you had your own stuff going on too.'

'My stuff is nothing compared to hers,' Aidan tried to protest, but Jase held him even more tightly.

'Yes, it's different to what's going on with Isla, but every child deserves unconditional love. And there's no point pretending it doesn't hurt like hell when you don't get it. But you've got it now. There are times when you drive me mad. Today's been a case in point.' Jase put a hand under his chin. 'But I honestly don't believe there's anything you could do that would stop me loving you. If you ever cheat on me, I'll hate your guts, and if I get the chance, I'll chop your balls off and have them made into earmuffs, but deep down I won't be able to stop myself from loving you.'

'*Earmuffs?*' Aidan was laughing now, and crying too, as his husband pulled him closer still.

'In a minute I'm going to kiss you, just to shut you up.' Jase grinned. 'But before I do, I need to tell you something. Ellen was great. I used a little white lie that an emergency had come up for you at work and she was so understanding. She really wants to help us, and I'm pretty damn sure she's the right person to do it. You must know there's no one else in the world I'd want to do parenthood with, but I'm not going to force you into anything either. All I need you to do is nod if you want me to set up a second meeting with Ellen.'

Aidan looked at his husband, and before he even realised he was doing it, he started to nod. Standing in front of him was his person, the one he wanted to share everything with. And if Jase believed in him, half as much as he said he did, that was enough to convince Aidan he was right, because there was no one in the world he trusted more.

* * *

'I need a glow up.' Wendy plonked herself down on the seat next to Aidan and Jase, in Danni and Charlie's back garden. 'And I feel like you two are just the guys to help me.'

'I think she thinks I'm Gok Wan and you're Tan France.' Jase looked at Aidan and winked.

'Or she thinks we're Trinny and Susannah. And with my inability to stick to the pre-baby diet, I'm certainly in danger of getting the boobs.' Aidan laughed, but turning towards Wendy, he could see she was deadly serious. 'What's up, my darling? You don't look like your usual self at all.'

'I feel like a bag lady. Look at me, I tried to make an effort, but I just look a state.' Wendy pulled at the 'cold shoulder' top she was wearing, which had sleeves with cut out sections. It was the kind of thing Aidan's mother had always seemed to favour on what she described as 'fancy occasions', for reasons he'd never quite been able to fathom, because they did nothing for her, but he wasn't about to confess to Wendy how much he disliked what she was wearing.

'You always look grand. You've got the biggest smile and—'

'That's exactly the sort of thing people say to someone whose got nothing else going for them.' Wendy sighed. 'I don't want to have the biggest smile. I want to have a banging figure and look ten years younger than I am. I want everyone to say Gary's punching above his weight, instead of wondering what he's doing with an old frump like me.'

'Right, what's going on?' Aidan put down his drink, signalling he meant business. 'Gary's over there at the barbecue with Charlie and Joe, laughing his head off and looking very much as though he feels like the luckiest fella in the world. And from what he's said ever since the two of you got together, I know that's true.'

'He told me he's happier than he's even been.' Jase leant forward in his chair. 'So whatever it is you're concerned about, you definitely don't need to worry about Gary not realising that all his Christmases have come at once.'

'It's just...' Wendy shook her head. 'Oh, ignore me, I'm being stupid.'

'Anyone need another top up?' Danni suddenly appeared behind Wendy, who thrust out her glass in response.

'Always.'

'You three looked like you were plotting a revolution as I walked over.'

'I was just after some advice on getting a glow up.' Wendy pulled a face. 'But I probably need Paul Daniels to pull off a trick like that, and he's been dead for years.'

'What a load of rubbish.' Gwen, who'd been chatting to Esther, on a neighbouring table, swivelled around in her seat, and Esther followed suit. 'What you need is a lesson in self-confidence. I went through that same thing when I hit fifty, and I wanted to cover up and hide.'

'*You*?' Esther nearly choked on her drink, and Aidan had to press his lips together to stop himself from laughing. It was almost impossible to believe that Gwen had ever lacked confidence about anything, but she shot Esther a look that said otherwise.

'I thought my best days were behind me, but I had no idea how good things could get if I just worked at it.'

'Is this where you tell me I need to get myself a gym member-ship, cut out all sugar, and give up alcohol?' Wendy wrinkled her nose. 'Because I don't think I can do that and there's no point anyway, it's not like I can turn the clock back. How can I feel anything but past my best, when my ex has got a woman who's five years older than our eldest daughter pregnant? A woman he met when, for once in his life, he covered for me at a college open evening when our youngest went to look round. And, if that wasn't bad enough, Gary's ex-wife is all over social media with her wedding pictures. She's lost forty pounds since they split, and got lip fillers and veneers. I went out and got myself some hair extensions, because I thought that might be an easy fix for looking and feeling younger. But my daughter said they look cheap and that they make me look, in her words, even older than I am.'

'Do you like them?' Gwen narrowed her eyes.

'I did, until she said that.'

'What everyone else thinks doesn't matter. The only person who can make you feel better about yourself is you.' Gwen stood up and took hold of Wendy's shoulders. 'You need to stand in front of a mirror and tell yourself all the things you like about the way you look. I couldn't even look at my reflection when I first started, and all I saw was stretch marks and dimply bits, and things that swung a hell of a lot lower than they should.'

'I can't think of anything I like about the way I look.' Wendy frowned.

'Neither could I, so I started with what I was grateful for. This body that I'd complained about, because bits of it were more floppy than perky, had carried my babies. It had also allowed me to work as a midwife for more than three decades at that point, and it had kept me healthy and well, despite the fact I often abused it. Once I started to be grateful for what it had done for me, I could see things I liked about it too. And once I got to that stage, there was no stopping me. One of the most liberating things I ever did was becoming a life model for an art group at the Three Ports College. I had to pose naked, and the first time I was terrified what the results might look like. But when the students were finished and the tutor asked for my opinion on their work, I could finally see my body through someone else's eyes. I was strong and beautiful, in a perfectly imperfect way. Nothing stopped me after that, and I wouldn't be doing all the things I'm doing now, if I hadn't gone through that phase in my life.'

'I'd rather sand my fingertips off with a cheese grater than pose naked in front of an art class at the Three Ports College, especially as my ex-husband's girlfriend works there now.' Wendy laughed for the first time. 'But I get what you mean.'

'I think what we need is a St Piran's night out.' Aidan looked at Wendy. 'We could go somewhere really classy, that we all need to dress up for. Don't get me wrong, I love a barbie as much as anyone, but we need a night out where jeans and a T-shirt just aren't going to cut it.'

'What about one of the fundraising balls at The Pavilion? The Friends of St Piran's had one last year, but they have loads of them.' Wendy's face lit up at the thought, and she wasn't the only one. It had been ages since Aidan and Jase had been on a night out like that. They'd been so caught up in their plans to start a family, and then in Isla's diagnosis, but they all needed to have some fun. There was nothing Aidan liked better than seeing Jase all dressed up for a big night out. Every time he saw his husband in a tuxedo, he fell in love with him all over again. And if it helped Isla feel as if life was back to normal for a night, too, that would be even better.

'We'd need twenty for a table at most of the events, I think.'

Esther furrowed her brow. The hospital had a large workforce, but there was a core group of staff who'd become closer, most of whom worked in A&E, or like Wendy, had some connection to it. 'With partners, we could probably stretch to a second table. I'm sure all the usual crowd would be up for it.'

'We'll have to ask Amy, Zahir and Isla too; it's such a shame they couldn't make it tonight, but I suppose some of us had to work.' Danni set the bottle she'd been carrying down on the table, and put a hand on her bump. 'I'm happy to be the designated driver and take as many as I can fit in my car, but when we work out the numbers, we could think about hiring a couple of minibuses.'

'I'll text Isla later and see what she thinks.' Aidan had no idea if she'd feel up to having a night out, but she needed the distraction more than anyone, and he was already determined to do whatever he needed to make it a special night for her.

'The way things are going, this might have to be mine and Charlie's hen and stag do, even if we have pushed the wedding back for a while.' Danni smiled. 'Because the chances of us organising a night out when this little one comes along are pretty slim, especially seeing as all of our potential babysitters would be on the guest list. That's if anyone even wants to volunteer for babysitting.'

'You can put our name on the list for a start; we're up for as many baby cuddles as we can get.' Jase's tone was light, but Aidan could see the yearning in his eyes. And suddenly picturing his husband with a baby in his arms held even more appeal than the idea of him in a tuxedo. He was made to be a father, and Aidan wouldn't let him down again.

# 18

Isla had managed less than three hours' sleep. She'd started doing research into whether the form of leukaemia she'd been diagnosed with, and whether the treatment she was due to start as a result, would affect her chances of a successful egg collection. But she'd ended up down an internet rabbit hole of conflicting advice and personal stories. The evidence suggested that the treatment wouldn't affect her long-term fertility, but that patients shouldn't get pregnant once they'd started taking the inhibitors, because it could harm the baby. Right now, there was no chance of her getting pregnant, unless it was an immaculate conception, because she hadn't even been on a date in well over a year. But what she couldn't work out was whether the treatment would affect the quality of her eggs and whether that meant she should go ahead with the egg collection before her treatment started, not just for Aidan and Jase, but to safeguard her own chances of having a baby one day.

The trouble was, she still didn't know whether they wanted her to be their donor any more. Aidan had told her not to even think about the egg donation until the doctors had monitored her first round of treatment, and assessed whether or not her body was responding to the inhibitors. But her research had made her question if that was the right move. If she ever wanted to become pregnant naturally, she'd have to stop the inhibitors, and the same would apply if she wanted to undergo egg collection in the future. If she was going to do it, she couldn't see the point in delaying. Although maybe it was Aidan's way of gently backing out of their plan. There'd been more questions than answers, ever since she'd got her diagnosis, and it was the reason why sleep had been so elusive even after she'd stopped trawling through the internet. But by the time she dragged herself out of bed after far too little sleep, she had at least made one decision.

As she pinged off an email to the fertility clinic, a reminder popped up on her phone, telling her she had an appointment at The Thornberry Centre in ninety minutes. She hadn't needed the reminder, even though the calendar on her phone seemed to be filled with appointments for blood tests and assessments. She was meeting her consultant again in three days' time, and she wanted to be in a position to tell Dr Yang about the decision she'd made to go ahead with egg collection. In the meantime, Vanessa had arranged an appointment for her with one of the counsellors at The Thornberry Centre.

When Vanessa had called to tell her about the appointment, Isla had tried to say she didn't need it, and that she had enough support 'in real life' not to need a stranger. She'd also tried to brush off the need to talk to anyone at all about how her diagnosis had left her feeling. After all, it was the 'best' kind of leukaemia she could have, according to Dr Yang. But Vanessa had clearly seen and heard it all before, and she hadn't been prepared to take no for an answer. She could tell that Isla wasn't taking this as casually as she pretended to be, and eventually she'd been forced to admit that her diagnosis had triggered some painful memories of her father's battle with his own health. What she hadn't confessed to Vanessa was that she couldn't talk to her family, because she was terrified about how it might affect them. And that the 'family' she claimed to have so much support from was really Aidan and Jase. She hadn't told any of her old friends yet, either, because they all knew her family and she didn't want to risk the news getting back to them, even if one of them thought they were acting the good Samaritan by getting involved.

She'd had dinner at her grandparents' place the night before, and Joy had fussed around her the way only a grandmother could, asking her if she was dieting again. Even when Isla had tried to insist, as she always did, that it was just a side effect of being on her feet for so much of the day, her grandmother wouldn't let it go. It was like she was some kind of bloodhound, sniffing out the fact that there was more going on this time, and Isla had almost buckled under the pressure. It was only when Grandpa Bill had noticed how uncomfortable she was getting, and had told his wife to stop nagging, that Joy had eased off. That hadn't stopped him taking Isla to one side afterwards, and quietly offering to gift her a regular monthly payment to '*help out*', so she could reduce her hours and get a bit more rest if she needed it. Isla was surrounded by people who loved her, but they were incapable of letting her sort out any problems she might have by herself.

The medication Isla would be taking when she started the inhibitors would be much easier to hide than chemo would have been, but going away with her grandparents to visit her mother and Lexi, after the babies arrived, still presented a risk. If she was stopped at customs and asked about her medication, the cat would be out of the bag. She wasn't ready to tell them yet, and she wasn't sure when she would be. But one thing she knew for certain was that she didn't want it to overshadow the joy they should all be feeling at the arrival of the twins. It was just one more reason why she wanted to go ahead with the egg collection, because her grandmother would definitely want to know why her plans had changed if she didn't. Isla knew how lucky she was to have a family who cared about her so much, but there was no denying it felt overwhelming at times. And maybe there was more she needed to say to the counsellor than she was prepared to admit.

Sitting in one of the waiting rooms in The Thornberry Centre would have been a wake-up call if Isla had needed one. No-one would have been able to tell that some of the patients in the waiting area had ever been ill, but there were others who wore the side effects of their treatment like neon signs, declaring to the world they were in the midst of a storm, with the kind of devastating impact that only cancer could wreak. There were people from a wide span of ages too, from the elderly couple gripping one another's hands in the far corner of the room, to the teenage boy in a wheelchair, whose lower left leg was missing, and who was listening to something on his headphones, whilst studiously ignoring his ashen-faced mother. Almost all the other patients had someone with them, except a woman who was furiously knitting, as if her life depended on it, the needles moving so fast they were in danger of giving off sparks.

'Rube!' The boy, who looked to be in his late teens and until that point seemed to have an expression set in stone, beamed with delight as Reuben came into the waiting room with a huge box in his arms. 'I spoke to the coach and now that we've got some sponsorship, he's going to look into starting a wheelchair rugby team.'

'That's brilliant, Ben, and I think we both know who their number-one player is going to be.' Reuben hadn't noticed that Isla was on the other side of the waiting room, and she wasn't planning to alert him to it. She couldn't take her eyes off him all the same.

'Ben Meredith.' A woman in a smart grey suit came out of one of the consulting rooms and called the boy's name, but as his mother went to stand up, he shot her a look.

'I told you, I'm going in by myself. I've got to start being more independent if I'm going to get back to uni.' When she still tried to protest, he held up his hand. 'Mum, *please*, we've talked about this.'

'Okay.' The woman sat back down with a thud, her eyes following her son's every move as he said goodbye to Reuben, and then slowly wheeled himself towards the consulting-room door, finally disappearing from view.

'Thank you for talking to him about the wheelchair rugby.' The boy's mother reached out to Reuben, and took hold of his hand. 'He's been broken-hearted since the op, thinking he'll never play sports again. But he's been in the home gym all week, since they said they're going to start a group at the club, working on his upper body strength. He wouldn't have spoken to the coach, or started to get excited about things again, without you and your sponsorship.'

'It was nothing, Sam, honestly. The sponsorship helps me out with my tax bill.' Reuben shrugged as if what he'd done for Ben really was nothing, but Isla had seen with her own eyes how much it had obviously meant to the boy. 'And he's too talented not to keep up his rugby.'

'I can't tell you how much happier he's been, and like he said, he's making plans to go back to uni now too. I'm trying to focus on the fact that he's got no evidence of disease at the moment, and that we're moving ahead now he's getting a prosthetic, but all of that was really hard to do when he was so down. Meeting you has made so much difference to him.' Sam squeezed Reuben's hand again. 'He's getting so independent again, and I'm sat here twiddling my thumbs. So I might as well go and grab myself a coffee.'

'Make sure you get yourself some of this before you go.' Reuben inclined his head towards the box he was carrying. 'I remember how I ate my mum out of house and home when I was Ben's age, and there's lots of good stuff today, including some strawberries. I know he likes those.'

'Thank you.' Sam stood up and planted a kiss on Reuben's cheek, before taking some things from his box. 'Can I get you a coffee?'

'No, thanks. Just go and enjoy having five minutes to yourself. I'll see you both soon.' It was only when Reuben turned away from Sam and set the box down, that he spotted Isla.

'Are you following me?' He grinned and her pulse seemed to quicken in the annoying way it always did whenever he was around.

'I was about to ask the same of you. Let's face it, you could reasonably expect to find me here, but I can't say the same of you.' Even as she said the words, she knew they weren't true. It was typical of what she'd seen of Reuben that he'd come along and donate produce to patients in the cancer unit.

'I come in a couple of times a week with leftover stock. On Tuesdays I leave a couple of boxes for the patients having chemo, and on Fridays I split them between the radiotherapy and counselling waiting areas.'

'The world would be a nicer place if there were more people like you in it.' The words were out of her mouth and hanging in the air before she could stop them, and a wave of heat flushed up her neck, staining her cheeks.

'Not half as nice as it would be if there were more people like you, but a one-off is even more precious.' From anyone else it would have sounded unbearably cheesy, the chat-up line of someone trying way too hard, but somehow Reuben made it sound as though he meant every word. Although that didn't stop her cheeks going even hotter. 'How are you doing?'

Reuben had taken the seat beside her and lowered his voice, but she could still feel the eyes of everyone in the waiting room on her. Even the *click clack* of the knitting needles had stopped, and she suddenly understood what it must feel like to be a goldfish in a bowl.

Isla glanced at her watch. 'I've still got fifteen minutes until my appointment, and I could do with a bit of fresh air.'

'Let's go then.'

The area outside The Thornberry Centre was probably the nicest part of the hospital. There was a pretty garden, with raised planters, in a hexagonal pattern, flanked by six benches. In the centre of the garden was a fountain and, at the furthest end from the building, a bronze anchor with a plaque beneath it, engraved with the word 'Hope'. Isla had sometimes sought refuge in the garden when she'd taken a break during a traumatic shift in A&E, and it had always filled her with a sense of peace.

'You made such a difference to that boy's life.' Isla sat on the third bench, and Reuben took a seat next to her.

'It was nothing special.'

'It was to him. And to his mum.'

'I'm only trying to repay what I've had. Sam's a single mum and it's been tough for her since Ben's diagnosis with osteosarcoma. I think he just needed someone to talk to who wasn't his mum, or a counsellor, and who was able to be a bit less emotional than the other people around him. When I had some tough times, and I couldn't talk to Mum or Anthony about them, I was really grateful that I had Jase and Aidan. Especially when my dad died.'

'I'm sorry, I wasn't sure what had happened with your dad, because Aidan and Jase have only really talked about your mum and Anthony.' Isla had told Reuben things that some of her closest friends didn't know. But now she thought about it, she hadn't really given him the chance to tell her anything much about his life. She'd assumed he'd had the perfect upbringing, because that was how everyone else's lives had looked when she was growing up, and she'd been envious that none of her friends had been forced to face the prospect of losing a parent. But Reuben had lost his dad too.

He sighed. 'I don't talk about him much, because for a long time he wasn't a part of my life. He left Mum when he found out I was on the way, and he was never really interested in seeing me. We had patchy contact from when I turned five, but he was always more absent than present.'

'That must have been hard.' Isla searched his face as she spoke. She was old enough now to know that the assumptions she'd made about how happy other people's childhoods were weren't always true. And she'd come to realise that losing a father who adored you was far better than having one who'd never cared, but Reuben shrugged.

'Not as much as you'd think. Anthony has filled a lot of that void and he's been incredibly good to me. Any gaps that were left were more than made up for by having Jase and Aidan, who were like the fun dads, balancing out the serious and stable side I got from Anthony. Then there was mum, and my grandparents. Honestly, no kid could have got more love than me.' Reuben smiled. 'It was when my father got back in touch on a more regular basis that things got a bit tougher. He was dying of liver cirrhosis, and I didn't know how to feel about him, or the fact he was dying. He was a stranger, who suddenly wanted this close relationship. There was such a lot of pressure and I felt guilty because part of me wished he'd never got in touch.'

'I can understand that. Watching someone slowly fade away is hard enough when you love them.' Isla swallowed hard.

'I was so confused and I felt like the worst person in the world because I didn't want to spend all my time with him, even though we did manage to get closer than we'd ever been. It was hard to talk to Mum and Anthony, because they were still so angry about how my dad had treated me. I spent a lot of time with Ricky in the final days, and Jase and Aidan would often come with me. I don't know what I'd have done without them, because they were the only people I felt I could be completely honest with. I knew it was hurting Mum and I felt terrible about that, but Ricky had no one else. It was such a sorry existence he'd had in the end, and I couldn't be angry with him any more. He'd messed up his own life, far more than he'd ever messed up mine. When he died, and I discovered he'd left me a substantial amount through a life insurance policy, the guilt I felt about not loving him the way a son should got even worse, and to counter that I started to talk about Ricky like he'd been some kind of saint. I clashed with Mum and Anthony, and even with my grandparents, but Aidan and Jase got me through that too. They listened and they didn't judge or project how they were feeling about my father on to me. I could so easily have blown the money he left me, but the uncs helped me get my head straight and decide what I wanted to do. It's how I was able to buy the deli. Being able to help a few other people out, because of the business, makes me feel better about what happened to my dad and that his life wasn't for nothing after all.'

Isla wanted to tell Reuben that his father's life had meant so much more than the deli because without him Reuben wouldn't have existed. But she managed to bite back the words. When she was around him, it was hard to remember what a mess she could create by crossing a line between them, and she had to keep reminding herself why it could so easily end up being a disaster. It was safer to talk about losing their fathers, than to allow how she felt about Reuben to creep into the conversation. 'Creating a legacy like that for your father is amazing, and it's what I still want to do for my dad. But I don't even know if Aidan and Jase want me to be their donor any more.'

'Have you spoken to them?'

'I've tried. Aidan just keeps telling me that the priority is for me to look after myself.'

'It is.' Reuben's eyes met hers and the look he gave her was so intense she had to drop her gaze.

'I might have a normal life span, or things might escalate quickly, to a point where it could be too late to do any of this. I don't want my life to have meant nothing.'

'It already means so much and not just to your family, or the patients whose lives you make such a difference too. You've got no idea how it felt for Aidan when you made that offer. He hasn't had the easiest of times with his family and I know that's affected his self-worth, but you will have helped change that. You're trusting him with the most precious gift you could give anyone, and I know that will have meant the world to him, and to Jase.'

Tears pricked her eyes, and Isla focused on some yellow flowers in one of the raised beds, so Reuben wouldn't realise how emotional she was. 'I do trust Aidan and Jase. It's what made the decision so much easier than being an anonymous donor, but I need them to understand that they're helping me as much as I'm helping them. I'm terrified that without them, I won't get to give my dad the kind of legacy he deserves and I don't want to risk waiting until it's too late. But I don't want them to feel like I'm forcing their hand either, because it's got to be right for them. I really wish I'd got through the egg donation, before I was given my diagnosis.'

'Just tell them what you've told me.' Reuben reached out for her hand, and her fingers curled around his, exactly like they had the first time their hands had touched, and it felt like the most natural thing in the world. This situation was already so complicated, and she'd told herself time and again that her attraction to Reuben should be left to pass, as it no doubt would eventually. She didn't even know for certain if he felt the same, although it often seemed like he did. Either way, she'd already discovered to her cost that sometimes she couldn't control what went on in her body, and all she could do was try to trust that everything would somehow work out for the best.

# 19

In the hours leading up to meeting Ellen for lunch, Aidan felt so nervous that even the thought of eating made him nauseous. So much was relying on him making a good impression, and he'd already messed up once. From the messages she'd sent since their first meeting, it was clear that Ellen had loved Jase on sight, just like everyone else did. That meant the only one capable of derailing her offer to be a surrogate was Aidan. For as long as he could remember, his go-to approach when meeting new people had been to try and make them laugh. He'd earned himself a reputation for his dry humour at university, and in every job he'd had since then.

'I feel like I'm going on a first date. The trouble is, I've been happily letting myself go for the past ten years, safe in the knowledge I'd never have another one of those.' Aidan turned to his side and sucked in his stomach, as Jase sat on the bed watching him. 'Now I've left it far too late to get in shape, so I can try to persuade Ellen I'll be a great role model for healthy living. I keep reading about the importance of starting weightlifting before I hit middle age, but I don't think lifting my own body weight out of the chair really counts.'

'She won't give a damn what you look like.' Jase was laughing, even before Aidan spun round with a look of outrage on his face.

'Well thanks very much!'

'You know what I mean. You look great, but that's not what she's going to focus on. She wants to know you're someone she can get on with throughout the pregnancy, and she also wants to know that you deserve to be a dad.' Jase reached out to Aidan. 'And everyone who meets you can work that out pretty quickly.'

'So I didn't need the Spanx after all?' Aidan raised his eyebrows, laughing too, as he closed the gap between him and Jase. All he had to do was convince Ellen that hanging out with him wouldn't be unbearable, which should be easy, because he'd never had a problem convincing anyone of that. Except for his father.

'It's been such a lovely afternoon, thank you.' Ellen kissed Jase on both cheeks, before turning towards Aidan and doing the same as they stood in the car park outside the restaurant. 'I was on board after meeting Jase, but now I know a baby would be so lucky to have the pair of you as parents. This will be my last time as a surrogate, and I'm so glad it's going to be for you guys.'

'We feel so blessed that you've chosen us.' Jase was beaming. The lunch couldn't have gone better, and they'd stayed talking for another hour, even after Aidan had settled the bill. If everything worked out, this would be Ellen's third surrogate pregnancy, and with two children of her own before she started her surrogacy journey, she'd made the decision to 'retire' at five. Aidan just hoped they'd be ready to go ahead when she was, because she might not want to hang around waiting if things weren't in place to proceed with an egg donor.

'As soon as I read your profile, I felt a connection.' Ellen had a wonderfully warm smile. 'And I meant what I said about you guys coming over for a barbecue soon. I think it's important for you to meet Andrew and the kids, because we're going to be part of one another's lives for a long time.'

'I hope he likes us.' Aidan wished he could just enjoy the fact that the meeting had gone so well, without the wave of anxiety that had almost immediately begun bubbling up inside of him. But it didn't work that way.

'Oh he'll love you, trust me.' Ellen made it sound as though her husband had very little choice in the matter, and that's exactly what she meant. 'But at the end of the day, what he thinks won't influence my decision. It's my body and I get to choose who I want to help become a family. And I've made my choice.'

'Thank you so much, it means more to us than we could ever explain.' Aidan hugged her, her response muffled against his chest.

'I know, but I feel so lucky to be able to do it for you. There's no better feeling than knowing you've helped create a new family.' She pulled away slightly and looked up at him. 'Which is why I understand your egg donor's determination to try and help you, even in the middle of everything else she's got going on.'

Aidan had explained Isla's situation, and had told Ellen that they hadn't decided how they were going to proceed. It was Jase who'd insisted they tell Ellen everything, and he'd asked if she had any concerns about carrying an embryo created with an egg donated by someone who'd been diagnosed with cancer. Despite the fact that Isla's consultant had confirmed there was no risk of passing the cancer on to a baby, Jase had told Ellen he would understand if the idea made her feel odd. Cancer could grow from one rogue cell, after all. But Ellen had been adamant that she didn't have any concerns. Her first surrogate pregnancy had been for a woman who'd had her eggs frozen after being diagnosed with cervical cancer, and who'd subsequently undergone a complete hysterectomy. Three years later, and in remission, she and her husband had longed to start a family. This was no different, according to Ellen. But Aidan had seen the look on his husband's face and he was certain he knew what Jase was thinking. It *was* different, because that woman had been desperate to use her own eggs, rather than a donor's. But Jase and Aidan would be using a donor anyway, so why not choose one without that kind of complication? On paper it would have made perfect sense to take the easy choice, but life wasn't a paper exercise and Aidan still couldn't let go of the idea of using a donor they knew well, and would be happy to have as a part of their lives.

'We'll let you know as soon as we can what's happening with the donor eggs.' The way Jase described it felt suddenly impersonal, like it wasn't a crucial part of the process. Except this wasn't just about an altruistic gesture, from some random person, it was about Isla, and Aidan had grown to care about her more and more. Despite his recent wobbles, he knew for certain now that he wanted to be a father, but he couldn't imagine leaving Isla out of the equation either. So he had no idea how he'd come to terms with it if Jase was determined to go another way.

'I'll text you when I get in about a date for the barbecue.' Ellen held up her hand in a final parting gesture, just before she slid into the seat of her car. There was nothing stopping Aidan turning around and following Jase to their own car, except he knew when he did that they were going to have to have a very difficult conversation. It was time to decide, once and for all, whether they were still going to accept Isla's offer of donating her eggs, and he wasn't sure he was ready to hear what his husband had to say.

* * *

Aidan looked at the text on his phone again and let go of a deep breath. Putting off the conversation with Jase wasn't going to solve anything, so he might as well get on with it. The problem was, he wasn't entirely sure how to interpret what Isla had said in the last message she'd sent him.

> I've had the go-ahead from the clinic and I'll be starting the hormone injections on Wednesday. I know you're worried about me doing this, but I promise it's what I want. The first five eggs are yours whatever happens, and we'll split the rest fifty/fifty. It's just a bit of insurance for me, but regardless of how the leukaemia progresses, this might be my only chance to make a baby xx

Isla was repeating what she'd said the last time Aidan and Jase had seen her, and they'd told her again that going through with the egg donation shouldn't even cross her mind right now, because she needed to concentrate on her treatment and start it as soon as possible. Only she'd been as adamant as she was well-informed, and she'd clearly done her research.

'If I need to go on to chemo, they won't let me pause to have egg retrieval, so I'm going to be doing this whether you want my eggs or not.' Isla had made it sound like she was offering him a pint of milk, but her voice had cracked on the next sentence, and she'd suddenly looked incredibly fragile. 'If that happens, having a baby might never be an option for me, because I might not be well enough. This might be the only baby I'll ever be a part of creating, and it's still so important to me to do that. It's giving me something to aim for, and a reason to look forward. But if you don't want to go ahead, I understand, and I can cover the costs of the treatment myself.'

'Of course we still want you to be our donor.' Aidan had known in the moment that he shouldn't be speaking for Jase, but his heart had ached looking at the woman standing in front of him, who'd seemed so alone. Focusing on the fertility treatment was giving her something else to think about, and it was the best chance she had of fulfilling the promise she'd made to honour her dad's legacy. It was only later when he'd replayed the comments that he'd started to worry just how attached to the idea of making a baby Isla might become, and he was scared of what it might do to her if it didn't work. Jase hadn't said anything afterwards about Aidan accepting her offer, but from what he'd said to Ellen, he clearly had doubts too. However difficult it was, they needed to talk about it, and come to a decision, because Isla's fertility treatment was starting in two days' time.

'That went great, didn't it?' Jase glanced at Aidan, and then looked back at the road, as they headed home from their meet up with Ellen.

'She's lovely.' Aidan took another deep breath, still unsure of what he wanted to say, even as the words began to come out of his mouth. 'But we need to make a decision about Isla; the clinic have given her the go-ahead and she starts the injections on Wednesday.'

'Right.' Jase's expression was unreadable, but there was a tiny muscle going in his cheek.

'You don't want to use her eggs any more, do you?' Something twisted in Aidan's chest. He couldn't imagine taking this away from Isla, but he couldn't deny he had doubts, too.

'I don't know.' Jase pulled into a passing place and stopped the car, turning to look at Aidan again. 'I don't know what the right thing is for any of us, any more.'

'Because of the cancer?' When Jase nodded, Aidan felt as if his heart had contracted. He knew better than anyone what it felt like to be considered not good enough, and it was as if they were rejecting Isla for something completely out of her control. 'It wouldn't affect the baby, and we've been told it's not genetic, so—'

'Oh God, no, it's not that.' Jase's eyes had gone glassy. 'What I'm scared of, is us using some of Isla's eggs, and if the cancer progresses, having taken away some of her chances of becoming a mum. How could we live with ourselves, if we do that? How are we all going to feel, if she never has a child, but we do? We'll have stolen that from her. I just don't think I can take that risk.'

'You are the kindest man in the world.' Aidan leant forward and kissed his husband slowly, before pulling away again. The realisation hit him, that if it ended up just being the two of them forever, he'd be okay with that. Far more than okay in fact, because he really had married the best man in the world. Jase was someone who always thought of others before himself, and who radiated the same kindness he carried in his heart. But Aidan needed to confess his own doubts, and he wasn't sure they came from nearly so pure a place. 'I've been worried too, but what I'm scared of is that she seems to be pinning everything on us having a baby. I've become so fond of Isla, she feels like a little sister to me in many ways and I really want her to be a part of our child's life. But what if the fertility treatment doesn't work? Right now, I just want to protect her and make sure nothing can hurt her, because she's going through so much and there's nothing we can do to take that away. But if the treatment fails, it's going to devastate her. It'll break our hearts too, but we'll have the option of trying again, with another donor if we have to. We can't let Isla stop her treatment to do that for a second time, but I'm worried about how she'll react to the idea that we might need to move on? I'm scared it'll break her, that she'll pull away from us and stop looking to the future the way she should. We didn't cover any of this in our counselling, because the stakes weren't so high back then, and we weren't pinning everything on this one egg collection being enough. I don't think I could give up on our dream, or the chance to try again, even if that meant saving Isla any more pain. But it's going to hurt her if we put a stop to things now, too, and I've got no idea what to do for the best.'

There was a rawness in Aidan's throat as he waited for Jase to respond. All of the pieces of the jigsaw should have been fitting together now that Ellen wanted to be their surrogate, only the picture emerging was nothing like the one they'd seen on the box and none of the bits were slotting together the way they were supposed to. Maybe it was a sign from the universe that they shouldn't try for a baby, except he knew they'd spend all their lives wondering what could have been if they didn't attempt to follow their dream.

'I don't either, but it's hard to imagine going ahead without her.' Jase shook his head. 'So what do we do?'

'I think we need to have some more conversations with Isla, and see how we all feel once we know whether her treatment is working. My biggest fear, if we pull the plug now, is that she won't let us support her with anything she's going through, and that's something I really don't think I could deal with. We've still got a bit of time. The plan was always to freeze Isla's eggs anyway and, whatever we decide, she'll have stored some eggs she can use in the future if she needs to.'

'The problem is, Ellen is on a timeline of her own. This is her last surrogacy and you heard what she said about wanting it all finished before her eldest starts secondary school. We've got eighteen months, so we can't put it off for long.'

'I know, but despite what Isla told us, I'm almost certain she can't afford the cost of having her eggs frozen on her own and I don't think the NHS would cover it, because she's not going through chemo. So, if we make a definite decision not to use any of them now, I don't think she'll be able to go through with it.' Aidan closed his eyes for a second, opening them to meet his husband's gaze. 'I know I'm asking a lot, but I want to help her with this, whatever we decide. She offered us an amazing gift, and we owe her this. If it means I need to take out a loan, or take on all the overtime going, to top up the IVF fund, then I'm happy to do it. Right now, the thing Isla needs more than anything, is to create a future she can look forward to, and I'm not taking that away from her.'

'You were so wrong when you said I was the kindest man in the world, because I'm married to him.' Jase pulled Aidan closer and hugged him tightly. Being in his husband's arms had always felt like the place he was meant to be, and Jase had made Aidan feel safer, and more loved, than anyone else ever had. That kind of love was the one thing Aidan had craved most in life. So he was prepared to do whatever it took, to give the man he adored what he wanted too. But for now, they'd agreed to take a step back from their own dreams, to focus on supporting Isla. Aidan hadn't thought it was possible to love Jase any more than he had ten minutes before, but that was something he'd definitely been wrong about.

## 20

Isla moved as quietly as she could, checking that the drip was functioning the way it should and replacing the electrolytes in her patient's body. Stuart had his eyes closed, looking peaceful for the first time since he'd been admitted, when he'd been clawing at his throat and choking, his eyes wild with panic. He was struggling to swallow and, with an obvious progression of his Motor Neurone Disease, he'd been in a lot of distress. Isla had found it traumatic, so she couldn't even imagine what it was like for Stuart. He'd been given pain relief which had helped ease his panic, and had allowed him to rest, which was why she was so keen not to disturb him now. Stuart's bloods had been taken and he'd undergone a full examination, but for now the only treatment was to address his dehydration. A specialist from the speech and language team would be carrying out an assessment on Stuart's inability to swallow, and they'd asked to see a copy of his advance care plan to see whether there'd been any discussion about the use of a feeding tube. The paramedics had said at handover that it was a carer who'd called for the ambulance, but no one had accompanied him, and there'd been no sign of any relatives yet.

Stuart must have been about the same age as Isla's father had been when he died, and the panic in his eyes when Isla had first seen him had been like an echo of the final stages of her father's illness too. In those last days, it wasn't clear if he'd even known who his family were. But despite losing his ability to communicate with words, it had been obvious when he'd opened his eyes that he'd still been able to feel afraid, and that had been the hardest thing for her to bear.

'Didn't want to wake up.' The words were hard to make out, but when Isla looked at Stuart, it was almost as if she could see them written in his eyes.

'I'm so sorry, I didn't mean to wake you.' She touched his hand for a moment, but his only response was to sigh.

'Enough.' It was just one little word, but it said so much, and it was as if Isla could actually feel the heart she'd superglued back together when her father had died shattering in her chest all over again.

Chloe, one of Stuart's carers, had arrived at the hospital about ten minutes after he'd woken up and spoken to Isla. The details of his advance care plan had set out that he didn't want a feeding tube, and Chloe had told Isla, and the rest of the team caring for him, that Stuart had been adamant he didn't want to prolong his illness. The progress of his MND had been relatively slow and he'd been living with the disease for more than three years already. According to Chloe, he had no living family, and most of his friends had drifted away since his diagnosis. Everything she'd said had broken Isla's heart a little bit more, and by the time

Stuart had been moved up to the ward, she'd had to go to the toilets to cry in private. Her tears were for her patient, her dad, and all that her family had gone through with the progress of his illness. But what she hadn't admitted, even to herself, was the drip, drip of fear – like a broken tap – that situations like this had triggered since her own diagnosis. It was nothing like MND, logically she knew that, and she also knew she was supposed to feel grateful that things weren't so much worse. But the not knowing how they would end up meant she couldn't turn off that dripping tap, no matter how much she might want to. Instead, she pushed the feelings down and made it all the way to the end of her shift, without anyone needing to ask if she was okay. They might have queried the redness of her eyes, if she hadn't pre-empted it by telling Amy that her hay fever was playing up, but she really thought she'd got away with it.

Amy had finished her shift at the same time as Isla, but she'd left the department first as Isla had needed to discuss the handover of one of her patients. She hadn't expected Amy to still be outside the shop, tucking into a huge piece of cake, when she'd gone to grab a drink before leaving.

'Oh my God, Isla, you have got to taste some of this pistachio cake Gwen has made, it's the best thing I've ever put in my mouth.'

'Well, I wouldn't go that far.' Gwen, who was the undisputed queen of innuendos, dropped one of her trademark winks as she made the comment, and Amy almost choked on the forkful of cake she'd just eaten. 'Danni and Charlie have asked me if I'd be able to make the cake for their wedding, so I'm trying out a few recipes and I need guinea pigs.'

'Come on skinny minnie, you can indulge just this once, because whatever diet you're on is working a bit too well, if you ask me!' Amy was already putting a slice of cake onto a paper plate, but when she looked up and realised that Isla had tears streaming down her face, she dropped it onto the table. 'Hey, what's wrong, and don't try passing it off as hay fever, because even I'm not that thick.'

'I don't, I can't...' Isla could hardly see through her tears and her head was throbbing with the effort of trying to hold them back for so long, but then Gwen slipped an arm around her waist.

'Right, come on you two, we're not doing this out here.' Within thirty seconds, Gwen had ushered them into the shop, behind the counter where one of the other volunteers was serving, and into the small stock room at the back, where much to Isla's surprise, there was a three-seater sofa. 'This is top secret, by the way, only the shop staff usually get to discover this space.'

'You do know I'm coming here whenever I need a break, don't you?' As Amy turned towards Isla, the grin slid off her face. As hard as she'd tried, Isla hadn't been able to get control of the tears this time, and they were still running down her face. 'Oh Isla, what is it? Has something gone wrong with the fertility treatment?'

'No.' She was gulping for air now, like a fish out of water and Gwen took charge again.

'Sit down, my love, and don't talk for a minute. Just breathe and keep crying if that's what you need to do. Then you can talk, but only if you want to. I'm going to get you a drink.' Gwen was true to her word, returning a couple of minutes later with a hot chocolate. It might have seemed an odd choice for the time of year, but she obviously knew what she was doing, because when Isla took a sip it was like a warm hug. Amy had sat next to her in silence, while Gwen was gone, giving her hand a gentle squeeze, which in itself was nothing short of a miracle, as there was little Amy hated more than silence; she usually talked non-stop.

'Thank you.' Isla's breathing was shuddery as she spoke, but the tears finally seemed to be drying up.

'You're more than welcome, my love; now, you take as long as you want. I can disappear back out to the shop if you want to chat with Amy in private, or you can both just sit here until you're ready to leave, if you don't want to talk at all.' The reaction on Amy's face to Gwen's words made Isla smile through her tears.

'I don't think Amy's ever going to forgive you if I follow that advice.'

'I mean you don't *have* to tell us.' Amy pulled a face. 'But isn't there a saying about a problem being smaller when you share it?'

'A problem shared is a problem halved.' Gwen shrugged. 'But you get to choose who you share it with.'

'I've got leukaemia.' Isla should probably have broken the news more gently than that, and Amy gave an audible gasp.

'Oh my God, I'm so sorry.' She enveloped Isla in a hug that almost knocked the hot chocolate out of her hands. 'But you're going to be okay. The success rate for treatment is really high and...'

'I don't think Isla had finished talking yet.' Gwen's tone was gentle as she interrupted Amy, but the words still stopped the younger woman in her tracks.

'I'm sorry, I'm sorry. You know I'm a motormouth at the best of times.'

Isla gave her a watery smile, and braced herself to tell the story she'd been trying to tell herself ever since the diagnosis. 'I'm lucky because it's chronic myeloid leukaemia, which as Amy says, has a high success rate of being effectively managed by medication that stops the overproduction of white blood cells. Just tablets for now, that's all.'

'There's no *that's all* about it.' Gwen sat down on the other side of Isla, fixing her with a look that made it difficult not to drop her gaze. It was going to be impossible to maintain eye contact, and keep trotting out the lines she'd just spun, making this sound like nothing, because Gwen was right, this wasn't nothing. 'A diagnosis like that would hit anyone hard. When did you find out?'

'Almost a month ago.' Isla's voice sounded so small, but as a sudden thought struck her, she grasped Gwen's wrist. Gwen had been friends with her grandparents for a long time and there was a good chance she'd feel they deserved to know. 'But I haven't told Nan and Grandpa Bill, and you can't tell them either. *Please*, you've got to promise me.'

Gwen's eyebrows shot up in surprise, but she was nodding. 'I promise not to say anything, but you really should, sweetheart, they'd want to be there for you.'

'I'm scared it will kill them. They've already had to go through losing their only son, and I can't put the burden on them that I could die too. Or on Mum and Lexi.'

'You could *die*? I thought you said you just have to take a pill.' Amy looked close to tears now, and this was exactly what Isla had been afraid of. But she'd started now, so she had to finish.

'There's a chance I could, if the inhibitors aren't effective and the cancer progresses through several phases. But even then there are treatment options to move on to, including chemo. It would only be if none of those things work.' Isla painted on a smile. 'We're a long, long way from that yet.'

'It's not just the chance of the worst-case scenario that's worrying you, though, is it?' Gwen was like some kind of all-seeing eye, and Isla shook her head.

'No, it's having to live with it that scares me most. The type of leukaemia I have is usually not curable, so it's a lifelong condition. Not knowing if and when things are going to change terrifies me. I saw Dad go through it, and watched what it did to everyone who loved him.' She sighed so deeply, it was as if someone had sucked all the air out of her body, and she had to take another shuddering breath before she could carry on. 'I thought I was doing better. I've been to a couple of counselling sessions, and I'd made the decision to go ahead with the egg donation, and to freeze some eggs for myself too. It's for insurance really, because if the leukaemia does progress, it might be too risky to delay chemo at that stage for a second egg collection. I thought I had it all straight in my head, but then we had this patient today, Stuart, who's been living with MND, and it brought back so many memories of what Dad had to deal with. I don't want to go through that, but more than anything I don't want my family to go through it again. I'm pinning all my hopes on counselling helping me to find a way of managing all those feelings, but I just don't know if I can. Not while I'm in a job like this. I've been avoiding seeing my grandparents too, because I'm scared I'm just going to blurt it out.'

'Do you wish you'd never been told that your father was ill?' Gwen was still looking at her in a way that meant she couldn't have lied, even if she'd wanted to.

'No, as awful as it was to know we were losing him, it also made me treasure every minute, in a way I wouldn't have done at that age, if I hadn't known we were on borrowed time. He always took every opportunity there was to make memories with us as well, and I think it helped us all to cope.'

'I've always thought that's the way we should all live, as if we're on borrowed time. It's what Barry and I have done ever since I came out of the other side of my horrible menopausal depression, determined to grab life and him, by the short and curlies.' For the first time Gwen laughed, and Isla found herself smiling again too. 'None of us know what's round the corner, my love, not really. No matter how much we might like to pretend to ourselves that we do. So, whatever you decide about telling your family, follow your dad's example and make as many memories as you can with the people you love. Hopefully your condition will remain stable for the rest of your life, but you'll never regret having done those things if you stay well. But you sure as hell might regret it if you don't, or if something else happens to take you away from them, or vice versa.'

'Gwen's right, we should all be doing that.' Amy put a hand on her arm. 'So no more excuses, you and me are booking that trip to Paris we keep talking about.'

'Why do I feel like you're using this as an excuse to railroad me in to holding your bag, while you pursue every good-looking man in a five-mile radius of the Eiffel Tower?' Isla was smiling, and Amy responded with a casual shrug.

'Can't something have a double benefit?' As Amy laughed, it was easy for a moment to forget everything that had been weighing her down, but as her friend started listing all the wonderful things they could do in Paris, Gwen leant forward and whispered in Isla's ear.

'Tell your family, you'll feel better when you do.' Isla gave an almost imperceptible nod, but she was already giving herself the excuse that she hadn't made any kind of promise. Part of her might be almost certain that Gwen was right, but she still had absolutely no idea if she'd ever be ready to put her family through something like this again.

# 21

'This is such an unexpected pleasure.' As Isla's grandmother set the tray down on the table, she repeated the same words she'd said when Isla had first arrived. She hadn't phoned her grandparents to say she was coming over, because it had been a spur-of-the-moment decision. What Gwen had said had weighed on her mind. Not just her comment about Isla being glad once she'd told them about her diagnosis, but also her advice to make the most of every moment she had with them, regardless of how she responded to treatment. No one was around forever, and they were two of her favourite people in the world, so she should be making the most of every moment with them. But it wasn't too late, and she fully intended to make up for lost time.

'I'd hate to see how much food you'd have brought in if you knew I was coming.' Isla grinned. There was a plate stacked high with biscuits and cookies, and another one with sausage rolls on one side and a brick wall of brownies on the other.

'You timed it well, coming on a day when I've been baking and your grandpa hasn't had the chance to polish everything off just yet.' Joy's tone was teasing, and her husband laughed.

'I did my best, but not even I can eat forty brownies in one sitting.'

'I told you that some of those are for the bake sale that Gwen is organising for the Friends' summer fundraising drive. So if you had eaten them all, you'd have had her and me to answer to!'

'Thank God I didn't then, because no man could survive that.' Grandpa Bill laughed again, and Isla did her best to arrange her face into a smile, but she was having the same trouble faking it as she'd so often had lately. The thought of her grandmother meeting up with Gwen and them idly chatting about life, without Gwen bringing up the fact that Isla had been diagnosed with leukaemia seemed impossible.

'This year would be particularly dangerous for you to cross Gwen, because she's on a mission to raise funds for another scanner.' Isla's grandmother sighed. 'One of the nurses on the orthopaedics ward was diagnosed with cancer after a scan that wouldn't have been detected any other way until it was too late. She'd have left her six-year-old son behind if it hadn't been caught in time. So, she wants to raise all the funds she can.'

'Cancer's the devil in a not-very-convincing disguise.' Grandpa Bill shook his head. 'It's pure bloody evil.'

'It is. Her husband was so terrified of losing her that the only way he could cope was to go out and run until he was almost fit to drop. He's doing a fundraiser for the scanner too, running three marathons in three weeks. Her dad, who's in his seventies, is doing one of them with him because he's so grateful for what the scan picked up and the fact that he's still got his daughter. There's nothing a parent fears more than losing a child.' Her grandmother's voice was thick with emotion, and Isla got to her feet, wrapping her arms around her nan, as Grandpa Bill did the same from the other side, encircling both of them in his arms.

'I'm so lucky I've got you here with me.' Joy leant her head against Isla's shoulder. 'That everyone is well, and we've got the visit to the twins to look forward to. I count my blessings a lot, but stories like that are a reminder to do it every day.'

'They certainly are, my love.' Bill squeezed them both tightly for a moment, but that wasn't the only reason Isla was struggling to catch her breath. There was no way she could tell them about her diagnosis now. It would cause them so much worry and she decided it was better to wait until she knew how the treatment was going before telling them. All she could do in the meantime was to hope, for her sake and theirs, that they'd never need to know at all.

* * *

When Reuben had invited Isla to go to the weekly get-together at his grandparents' house, she'd told him not to be so silly. Meeting the family was something you did way down the line in a relationship, and they weren't even in one. She could admit now that they were friends, fast becoming very good ones, and circumstances had meant they'd shared confidences with one another that no one else knew. But it had never crossed the line into something else, although she'd have been lying to herself if she'd pretended she hadn't thought about what it might be like to kiss him. But they hadn't and if she ever did decide a relationship was worth risking her heart for, it certainly wouldn't be at a time when she was going through so much other stuff. And it wouldn't be with someone whose friendship she'd miss as much as she'd miss Reuben's, if it all went wrong. So meeting the family seemed like an odd thing to do.

'My family love meeting my friends, and you're not just that.' When he'd looked at her, she'd wondered if he was going to make a move, her body reacting as if he was already touching her, as she desperately tried to persuade herself it would be a mistake. Except her body and her brain seemed to have gone their separate ways. But he hadn't crossed the line, and the only contact had been a light touch on her arm. 'You're already family in a way, and you're going to be around us a lot after Jase and Aidan have their baby. So why not get meeting the rest of us out of the way now? I would say we're a perfectly normal family, but I'm not going to lie.'

He'd grinned then, that disarming smile of his that had made her feel like there was some kind of connection with him from the first day they'd met. He probably had that effect on everyone, but either way it made it impossible for her to resist his invitation. She'd double-checked with Aidan, who'd seemed delighted about the idea, and now here she was.

'You needn't have bought anything. We're just so glad you've finally come to visit, darling.' Reuben's grandmother, Lin, planted a big kiss on her cheek after Reuben finished his introductions, and Isla had given Lin the chocolates and wine she'd brought with her. 'I've heard so much about you from Aid and Jase, and of course, Rube. Come through, come through. Everyone else is in the living room already. It's Tash's birthday, so you've picked the perfect occasion to join us.'

'I'm sorry, this might be a bit full-on.' Reuben whispered the words to her, before his grandmother started to hug him too. He'd explained that it was his mum's birthday, so she'd brought along some chocolates for Tash, too. What she hadn't realised was that she'd be getting a gift. After another round of introductions, Lin gestured towards a two-seater sofa, with two packages in brightly coloured wrapping paper on the coffee table in front of it.

'Right, you two sit over there, you can see where your presents are.'

'I forgot to tell you about this. It's a family tradition that no matter whose birthday it is, everyone gets a gift.' Reuben rolled his eyes, but he was still smiling.

'It's all Jase's fault.' Tash gave her younger brother a playful nudge. 'When he was little he'd go into absolute meltdown when it was my birthday and he didn't get any presents, so Mum started buying him something small to stop him from sulking and the tradition just grew from there.'

'These days it's only a bit of fun.' Lin shrugged. 'Just a token gift to make everyone in the family feel included in the celebration.'

'You're a part of the family now whether you like it or not.' Jase raised his glass. 'Although, after the gift you offered us, I think the bath bombs, or whatever delight you've got in your package, are going to seem like a poor exchange.'

'I'm expecting socks as usual.' Reuben's grandad, Ray, laughed, earning himself a stony look from his wife.

'If you cut your toenails a bit more regularly, so they didn't poke holes in the front of your socks, I wouldn't need to buy them so often.'

'Maybe you should have bought him some toenail cutters?' Tash pulled a face. 'It's just a good job we're not eating yet, because it would put poor Isla off her food.'

'Ray would need a belt sander for those things, anyway.' Aidan's words were met by a chorus of laughter, even from his father-in-law, although he also threw a pillow in his direction. They were so much fun to be around, and the love they had for one another was evident. Isla found herself watching Aidan a lot of the time, noticing how comfortable he seemed in the heart of his husband's family. He'd told her how strained things were with his own relatives, and it was lovely to see he'd found a second family who clearly adored him as much as he did them.

When Isla had eventually opened her gift, she'd discovered that it wasn't socks, or bath bombs. Instead, there was a mug, with the words *'I make families, what's your superpower?'* written across the front. Tears had pricked her eyes and she'd felt a huge rush of affection for everyone in the room. If everything went well and Jase and Aidan got their dream of becoming parents, the baby was going to be incredibly lucky to be a part of this family. When she'd thought about the prospect of potentially losing her own fertility, the idea of preserving her eggs had felt like a huge priority. It was strange, when she'd always feared how vulnerable it would make her to love someone enough to want to start a family with them, but she couldn't deny any more that a big part of her wanted that. Only now she wasn't sure she could ever risk having a child, not when there was no guarantee of how her leukaemia might progress. She'd always had this habit of allowing her brain to race too far ahead, and imagine scenarios she might not ever have to face. It was something she was working through with her counsellor, who'd assured her that her feelings would settle down once she'd processed the shock of her diagnosis. But the truth was, ever since she'd realised there was absolutely nothing she could do about her father's illness, she'd always been frightened of things she couldn't control, and her own diagnosis had brought so much of that back.

'Are you okay? Sorry if this is a bit much.' Reuben leant closer to her as he spoke and the confusion spiralling around in her head whipped up into a frenzy. She really liked him. There was no point in pretending, but wanting something didn't always mean it was a good idea. And she still didn't know if he saw her as anything more than a friend, who also happened to be donating her eggs to his uncles. He might feel weird about that too, even if he did like her. It was all so complicated, and she needed to talk some sense into herself, but it was very hard to do that when Reuben was sitting so close.

'Your family are lovely.' It was on the tip of her tongue to say 'you are too', but somehow she managed to hold back.

'Well, I've promised Nan I'll go and get the barbecue started, so you can either stay in here and face the inquisition that will no doubt start as soon as I leave, or you can give me a hand.'

'I'll come with you.' It would probably have been safer to steer clear of spending any time alone with Reuben, but she didn't seem to be able to help herself.

Ten minutes later the barbecue was lit, and the coals were beginning to do what they were supposed to.

'Do you want to see the most magical place on earth?' Reuben turned towards her and she wrinkled her nose.

'Are you offering to take me to Disneyland?'

'Maybe one day.' As he looked in her direction, she swore she could feel the blood pulsing through her veins. She was on dangerous ground, because if he touched her now, no amount of telling herself this might be a stupid thing to do was going to make any difference. 'But for the time being, I was going to show you the part of the garden where Nan and Grandad convinced me there were pixies living, when I was a kid.'

He took her hand, making the blood rush even faster, and led her towards the bottom of his grandparents' garden, where a semi-circle of huge oak trees separated their property from the farmland behind it. All the trees had little wooden doors nailed to the base of the trunks.

'Grandad made the doors, and Nan used to hide stuff among the trees and the flowers around them, telling me they were things the pixies had left behind. They'd tell me stories about them, and I spent every spare moment down here, desperately hoping to catch sight of one.'

'I bet that was amazing.'

'It was, and I had the best childhood, because I was the focus of everyone in the family, so I never really missed having a dad around. It must have been so much harder for you, with your dad's illness being such a big part of your life growing up.' Reuben took hold of her other hand, and they were standing face to face, so close she could feel him breathing.

'I was lucky too and I had grandparents who stepped up, as well. My nan was amazing and when Mum really wasn't coping well, she was the one who gathered me and Lexi up, and focused all her energies on us. She's the person I most want to be like and even though there's no genetic link between us, she taught me more about what family means than anyone else. That's why I don't have any concerns about donating my eggs to Aidan and Jase, because Aidan understands that too, that family is the people who love you most, not just the ones you share some DNA with.'

'You're not like anyone else I've ever met. You're going through so much, but you still want to help other people. I've been wanting to say this for a long time, Isla, and I know it's going to sound like a line you've heard a hundred times before, but I can't stop thinking about you.'

'I haven't heard it nearly as often as you might imagine.' Despite the nerves fluttering in her chest, she managed to laugh. Reuben might well be one of those people who fell for someone easily, but it had never happened to Isla before, and for once in her life she was going to feel the fear and do it anyway. Dropping his hands, she put her arms around his waist, pulling him closer, before announcing her intention. 'And because of that I'm going to kiss you now, if that's okay?'

'I think I can live with the idea.' Reuben grinned again and, as she pressed her lips against his, all the chatter and worries about the future that had been racing through her head were silenced. It was just the two of them, and this moment, and the best kiss she'd ever had in her life. Nothing else mattered, nothing else even existed, and she never wanted it to stop.

Like all good things, the kiss eventually had to end, because if it hadn't, Isla wasn't sure she could have been responsible for her actions. As welcoming as Reuben's family were, she doubted they'd have been thrilled to find her tearing off his clothes in the magical pixie garden they'd created for him when he was a child. She wanted to blame the hormones she was injecting into her body in preparation for the egg collection, but she was past trying to delude herself now. Her feelings for Reuben had grown from a powerful initial attraction to something much deeper, and pretending they hadn't wouldn't make them go away. Instead, she was trying not to overthink it and just see what happened. This was one more thing she couldn't control, which scared her, but she had a strong suspicion it was already far too late to protect her heart.

'Do you want to stay out here and be my barbequing buddy?' Reuben entwined his fingers with hers. 'I know everyone wants to talk to you, but it's nice having you to myself for a bit. At least until they all start coming out here asking when the food's going to be ready.'

'I'd like that.' The fact that Reuben was making no attempt to play things cool made her like him even more.

'Great, wait here. I'll go and get us some drinks.' He kissed her again, much more briefly this time, but her body still tingled with anticipation. 'I'll be right back.'

'I'll see if I can be the first one to spot a pixie.'

'Listen, I *really* like you, but if you're the first one to spot one, after all the years I spent trying, I might not be able to forgive you.' Reuben attempted to give her a serious look, but then he broke into a smile. 'Just don't tell me if you see one.'

'I promise to take it to my grave.' It was only a throwaway line, but Isla shivered as Reuben disappeared. She had to stop focusing on the worst scenario, and make the most of every moment, the way Gwen had told her to. But it was harder than she wanted it to be to not let unwanted thoughts creep in. Maybe concentrating hard, in the hope of finally spotting a pixie, really was the way to go.

It couldn't have been more than a minute or so since Reuben had gone inside, and Isla was crouching at the base of the furthest oak tree, out of sight, trying to read the tiny hand-carved inscription on the door, when she heard voices. She'd have recognised the first one anywhere.

'So, what's it like turning forty-nine?' Aidan's voice had a gentle teasing tone to it.

'Much the same as being forty-eight so far, but I'm going to have a bloody big party next year, that's for sure. And hopefully I'll finally have a little niece or nephew to share the day with. I can't think of any better gift than being an auntie.' Tash sounded really excited by the prospect, but Aidan's response was far more measured and downbeat.

'I'm not sure how quickly it's going to happen.'

'I thought the meeting with the surrogate went well?'

'It did.'

'So, what's the problem?'

'We're just not sure if using Isla's eggs is the right thing to do any more. It might be better to wait and find another donor, but I've got no idea how long that's going to take.' Isla felt as though she'd been winded. Aidan had been having doubts all this time, but he hadn't had the guts to tell her. Suddenly she had no idea whether he'd meant any of the things he'd said since her diagnosis, and even the ground beneath her feet no longer seemed as solid as it had.

'Come on you two, you can't hide out here!' Ray's voice suddenly filled the air. 'Lin's got her sister on FaceTime, and Auntie Pat wants to wish you a happy birthday.'

Waiting until she was sure they'd gone inside, Isla stood up, all the blood rushing to her feet as she did, forcing her to lean against the tree she'd been crouching next to. Aidan and Jase were clearly having doubts they'd never shared with her about using her eggs, and her mind was already racing ahead and coming up with all sorts of reasons why that might be, but none of them were good.

**22**

———

Reuben had wanted to leave with Isla when she'd told him she didn't feel well. The barbecue had just been getting underway and it had taken all her powers of persuasion to convince him to stay, by telling him she had a migraine coming and just needed to go to bed to wait it out. He'd looked doubtful, and Aidan and Jase had fussed round her too, offering to drive her home, but the last thing she'd wanted was to be stuck in a car with one of them, feeling as if all their plans were unravelling because of her. She couldn't help the fact she'd got leukaemia, but she hated the consequences almost more than the illness itself. She'd heard the pain and disappointment in Aidan's voice, and her illness was already changing things, and curtailing her plans, just like she'd feared it would. All of her determination to try and follow Gwen's advice, to grab life while she could, felt impossible now. How was she supposed to grab life, when the leukaemia was already preventing her from being able to do the things she wanted most.

The day after the barbecue was always going to be a difficult day, because it marked the anniversary of her father's death. It wasn't an event that was celebrated, the way they still celebrated his birthday, but they always remembered it in some way. There'd be another trip to the cemetery with her grandparents, and they were having lunch in his favourite pub together afterwards. In the evening, her mother would FaceTime them all, and they'd no doubt exchange some memories of the man whose absence was no less painful after six years, than it had been when they'd first lost him.

She'd woken up in the morning to missed calls from both Aidan and Reuben, who'd left voicemails checking how she was, and texts after that, asking her to get in touch to let them know she was okay. She'd replied to both of them, saying she was fine, and apologising for bailing on the barbecue. To make sure neither of them suddenly turned up, she also explained that it was the anniversary of her father's death and that she was off work for a couple of days, but she'd be in touch after that. She had no idea what she'd say to either of them when she saw them, but that was a worry for later. She had to get through the day with her grandparents first. They'd never have expected her to be upbeat, given the significance of the date, but that didn't stop them realising something was wrong.

'You haven't eaten anything.' Her grandmother laid a hand over hers, as they sat in the pub. 'I know this is a tough day, my love, but your dad would have hated seeing you like this.'

The guilt bubbling up inside Isla threatened to spill over, because she felt like the worst kind of fraud. It was an awful thought, but she hadn't realised until she'd overheard Aidan talking to Tash, just how much the egg donation meant to her. Doing it wasn't just about helping Aidan and Jase, or even creating a legacy to honour her father, she was doing it to make her own life mean something too, and that was the part that suddenly felt more important than it ever had before. Yet she'd sat in the pub, letting her grandparents believe that the blackness of her mood was entirely down to the anniversary of her father's death.

Even after she'd followed them back to their house to wait for her mother's call, she felt as though a black cloud was hanging over her, which she couldn't shake off. Isla could almost hear Gwen whispering in her ear again, that she'd feel far better if she told her grandparents everything. But her decision not to share her diagnosis, meant she couldn't even explain what had happened with Aidan and Jase, and why her plans to donate her eggs would probably come to nothing. At least three times she'd opened her mouth to tell them she had leukaemia, but something had stopped her every time.

'Is that your mum already? She's early.' Her grandmother snatched up the iPad as the ringtone for the FaceTime call filled the air. The poor woman was probably giddy with relief at having something to break up the dark mood, which Isla seemed to be trailing around with her.

'Hello! You're never going to guess what.' As soon as her mother's face appeared on screen, Isla knew something big had happened. She was laughing and crying and, as she turned the iPad slightly, Isla's heart seemed to skip a beat. There, behind her, were Lexi and Josh, each with a tiny baby in their arms. Even though it was a picture that needed no narration, her mother did it anyway. 'They're here! And everyone's safe and well, and it's just been the most incredible day ever.'

Her mother burst into tears again at that point, and it was left to Josh to explain what had happened. Lexi's waters had broken just after midnight US time, but she hadn't gone into labour. When she'd arrived at the hospital and was scanned to check the position of the babies, it turned out that twin one had moved into a transverse position. After that, everything had happened quickly and they'd made the decision not to call the rest of the family in the UK, until they knew the babies were okay, to avoid causing them any unnecessary worry. The babies had been born by caesarean, two weeks earlier than planned. Thankfully everything had gone well and the first twin, a little girl, who they were naming Nicole, in honour of her grandfather, had arrived just before her brother, whose name was Theodore. Lexi had told Isla that she'd considered calling her son Nicholas, but that name would always belong to their father.

The arrival of the babies had lifted Isla's mood in a way nothing else possibly could have done and as the family excitedly talked about all the things they were going to do when they went out to meet the twins in just three weeks' time, she was already looking to the future again. Aidan and Jase might have decided against using her eggs, but that didn't mean she might not want to use them herself one day and she didn't want to write off the possibility. She was still mulling it over much later, when she got a second call from her mum.

'I just wanted to make sure you're okay, sweetheart? You didn't seem quite yourself earlier.' Her mother's voice was warm, and Isla found herself wishing, for the hundredth time, that they weren't so far apart. 'I know how much Lexi wishes you could have been here, and I know missing out on seeing the twins arrive has probably been tough on you too.'

'All I care about is that everyone is okay, but I can't wait to meet them.' Isla meant what she said, but a part of her had to admit her mother was right that this was hard. Not because she'd missed out on seeing the twins arrive, but because any journey to motherhood she might make wasn't going to be easy. It would mean pausing her treatment, or trying a different medication while she was pregnant. Everything she'd read suggested she could have a baby, and that pausing her treatment shouldn't have irreversible consequences. But nothing about it would be 'normal' and the usual pregnancy fears would be far more intense. Even if she was lucky enough to get the family she now knew she wanted, she'd never be able to just get on with life as a mother, taking her health for granted the way other people did, and assuming she'd always be there for her children. Why couldn't she be like Lexi and everyone else? She didn't want to have CML, and she didn't want it hanging over her head for the rest of her life. She wished she could be one of these saintly people she'd seen on the Instagram accounts she'd started following, about living with cancer, who used the phrase 'why not me?' She was still angry that it had happened to her, after everything her parents had done to try and safeguard their daughters' health, which meant asking 'why me' was something she hadn't managed to stop doing yet.

'Oh Isla, they're beautiful.' Her mother was obviously already head-over-heels in love with her grandchildren. 'And I can't help thinking they were born on your dad's anniversary for a reason. All these years of pain, even before he died, and never feeling like I could look forward to the future, because it was so goddamn terrifying. Only now I can, because Nicole and Theodore are the future. I know it sounds crazy and, maybe it's the sleep deprivation, but it feels like a bit of a rebirth for me too.'

'I'm so happy for you, Mum, and I'm so glad they're here.' Isla was just grateful that her mother had called instead of FaceTiming, because she hadn't been able to stop her face from twisting in pain at how unfair all of this was. There was no happy-ever-after, at least, there wouldn't be if she told her mother the truth about her diagnosis now. It would take Clare right back to the place where she'd spent so many years of her life, fearing with every breath she took for what the future might bring. She couldn't do it, and when they finally ended the call, Isla curled up into a ball on her bed. Burdening the people she loved most with the news of her diagnosis was more unthinkable than ever. She'd been able to cope with that, by leaning on Aidan and Reuben, but she wasn't sure if she could do that any more either. Aidan and Jase needed to push ahead with their plans to have a baby, and the truth was her head was in far too much of a mess to get any more involved with Reuben. Maybe it was for the best, because it would have hurt like hell to be on the periphery of things, when Aidan and Jase took the next step towards parenthood without her. It would probably be less painful to stay on in the States when she went to meet the twins, but she had no idea if that was even an option with her diagnosis hanging over her head. Getting the health care insurance she needed for permanent residency, when she required treatment for the rest of her life, could well be impossible. And it was just one more choice she might never get the chance to make.

Aidan had been trying to talk to Isla on her own ever since the barbecue. Despite her responses to his messages claiming that everything was okay, he was really worried about her. But when he'd said he was going to go round to check on her, Jase had talked him out of it, pointing out that she knew they were there if she needed them, and the last thing they should do was make it feel like they were putting any kind of pressure on her, even if it wasn't intended that way. But it hadn't stopped Aidan worrying, and he wasn't the only one.

Reuben had come to see him and Jase the night before, anxious that he'd blown his friendship with Isla by finally admitting how much he liked her. Jase had been the wise oracle again, telling his nephew that it was obvious to anyone who saw them together that Isla liked him just as much. But she had a lot going on, no one could deny that, and what they all needed to do was to give her space. If Reuben was finding that half as difficult as Aidan was, his nephew had his sympathy, because the urge to reach out to her, and try to make everything better, was almost overwhelming. Except Jase was right. No one could do that, and knowing Isla, she'd end up trying to make them all feel better about it instead. She'd even pulled out of the fundraiser at The Pavilion, two days after Tash's birthday, just hours before the event was due to start. There were whispered conversations between those who knew about her diagnosis, and who were concerned about why she'd cancelled. Amy had reassured them that Isla was fine, and that there'd just been some family stuff going on which she needed to focus on.

It wasn't until the first time they were on shift together after the barbecue, he'd overheard Amy congratulating Isla on the birth of her niece and nephew, and he tried not to feel hurt that she hadn't told him they'd arrived. He suspected it had been another attempt from Isla to protect him, worrying that talk about new babies would be hard for him to hear. He just hoped she knew him well enough to realise he'd be happy for her, and her family. A part of Aidan was frustrated too, that Isla was still putting everyone before herself. Worrying about how he might feel hearing baby news was typical of her, but she was shouldering the worry of her diagnosis because she desperately wanted to save her family any pain. That might be admirable, but she was in danger of hurting herself in the process. Everyone needed someone to lean on at times, and he was almost certain her family would want to support her given the choice. That's what families were for; the good ones at least.

If Jase had been there, he would have told Aidan he was being overly sensitive, because of the message he'd got from his mother that morning, asking him if he was planning to come over for his father's seventieth birthday celebrations. She'd also asked Aidan to send over any photographs and memories he had of special times he'd spent with his father, to go in the slide show his oldest sister was putting together for the party. His mother clearly had no idea how strained his relationship with his father had been for years, or at least she pretended not to. The anger May had told him their mother felt towards Sean had clearly dissipated, and she kept saying she wanted things to go back to 'how they were' before his last visit, as if they'd been fine up to that point. But there were no special moments he'd had with his father, let alone any precious photographs, captured in the twenty years since Aidan had left home.

Thankfully it had been a busy shift, without too much time to dwell on anything, but without any life-threatening admissions to the department either, which could break his heart in an entirely different way. But then a cardiac call had come through on the hospital's dedicated number.

'There's been a suspected cardiac arrest in The Sycamore Centre. A forty-three-year-old male, who'd brought his daughter in for an appointment, suddenly keeled over. Two of the staff from the centre are already doing CPR, but they haven't been able to find a pulse.' Aidan relayed the information to Zahir, and the well-oiled machine that was the A&E department swung into action.

'We need a trolley, oxygen and a defib over there now and I want you and Isla to come with me. If he's asystole, we'll need to give him adrenaline to try and restore his heart to a shockable rhythm.'

'We're on it.' Aidan exchanged a look with Isla who nodded. It would be quicker for them to go to the patient, rather than for him to be moved to A&E. They were the designated staff on shift, who'd undergone the necessary training to respond to in-hospital cardiac arrests. Once the patient was stabilised, they'd be able to transfer him, but for now the priority was to get his heart working again. At times like this, being a part of the team was almost like a well-choreographed dance, where everyone knew their steps and no one missed a beat. It meant the three of them were over at The Sycamore Centre within minutes. Joe and Chooky were working on the patient when they arrived, desperately trying to save his life, but the look on their faces said it all. Aidan knew it was almost certainly over, even before he took in the grey pallor of the man lying on the floor of the waiting room, protected by a makeshift screen. All of the other patients had been moved out of the waiting area, and only the sound of a child crying could be heard in the otherwise eerie silence of the room.

'That's Mark's daughter; one of the nurses took her into a consulting room when her dad collapsed.' Chooky looked close to tears as her eyes met Aidan's. Joe was still performing CPR, and he shook his head when Zahir offered to take over.

'I can't feel a pulse either.' Zahir frowned. 'But I think we should attach the defib to check.'

'Did his daughter see what happened?' Isla's voice caught on the words and it made Aidan's chest ache when he looked at her – she knew just how much this would hurt. Aidan had never had to face something like that, and yet it felt in some ways as though he'd been grieving the loss of his father for years.

'She did and she was screaming at him to wake up.' Chooky gave a shuddering sigh, as Aidan affixed the pads for the defibrillator. Moments later, the monotone voice of the machine stated that no shock was advised.

'He's asystole.' Zahir shook his head again. 'I'm going to administer some adrenaline and then we can check again. If that doesn't work, we can try moving him to resus, or...'

'We might have to call it.' It was Aidan who voiced words that no one wanted to say. The idea of taking the man through the hospital, as they tried to continue CPR, while everyone they passed had a ringside seat, was unbearable. The chances of bringing him back, if the medication and ongoing CPR didn't work, were almost negligible, and the colour of his skin suggested he'd been gone before they even got there.

'We might have to, but let's give it all we've got until then.' Zahir touched Joe's arm. 'You need to let Aidan take over now, you can't keep this up.'

'Okay.' Joe finally stepped back as Aidan took over, while Zahir administered the potentially lifesaving medication, and instructed Isla to check whether anything had changed.

'Any pulse?'

'No, shall I see if the defib can pick up a trace?'

'Okay.'

Aidan was certain he wasn't the only one holding his breath as they waited for the verdict, but the monotone voice came back with the same conclusion: no shock advised.

It was a cycle that was repeated as they continued CPR and further doses of adrenaline. A specialist from the cardiac team arrived about ten minutes after the team from A&E, and she and Zahir discussed the use of other medication, but it was increasingly clear that nothing was going to work, and that Mark had probably been dead before he hit the ground. Even on the tiny chance that the other medications made a difference, the likely damage to Mark's brain would be catastrophic.

'I think we need to call it. Everyone in agreement?' Zahir looked around, and every single person gave their agreement to the decision not one of them wanted to make.

* * *

'Whoever said tea can make everything better was a liar.' Chooky put down the cup she'd been holding.

'I don't think anything could make us feel better after that.' Joe swallowed so hard Aidan heard it. 'I wish we could have done something more. It seems impossible to think he was standing there one minute, talking to Chooky about his daughter's next appointment, and the next he was just gone.'

'Hopefully he didn't know anything about it.' Aidan was desperately searching for a tiny ray of light in the midst of something so awful as they all sat around a table in the hospital restaurant, half an hour after Mark's body had been removed from The Sycamore Centre.

'His daughter did though.' Isla's voice was small, and she was biting her lip as Aidan reached out to take her hand, hoping it might offer some kind of comfort.

'That's the worst part of it all. She's got a lot going on with her mental health as it is, and this is going to be really tough.' Chooky wrapped her hands around the tea she'd abandoned moments earlier. 'It's so unfair.'

'It is, but it's really made me think.' Joe adjusted the position of his glasses. 'I've been doing my best to be sensible and wait whatever the allotted amount of time is supposed to be before asking Esther to marry me, but I don't want to do it any more. After what happened with Lucas, I promised Danni I wouldn't rush things and put any pressure on Esther to take a next step she might not be ready for. But how can I know if I don't ask? I don't want to miss out on having a single day I could have had with her. My sister might not be very happy, but I'm going to ask Esther to marry me. I'll just tell her that she can say no as many times as she likes until she's sure she's ready.'

'That's great, Joe!' Aidan clapped his friend on the shoulder. The pain Esther's ex-fiancé had caused her was the stuff of legend around the hospital, but it was easy to see how happy Joe made her. And sometimes you just had to ask the question, even if you couldn't be certain you'd like the answer. As Aidan looked at Isla, he knew there was a question he needed to ask her too, but now wasn't the time to put her on the spot. They needed privacy to talk about it, and she needed time to really think about her answer. For now, he'd have to try and find the words to help her realise that whatever she decided would be okay with him. The words he was about to say were directed at Joe, but he hoped the sentiment resonated with Isla too. 'Sometimes you have to be honest about what you want, even if that means going back on an agreement you made when things were different.'

An unreadable expression crossed Isla's face as he spoke, and he put his arm around her, hugging her tightly, hoping she'd understood what he meant, and silently praying he hadn't thrown away the best chance there'd ever be for him and Jase to become parents.

## 23

Isla had seen patients younger than Mark die before, and it was always hard to get that image out of her mind, but the reason she knew she'd never be able to forget him, was because she could still hear the sound of his daughter sobbing when she got back to her flat. She'd cried until she felt as though she had no tears left, when her own father had died, and she'd known his death had been inevitable, although sooner than they'd expected. But there hadn't been heart-wrenching shock to accompany the pain of losing him. For Mark's daughter it would be different. His death had been completely out of the blue; her father was there one moment, and then just gone, without any warning. It was no wonder witnessing that had made Joe rethink his own life, and reassess his priorities.

It had made Isla think too. As an A&E nurse, she knew that tomorrow wasn't promised to anyone, but since her diagnosis she'd forgotten that, and she'd suddenly felt as though she was the only person in the world who had no guarantees for the future. But that wasn't true, and in the wake of Mark's death, when her thoughts had returned to his daughter again and again, she realised that what she wanted was a partner and a family of her own, despite her fears. Her grandmother had always said that grief was the price of love, but it was a price she'd been willing to pay ten times over to have had her son. Isla hadn't really understood it before, but to have been loved the way Mark and her father were loved, meant they'd had lives worth living, even if they'd been cut far too short. And she didn't want to miss the chance of building her own family with someone she loved that much.

It had made her realise something else; she'd been living half a life for far too long and fear had made her self-sabotage her own happiness. She'd been so scared of loving someone new, in case she lost them, but what was the point of a life without people to love? She had to stop living in fear and she had to find a way to stop living for everyone else too. Maybe it was time to get selfish and work out what she really wanted and how to get there. It sounded easy in principle, but letting go of long-held fears wasn't something that could happen overnight, and she still didn't know if she could tell her family about her diagnosis. At least not yet. The anger she felt about having CML kept bubbling close to the surface, and sometimes she felt as if she was trapped in a maze, trying to work out how to move in the right direction, but finding barriers in her path at every turn. She couldn't help wondering if it would be easier trying to navigate all these difficulties with someone by her side, but when she thought about that she could only picture one person. And Reuben didn't need her dropping her messy life into his lap. She had to work this out herself, and stop pretending she was happier hiding from the prospect of love, just because of the risk it brought.

The chance to build a family was what Aidan and Jase wanted too. But she'd heard what Aidan had said about people needing to do what was right for them, even if it meant going back on an agreement. He obviously didn't want Isla to go through with the egg donation; he'd said as much to Tash on the night of the barbecue, but he was too nice to come out and say it. So she was going to make it easy for him and Jase and give them the chance to walk away without having to be the ones to pull the plug on the process. All she had to do was tell them that she'd changed her mind, and to promise to find a way to repay them for the treatment she'd had so far, and the cost of freezing her eggs. She could stop the treatment and talk to her consultant about the possibility of a referral to an NHS-funded clinic, but that would have made everything that had happened so far completely pointless and it would delay her starting the inhibitors for even longer. At least this way she might eventually be glad she'd made the decisions she had. It sounded so logical when she thought of it like that, and she had no idea why it felt as though she was grieving the loss of something she loved.

Within an hour of getting home from work, Isla had started a loan application – she wanted to have all the plans in place when she told Aidan she wouldn't be going ahead. Making it business-like was the best chance she had of taking the emotion out of it, but her head already ached from trying not to cry again, and she had no idea how she'd get through the conversation when she was face to face with Aidan.

She was just trying to calculate the sum of her total monthly outgoings, the spreadsheet swimming in front of her eyes, when there was a knock at the door. It was already eight-thirty, so it wouldn't be a visitor. It was probably just the pizza delivery guy, getting confused by the numbering system in the chapel flats again.

'Reuben.' Seeing him standing there took her breath away, and not just because she was so surprised that it was him.

'Sorry, I know it's late just to drop by, but I was passing and...'

He shook his head. 'That's a lie. I wasn't passing at all. I knew you were working today, and I was at Aidan and Jase's house when he got in. He said you'd both had a tough day and I wanted to check you were okay. I thought if I called first, you'd just say you were fine.'

'I've been doing that a lot, haven't I?' There was something about him that made it almost impossible to keep up the pretence and, when he nodded, she stepped back and opened the door a bit wider. 'Come in.'

'I've bought you some sunflowers, and some strawberries. Nan made you a lemon drizzle cake she wanted me to drop round, and you left the cup she bought you behind.' Reuben set everything down on the kitchen counter, and Isla picked up the mug.

'I can't accept this.'

'I know it's probably a bit cheesy, but she means well.'

'No, it was lovely.' Isla dug her fingernails into the palm of her hand to distract herself from the emotion bubbling up inside her again. She had to convince him that the decisions she'd made were what she wanted, and he was never going to believe that if she started to cry. 'It's just that what happened today made me realise some things. I can't go ahead with the egg donation, because it's not what Aidan and Jase want...'

'What do you mean it's not what they want?' He furrowed his brow. 'They've barely talked about anything else since you made the offer.'

'But things changed when I was diagnosed. I tried to pretend they hadn't, but the truth is they changed for me too, and I don't think it's what any of us want any more. I heard Aidan telling your mum that they were having doubts.'

'They're probably just worried about you, and I know they're happy to wait until you're sure you're ready.'

'I know, but my head's such a mess at the moment, and I've probably attached too many of my hopes for the future to Aidan and Jase's plans. It started to feel like it might be my only chance of ever having a baby. I don't know if that's what freaked them out or not. But if it didn't, it should have, because if I'd said that to the clinic they'd never have let me go ahead.' Isla gripped the handle of the mug, enjoying how sturdy it felt.

'Anyone would have been knocked sideways by what you've been through.'

'One day I'm certain of what I want and what I think, and the next day I'm not.'

'Are you still talking about the egg donation?' Reuben's eyes never left her face, and a huge part of her wanted to say that her feelings for him were the one thing that hadn't wavered. But she'd meant what she'd said about him deserving more than to be caught up in the chaos.

'I don't want Aidan and Jase to wait around while I see if I can sort my head out, and go back to being the person I was before I had my diagnosis. And I don't want you to have to do that either.'

'I didn't even know the person you were then. It's the you now that I want to be with, however messy that might be.' He was so close she could have reached out to him, and made everyone and everything disappear again, but it would all still have been waiting for her on the other side. It wasn't fair to drag him along for the ride. If they'd been together years when she was diagnosed, it would have been different. Relationships were all about accepting the bad times as well as the good. But right now, she wasn't sure she could offer him anything good.

'I need to concentrate on myself for the time being, I'm sorry.' She pushed the mug across the worktop towards him, her throat burning with the effort it took to say the words, when deep down all she wanted was for him to stay. 'You might be the loveliest person I've ever met, Reuben, and I've got a feeling I'm going to regret this one day. But it would be far worse if I didn't do this, and you ended up being the one who was filled with regret. All I can offer is friendship, but I'm not even sure I'll be that good a friend right now.'

'Nothing I say is going to change your mind, is it?' He sounded defeated and she should have been pleased that he was giving up without too much of a fight, but the regret she'd told him she might feel one day was already flooding through her. She just couldn't let him see it.

'No, but I need to ask one more thing that I've got no right to ask you.'

'What is it?'

'Will you tell Aidan and Jase that I'm sorry, but I just can't keep the promise I made? I'll pay them back for everything, so they can go ahead with another donor straight away.'

'Is that what you really want?'

'It is.'

All Reuben offered in response was a nod, but she knew he'd keep his word. For his uncles' sake, if not her own. He didn't turn back as he headed out of the flat, and the click as he shut the front door behind him seemed to echo across the room. The tears that Isla had fought so hard not to cry, slid silently down her face. And when she took out the injection from the fertility, and jabbed it into her leg, she didn't even feel the needle go in. She was already in far too much pain.

\* \* \*

There was something hypnotic about the fountain outside The Thornberry Centre. It was the way the water danced up and out, cascading like diamonds hanging from a chandelier, before re-

joining the larger body of water and being re-formed into something entirely different. It was a process Isla felt she needed to go
through, physically and mentally, and the counselling session
she'd just had was another step along that road. As soon as the
egg collection was complete, she'd start her treatment with the
inhibitors, which would hopefully change things in a physical
sense too.

She'd ended up talking to the counsellor about Reuben far
more than she'd expected to, as well as working through her feelings about pulling out of the egg donation. Just like Reuben, the
counsellor had asked her if she'd spoken to Aidan and Jase about
her interpretation of their feelings, and she'd been forced to
admit that she hadn't. When the counsellor had asked if she
sometimes used avoidance to prevent herself from getting hurt,
or if she pulled back from things she really wanted, before
anyone else could, in order to feel she had some kind of control,
she'd had to admit both suggestions were true. Unsurprisingly,
the counsellor had linked it all back to growing up with a father
she'd known she was going to lose. That had been the ultimate
lack of control, and it was why she'd tried to choreograph her life
ever since, to avoid getting hurt, by pulling back from any situations where there might be a risk of that.

Isla's counsellor, Jayne, had agreed that her diagnosis had
almost certainly triggered the kind of out-of-control feelings she
hated, and had suggested that their next step was to develop
strategies to try to manage that, without it becoming self-destruc-
tive. Jayne had kind eyes and a gentle manner, and she was far
too nice to point out that Isla had already pressed the self-
destruct button more than once. She hadn't needed to, because
the moment Reuben had walked out of the flat, Isla had wished
with all her heart she could take back the things she'd said. She'd
been telling the truth when she'd told him she was a mess, the

lies had only come when she'd said she didn't want anything other than friendship. Telling herself she'd done that for his sake had made her feel a tiny bit better, but when Jayne had pointed out that he was a grown man, who didn't need protecting, and that it was just Isla protecting herself again, she'd had to admit that was true too.

The droplets of water in the fountain got second chances all the time, and she was still staring at it, holding on to the hope that she might too, when she heard a voice behind her.

'It's so peaceful here, isn't it?' It was Sarah Vardy, instantly recognisable, yet somehow looking entirely different than before. She was thinner, and there were dark shadows under her eyes, but she seemed far less anxious than she had in the past. She was well-groomed and elegant too, with no sign of the woman who seemed to have given up on even basic hygiene after the death of her mother.

'It's lovely. How are you doing?' Isla turned slightly, as Sarah joined her on the bench.

'I'm dying. It's a glioblastoma and I've decided not to have any treatment, other than counselling.'

'Oh Sarah, I'm so sorry.' There were never any right words at a time like this, and Isla instinctively hugged the older woman close to her. For a moment they didn't speak; the only sound was the fountain in front of them, and then Sarah pulled away.

'I'm sorry too, but it's weird, because the thing I'm most sorry about is not that I'm dying, it's for all the years I wasted fearing it.' Her eyes had filled with tears, and she dabbed at them with the crumpled tissue that had been balled up in her fist. 'I spent so long being terrified of cancer and it stopped me living my life. Fifteen years ago, it stopped me saying yes to going travelling with the only man I've ever loved. My mum begged me to go and to enjoy my life while I was young enough to do so. I could have had fifteen amazing years with him, seeing the world. Instead, I stayed inside the walls of my house, thinking I'd be safer there than anywhere else, and the only places I travelled to were hospitals. When my mother was dying, she told me her biggest regret was that she'd never got to see me find happiness. That's what I'm sorry for. I cheated myself out of so much because of a fear of something I could never have controlled. All that hiding away and playing it safe, and I still got cancer anyway. It's bloody ironic, isn't it?'

'None of it's fair and you can't blame yourself for not taking those chances, because you were battling a different kind of illness then.' Isla desperately wished she could do something to change the outcome for Sarah, or to give her back even a tiny bit of what she'd missed out on, but nothing could.

'It's partly my fault, because I didn't take the help that was offered to me to try and deal with my fears, as much as I should have done. I refused the medication and some of the therapies. I think it became so much my norm, I was scared of letting it go, because who would I have been without it?' Sarah closed her eyes for a moment, and Isla tried not to see the parallels between her own life and the woman's sitting next to her, but it was impossible. Isla's behaviour might have been nowhere near as extreme, but she was saying no to things she wanted because she was scared of getting hurt. Except nothing could hurt her more in the end than looking back at a life and feeling all those years had been wasted. There was no point in protecting herself, if it meant she didn't really live, and if she didn't get to experience the things that mattered most in life. It was the same message Gwen and Jayne had tried to give her. Nothing was guaranteed, her patients taught her that every day, and when her time came – whenever that might be – she didn't want to be like Stuart, alone in the world, apart from a carer who was paid to be by his side. She wanted people around her who loved her as ferociously as she loved them. And all she could do was wish the same for Sarah.

'There's no easy fix for that kind of fear.' Isla squeezed the other woman's hand. 'Have you got people around, giving you support?'

'My sisters have been great. I've driven them mad over the years, but they both dropped everything to be with me when I got my diagnosis. They're taking it in turns to stay with me and they've been helping me to look my best, because it helps me feel a bit better too, but I'm giving them both the next week off.' Sarah smiled; the look of serenity that had been on her face when she'd first arrived was back in place. 'Craig, the guy from all those years ago, got in touch after I put something on Facebook about my diagnosis. He came to see me, and we talked all night. He said he wanted to take me to his favourite places around the world and show me all the things he wished we'd seen together. So, he's taking me to Paris. He's hired a camper van so we can stop whenever I need to on the drive down to Kent, and then we'll get the ferry over to France, before driving on to Paris. He wrote all the time when he first went off travelling and I remember getting the postcard he sent me, with a picture of the Eiffel Tower on the front, and wishing to God I'd been brave enough to go. Now I'm going to get to see it, with Craig.'

'That's wonderful, Sarah, I'm so happy for you.' It was a ray of hope in all that had been lost, and Isla managed to smile through the tears that were blurring her eyes.

'He told me I was the love of his life, and I know he was mine. Not everyone gets to have that kind of love in life, so that's something, isn't it?'

'I think it's everything.' As Isla put her arms around Sarah again, the battle to stop herself from giving in to tears was well and truly lost.

## 24

The calls from Aidan's family had become much more regular since the day he'd stormed out of the pub. His mother called at least once a week and sent regular parcels containing things that couldn't be bought outside of Ireland, including the Jacob's Coconut Creams that Jase had fallen in love with on his first ever visit. Aidan's brother, Niall, had set up a WhatsApp group for all the siblings and their partners, where they regularly exchanged family photographs and checked in with how Aidan and Jase were doing. It might not seem a huge deal that Jase had been added to the group, in the same way his siblings' spouses had, but it felt like a massive step to Aidan. The funny thing was, since he'd made it clear he wasn't getting involved in his father's seventieth birthday celebrations, they all avoided mentioning Sean, and his mother acted as if her husband didn't exist during her calls. It was probably easier that way; it certainly hurt Aidan less to pretend he didn't exist. He could accept that the rest of the family still loved his father, because deep down he did too. He wished he didn't, but life was rarely as simple as he wanted it to be.

Ever since her visit, Aidan's relationship with May had made huge strides in getting back to how it was when they were children. She'd already booked a week in an Airbnb in Port Kara, so that she and her family could spend some quality time with Aidan and Jase in the next school holiday. When he'd tried to insist that she come and stay with them instead, she'd been adamant that they shouldn't impose, because there was no way of knowing where they'd be up to in their treatment at that stage, and they might need some space as a result. She was so empathetic and understanding, and had become their number-one cheerleader almost overnight. So it was no surprise to see her number flash up on his phone when it rang one evening, just after he'd finished work.

'If you're calling me to suggest another parenting book, Jase already has them all. He must do by now because we're spending more on books than on our mortgage!' It wasn't strictly true, but sometimes it felt like it.

'It's nothing like that. I wanted to tell you something before someone else does, or you see it online.' May's voice sounded strained and the tightness in Aidan's chest that always appeared when he feared bad news was making it hard to catch his breath.

'What's wrong?'

'It's Cian's father, John. He's dead and Da was the one who found him. He'd gone missing, and Da and some of the others from the pub went looking for him. John was in there almost every night, drinking far too much. It was always worse at certain times and yesterday was Cian's—'

'Birthday.' Aidan cut his sister off. He'd marked the occasion in his own way, raising a toast to his old friend and making the same promise he always did: to try to live a life Cian would have been proud of. It wasn't a date that ever slipped by unnoticed for him, and it seemed that John had been far more affected by his son's death than Aidan had realised. For a long time, he'd held hatred in his heart towards Cian's parents, but no one had come out of what had happened to him unscathed.

'I knew you wouldn't have forgotten.' May sounded like she was struggling not to cry. 'Da's friend Jimmy was in the pub too, and he said that John's drinking was even heavier than usual and that some of them offered to get him home. John insisted on getting some air first, but he didn't come back and they thought he'd decided to head off on his own. It was only when his wife called Jimmy, to ask if he'd seen John, that they realised he hadn't made it home. That's when they started looking for him. Da eventually went to the church and found John slumped on the ground, close to Cian's grave. He was already cold, but Da still tried to bring him back. It must have been awful, and Mammy said that the look on his face when he came home was heart-breaking.'

'Oh my God, that's terrible. Such a lot of wasted life that could have been avoided.' Aidan closed his eyes for a moment. Picturing Cian's face as it had been, back when they'd spent all their time hanging out together, bonding over a part of their identity that had tied them together like brothers. There'd been so many missed opportunities for Cian's parents to prevent the tragedy that had cost them their son, and that had now cost Eileen her husband. Someone always needed to reach out first, before it was too late, and sometimes that first step was all it took. 'Do you think I should talk to Da?'

'He's closed himself off, he's barely saying two words to anyone and I wouldn't want you to think, if he doesn't want to talk, that it's a personal thing against you.' May let go of a shuddering breath and Aidan tried not to over-analyse what she'd said. There was a chance she was trying to protect him, because she knew their father had no interest in trying to rebuild a relationship with his youngest child, but he was going to take her words at face value for now. Their father had been through something traumatic and this wasn't about Aidan.

'I'll send him a message and if he wants to call me he can, if not...' He had no idea how to finish the sentence, but he didn't need to. May understood.

'I wish I'd known what you and Cian were going through back then, I could have done more to help and I'll never forgive myself for that.'

'Don't say that. I spent years wishing I'd done more to help Cian, but we can't change the past, all we can do is try and learn from it.' Aidan breathed out slowly. Reaching out to his father was the right thing to do, despite the fact he'd told himself there'd be no more chances. Cian and John had never taken the opportunity to say the things that needed to be said, and they'd lost their lives because of it. Aidan's father might never say the words he wanted to hear either, but he wasn't going to be the one to prevent his father from having the chance. It was down to Sean now.

* * *

Isla telling herself that she couldn't lean on Reuben was one thing, but actually following through on that promise was a lot harder. He'd seemed so sad when she'd sent him away, turning down the chance of starting a relationship with him that a huge part of her had desperately wanted to take. She wondered if he'd ever want to speak to her again, but then he'd called the day after, just to check in, so he'd said. That's when she'd found herself telling him about Sarah, the tears flowing again as she recounted the regrets the older woman had shared with her. He'd listened and empathised, eventually asking Isla if she'd found the conversation with Sarah even more difficult because of what she was going through. She'd admitted she was determined, regardless of how the CML progressed, never to end up looking back on a lifetime full of regrets and missed opportunities.

'Talking of not living with regrets, I know you don't want us to be any more than friends, but I don't want to lose your friendship too, because I was an idiot and told you how I felt.' Reuben's voice was low, and she almost cracked then, and told him she felt things for him she'd never felt before. But she had to remember the promise she'd made not to drag him into the middle of a mess she was still a long way from sorting out. Isla couldn't deny she'd missed him, though, from the moment he'd walked out of her flat, and she couldn't bear the thought of him not being a part of her life in some capacity.

'I'd like to stay friends.' She wondered for a moment whether he could hear the lie in her voice. It wasn't what she wanted, but she'd made a vow to focus on getting her life back on track, and becoming romantically involved with Reuben could so easily disrupt that, especially if it didn't last.

'How about we go out and do something together? Strictly platonic, of course, and I promise not to say anything that crosses the line of our friendship, as long as you promise me something too.' There was a slight teasing tone to Reuben's voice, and she had a feeling she was going to have to work every bit as hard not to cross that line. But she'd manage somehow. After all, she'd got very adept at hiding how she really felt just lately.

'What do you want me to promise?'

'That we won't talk about the fertility treatment or the CML. It'll be just you and me, having fun, two friends together.' He emphasised the last part and she found herself nodding, even though he couldn't see her.

'I think that sounds like a fair deal, What did you have in mind?'

'Axe throwing.' This time his voice was completely deadpan and she couldn't help laughing.

'We're going axe throwing? Are you sure that's a good idea? I've got a lot of pent-up rage.' She'd meant it as joke, but Reuben still had that knack he'd always had of getting things out of her, even when she'd fully intended to keep them to herself.

'That makes it the ideal activity then. It's at that new bar in Port Tremellien, The Games Room. You can do axe throwing, crazy golf, beer pong, and there's even some karaoke booths.'

'I think you might decide you'd rather I threw an axe at your head than have to listen to me sing.' Isla was already grinning at the thought. It sounded like the perfect night out, doing stupid things and having the kind of fun she couldn't remember having in a long time.

'Are you free tomorrow evening? I can pick you up at six.'

'I'll look forward to seeing you.' It was the kind of thing friends said to each other all the time and there was no reason he should read anything more into it, even if she had to admit to herself that her longing to see him didn't feel much like friendship.

## 25

'Okay, that's three games down, one to you and two to me.' Isla smiled and it was almost as if she could feel her eyes twinkling. She'd forgotten what it felt like just to have fun, but Reuben had served it up in style, and now they were about to tuck into Sloppy Joe sliders, along with The Games Room's house special cocktail, which looked remarkably like a piña colada, although they'd both gone for the alcohol-free option. Isla hadn't wanted to confess that she didn't have a choice because she was taking the fertility medication, so she pretended it was in solidarity with Reuben, who was driving.

'I'm going to be the victor in the karaoke booth.' He grinned and something in her chest felt as if it had fluttered in response. But she wasn't thirteen any more, watching the *Twilight* movies, and fantasising about finding her very own Edward. That was the last time she'd felt like this, and when she looked at Reuben it had all the intensity of a teenage crush. So she dropped her gaze and swirled the straw around in her drink.

'Can you actually *win* at karaoke?' As she asked the question, she forced herself to look up again and meet his gaze, the fluttering sensation picking up pace as he laughed.

'You can certainly lose.' Reuben dropped the perfect wink. 'But as it happens, there's a monitor in the booths that picks up how much each person stays on pitch and you get a score at the end. It's a bit like *Just Dance* for singers.'

'Well, I hope you're ready. I might have downplayed my abilities before, but I've been told more than once that I've got a powerful voice.'

'You do know that's just a polite way of saying you're loud and tuneless, don't you?' Reuben laughed again, as she poked out her tongue. This had been just what she needed, and there was nowhere else she'd rather have been.

* * *

Reuben had scored a pretty impressive 76 per cent with his rendition of 'Texas Hold 'Em' and he raised his eyebrows as Isla moved past him to choose her song.

'Beat that if you can!'

'Oh, I fully intend to.' She'd smiled as she scrolled through the choices, and a karaoke classic she'd sung with her mum and sister at family parties caught her eye. It was cheesy and maybe even predictable, but she knew the song had meant a lot to her mother during difficult times.

'Okay. You've chosen "I Will Survive", so you're going old school with the original karaoke song.'

'You're just worried because you know the games' score is about to be three to one, to me.' Isla took a deep breath as the intro to the song began. But once she started singing, she forgot any embarrassment she'd anticipated at Reuben hearing her tuneless rendition, and she belted the song out for all she was worth, picturing her mum and the rest of the family. It was for all of them, and everything they'd survived. By the time she was finished, her eyes were blurred with tears, but she wasn't sad, she felt stronger and more powerful than she had in a long time. At least until she saw her score: a very mediocre 48 per cent.

'Oh God, I'm the loser.'

'No, you're not. You've just given everything to the song you were born to sing.' Reuben took hold of her arms. 'You've survived so much difficult stuff already, and you won't just survive what's going on now. You'll thrive. All the things you've been through have made you the amazing person you are, and everything that's happening now is just going to be a part of your story.'

'Thank you.' He was the kindest, most genuine person she'd ever met and in the confines of the booth their bodies were almost touching, all of which resulted in an almost unstoppable urge to kiss him again. Instead, she let go of another long breath. 'Not just for what you've just said, but for everything, it really has been the best night.'

'It has, hasn't it?' She couldn't work out if she was imagining the slightly wistful note in his voice and she wanted to say there was one thing that would make it even more perfect, but she couldn't break the promise she'd made and the only thing she could do was change the subject.

'We do need a tie-breaker though. How about we race each other to the bottom of one of their fudge brownie sundaes?'

'It's a deal, and shall we agree that whoever takes the overall win gets to choose where we go next time?' As Isla nodded, she did something else she'd promised herself she'd do more of, and counted her blessings. Having someone in her life like Reuben made it feel as if she'd already won. He might be just a friend, when deep down she wanted so much more, but he was already a part of her life she couldn't imagine living without.

* * *

Isla was shaking as the FaceTime call connected. She'd contemplated telling her nan and Grandpa Bill about her diagnosis before her mum and sister came online. But this was going to be hard enough, and she didn't want to go through it twice.

'Oh my goodness, look at those two! They're already changing so much.' Isla's nan clapped her hands together in delight, when Lexi appeared on the screen, with the babies cradled in the crook of each arm. Her mother was on one side, and Josh on the other.

'They really are, Nan, and we can't wait to see you. Just over a week to go now!'

'I'm just trying not to think about how quickly the three weeks you're over here for are going to go by.' Clare pulled a face. 'Sorry, sorry, I know I'm being a Debbie Downer, worrying about the end of everything before we've even had a chance to enjoy it.'

'That must be where I get it from.' Isla hadn't meant to blurt the words out, but they were churning inside her, making her feel as though she might be sick. 'I've got something to tell you all.'

'You're not pregnant too, are you?' Clare's eyes widened, but Lexi just laughed.

'She'd actually have to start seeing someone for that to happen.' Suddenly her expression changed, mirroring the shock on their mother's face. 'Unless you've decided not just to donate your eggs, but to be the surrogate too.'

'Oh Isla, please tell me you haven't, not without talking it through first.' Her mother leant closer to the screen and everyone started talking at once, voicing an opinion on whether or not she needed anyone else's permission to become a surrogate.

'Stop, stop. It's nothing like that.' Isla took a deep breath, the words she'd dreaded saying rushing out on the exhale. 'I've got leukaemia.'

Once they were out, there was no taking them back, and the ten minutes that followed were a whirlwind of tears, and questions, and reassurances that it would all be okay. Everyone had cried, even Josh, who Isla had no idea would have been as affected as he was. It was another reminder of just how much love she was surrounded by, and how lucky she was. But it was the wisdom of her grandmother that had calmed her mother's near-hysteria in the end.

'I know this is a horrible shock, Clare, and we all wish Isla didn't have to go through this. But every day is a gift, and you and Nicky learnt to treasure that. Knowing he'd eventually develop Huntington's didn't stop you planning things, it meant you were able to create the best life possible and Nicky never missed a single opportunity to make a memory with the people he loved. He's been my inspiration to do that, and I learnt far more from my son than I ever taught him. So that's what we all need to do: hope for tomorrow and plan like it's going to come, but live for today. Most people don't, because they haven't had the privilege of learning from someone like Nicky, but we all did. And that's why, even though Isla's going to be just fine, she'll get to do everything she should be doing, and make the most of every opportunity that comes her way.'

If Isla hadn't known better, she'd have been convinced that Gwen had already spoken to her grandmother, because their sentiments were much the same. But the truth was, it was a wisdom that came with age, and from having lived a life with ups and downs, sorrow and joy, and a realisation that the best type of life wasn't always the longest, but the kind that was measured in love.

# 26

When the clinic phoned to confirm Isla's final scan before the egg collection, it was clear they had no idea that the plans had changed. The nurse asked if Aidan or Jase would be coming in with her, and whether there'd been any rethink on attempting to create embryos for freezing with the first five eggs, or simply freezing all the eggs for fertilisation at a later date. The research Isla had done suggested there was a slightly better chance of embryos thawing more successfully than unfertilised eggs, but it wasn't even an option on the table any more, given that Aidan and Jase didn't want to go ahead. Either they hadn't told the clinic about the change of plan, or they were still too worried they'd hurt Isla by pulling out of the arrangement, which would mean Reuben had lied when he'd said he talk to them about it.

She tried not to fan the tiny spark of hope flickering inside her, that Aidan and Jase might have decided they still wanted to go ahead, because she'd never once wavered on that. She might have made a mess of things by fixating on it being her only chance of having a child, but she knew now that wasn't true. The odds of her managing her condition were hugely in her favour, and the biggest barrier to her having a family of her own day would be if she decided to stand in her own way. But she wasn't going to be like Sarah Vardy, Isla was going to start taking risks with every opportunity that came along, and the first one had arrived when she'd got that call from the clinic.

'Is everything okay?' Reuben sounded breathless when he answered the phone, but just hearing his voice gave Isla a warm glow.

'I'm fine.' She tried not to read too much into the fact that it sounded as though he really cared. She'd done nothing but try to push him away, and yet he'd still fought to be a part of her life and it genuinely seemed to matter to him that she was okay. 'I just had a call from the clinic asking me if anything has changed with the plans for the eggs I'm donating...'

'I'm sorry.' Reuben sighed. 'I couldn't tell them, because I know it's not what they want, and I needed to be sure you meant it before I said anything.'

'What makes you think I didn't mean it?' She kept her tone light. There was no accusation, she genuinely wanted to know what had given it away to him, before she'd fully realised it herself.

'Because I don't think anything you've done since your diagnosis has just been for you. I might not have known you for long, but from what I've seen, I've got a feeling that's been the case for most of your life. You became a nurse to repay the care you saw your father given. You stayed in Cornwall to make sure your grandparents didn't feel abandoned after he died, and you stepped up as an egg donor because you knew how badly Aidan and Jase wanted to be parents. You wouldn't have chosen to walk away from that, unless you thought you were doing it for their benefit.'

'I'd only just started to work that out myself the night you came round to the flat.' Isla had really believed she'd hidden her motives well, and the accuracy of Reuben's interpretation made it hard to catch her breath. This man, who she'd only known for a handful of weeks, seemed to know her better than she knew herself. It was scary and exciting, and she had no idea whether she'd pushed him away one too many times, but she wanted to find out. And she was about to take another big risk. 'Do you know why I asked you to leave that night, and said that all I could offer you was friendship?'

'Because I'm a terrible kisser.' He laughed, and she did too, because neither one of them could have had any insecurity about the kiss they'd shared. It had all the magic you read about in novels, or watched in movies, but knew never existed in real life. Except it did.

'You're not bad.' She loved how easily she could laugh with Reuben, but suddenly it felt as though her heart was in her mouth. It was time to tell the truth, and just because she knew she needed to take the risk, it didn't make it any less scary. 'I pushed you away because I was afraid. I was frightened that, if I let you get close enough, you'd hurt me. Or I'd hurt you, because something or someone would come between us, even if we didn't want it to. And there are so many things we're powerless to control.'

'You do know that no one can ever start a relationship without that risk, don't you?' His tone was gentle.

'It took me a long time to realise that, but I've decided I want to be a risk taker from now on.'

'That might be the best news I've ever heard.' Reuben laughed again and it gave her the courage to ask another question.

'I was wondering if you might be willing to take a risk with me?'

'What were you thinking, sky-diving, or bungee jumping?' The familiar teasing tone was back in his voice now, and she couldn't stop smiling.

'I know you won the sundae-eating contest, but I was thinking maybe dinner and a movie to start with? Only not just as friends this time.'

'That sounds perfect. When?'

Isla had wasted too much time already and she'd be going away soon, so she didn't want to wait. 'Are you free later?'

Luckily it seemed Reuben was just as keen. 'I'll close up the shop and come around now if you want me to.'

'There's something I need to do this afternoon, but I'll be done by the time you close up and then I'm all yours.' A day or so before, she wouldn't have believed she could ever be as upfront with Reuben as she was being now. But this was the start of the new Isla, and she owed it to patients like Sarah, Stuart and Mark, to go after what she wanted.

\* \* \*

Aidan hadn't been expecting a message from Isla asking to meet. He'd been checking up on her regularly since the barbecue, but he deliberately hadn't mentioned the egg donation. Even asking the question made it feel like he was putting pressure on her. It was hell, worrying about what she might be going through, and having no idea where it left his and Jase's hopes of becoming parents. She was his friend, and he wanted to support her, but any doubts he'd had about becoming a dad had disappeared when he'd realised their plans were unravelling. He and Jase had even begun to look at other options for egg donation, and they'd been planning to call the clinic after the weekend, to see how they might be able to proceed. He had no idea what Isla was going to say to him, and the strangest part was he didn't even know what he wanted it to be.

'I got you a latte, I hope that's okay.' Isla was already sitting at a table in The Cookie Jar café when he arrived. When she'd suggested they meet there, he couldn't help wondering if she knew he'd sat at the very same table during the infertility support group, questioning which route to parenthood would be best for him and Jase, scared that none of them might lead where he wanted them to go. It had felt like they'd got so close for a while, but now he was right back in that place again, not sure whether he and Jase would ever get the family they longed for.

'Thank you, that's perfect.' He glanced at Isla; she looked well and, whatever it was she wanted to say, that gave him a reason to smile as he sat opposite her. 'How are you? You're looking really good.'

'I am good, but I don't want to sit here making polite small talk when there's something far more important that needs to be said.' Isla's eyes were fixed on his. 'Do you and Jase still want me to donate my eggs? I heard you talking to Tash about having doubts, and the day we lost that patient in The Sycamore Centre, you said sometimes you have to do what feels right, even if that means going back on something you've agreed.'

Her words had come out in a rush, and had completely caught Aidan off guard. He didn't know what any of this meant, and he still couldn't read her expression. All he could do was answer her honestly. 'I did say that, because I wanted you to know that it's okay to change your mind. But the doubts I was having when I spoke to Tash weren't about me and Jase going through with it, although I've got to admit I had some wobbles. But I was more worried about you delaying the start of the inhibitors. I felt better about it when you said you wanted to freeze eggs for yourself too, but then you started talking about this being your only hope of having a baby and it scared me how much you were fixating on it, and how you might feel if it all went wrong. But none of those things were why we were having doubts.'

'Why were you then?'

'Because using any of the eggs you donate makes it feel as if we're shortening your odds of having your own baby later on. The more eggs you've got, the more chances you'll have.' Aidan knew it was the right thing to do, but it still hurt to let go of the dream. The reason that Isla being their donor had felt so right from the outset was because they knew her. They also knew she'd allow their child to be a part of her life, but that she'd never overstep the mark. She understood what it was like to be a child born as the result of a gift like that, and that not everyone in that position wanted the same thing. There was no guarantee they'd get that from another donor, and it was hard to walk away from the dream they'd built around the woman sitting opposite him.

'I'll have plenty of chances.' Isla set down her cup and took hold of one of his hands. 'I freaked out when I got the diagnosis, convincing myself that my life was going to mirror my dad's. I panicked, and I didn't hear what the doctors were saying about living with CML, rather than dying from it. All I fixated on, was that it probably won't be cured. But the odds are that I'll have a normal life span, and be able to do all the things I want to do, as long as I don't let the leukaemia define who I am. But I need to know if you think that's true, that you believe the inhibitor meds are going to do their thing, and that I'm going to be okay.'

'Of course I do.' Aidan wasn't just saying it to make her feel better. He'd known about CML from his training, but he'd done countless hours of research since Isla's diagnosis, and he'd been incredibly relieved to read just how manageable her condition was likely to be.

'Well prove it then.' Isla raised her eyebrows.

'How?'

'By letting me donate all of the eggs from this collection to you and Jase. I've had my scan and I've got three follicles that have got to eighteen millimetres. The drugs have worked as well as we could possibly have hoped, and the results suggest I'm at the ideal stage for the trigger shot and egg collection. I just need to know whether those eggs have still got a home to go to.' Isla put her hand over his. 'Because if you think I need to freeze them all for myself, it tells me you don't really think I'm going to have every chance of doing this all the old-fashioned way, one day.'

'I think you're going to be able to do whatever the hell you put your mind to. I don't know what's happened since I last saw you, but whatever it is I like it.' Aidan laughed, barely able to believe that their plans might be back on track, but he knew how much he wanted them to be, and it felt as if a huge weight had been lifted off his shoulders.

'So, is that a yes?'

'Too bloody right it is.' Aidan got to his feet and scooped her into his arms, wishing he could find a way to explain just how much her gift really meant to him and Jase. But they'd just have to prove that to her if they were lucky enough to have a child. And he suddenly believed that was going to happen too. Right now, almost anything seemed possible.

## 27

When Isla had asked Aidan to go in with her for the egg collection, he'd been incredibly touched. It had also allowed him to focus on her, instead of worrying himself sick about whether the procedure had worked. He couldn't go in with her, but at least he was there to hear the results when she recovered from the sedation. Jase was the one who'd been left at home, pacing up and down like the expectant father they desperately hoped they'd soon become, waiting to hear how many of the eggs were viable for the next stage of the process.

'Twenty-eight.' When the news had come in, Aidan had felt like whooping and high-fiving in exactly the same way his brothers and their father would, when their footie team scored. The decision was made to freeze half the eggs, and to attempt to create embryos from the remaining fourteen. It sounded like a huge number, and Aidan suddenly had visions of him and Jase having enough children to create their own football team. But each stage became another waiting game and once the mature eggs were combined with Aidan's sperm, the wait was on to discover how many of the eggs would fertilise. Every step was fraught with worry and doubt, and Aidan was more grateful than ever that he'd set up his journey to parenthood page online. It was a place where he could share what was going on and express some of his deepest fears – like the possibility of none of the eggs fertilising – without having to put that burden on Jase, or Isla.

As it turned out, when the eggs were checked on the day after retrieval, eleven of the fourteen had fertilised. It was still enough for a football team, but there'd no longer be any reserves. After that, the wait was back on, to see whether the eggs would develop into viable embryos, and their clinic made a decision on day five about which eggs were suitable for freezing.

'Seven.' Jase had been thrilled when he'd recounted the news from the fertility nurse. They were back to a football team with a couple of reserves, but this time it was for five-a-side. Aidan had known he should be grateful, but the dwindling number had been in direct contrast to his growing anxiety. It was only when he'd updated his page, that he'd started to feel better.

'IVFmumma85 says this is the best result we could have hoped for, and not to forget that we've still got fourteen eggs on ice we can use if we need to.' Aidan read out the latest comment to Jase, as he scrolled through the feed.

'She's right, but I've got this feeling we're not going to need them. Just look at those cells.' Jase grinned at the photograph that was now the profile picture on their Facebook journey to parenthood page. It was of the divided cells in the highest-grade embryo the clinic had frozen for them. And they'd select some to be thawed, once Ellen was ready for transfer. Both he and Aidan carried the same picture in their wallets; it was the closest thing they had for now to a photograph of their child.

'There are so many lovely, supportive comments,' Aidan called out as Jase headed to the kitchen to make them both a cup of tea. When he'd decided to share their story, he'd made a conscious decision to ignore the not-so-nice and frankly down-right horrible comments, that were an inevitable consequence of going public. So, instead, he deleted unkind comments, banned certain phrases, including the word 'abomination', which had been a favourite of his father's in reference to Aidan's sexuality, and blocked certain users from being able to comment at all. There would always be the people who wanted to spread hate, but what he chose to focus on was that there were far more people who wanted to send love and support. It was like focusing on how many embryos they did have, rather than how many eggs they'd lost, and all they needed was one to make it to the end.

'Oh my God.' Aidan had looked at the username three times since the thumbs up had appeared under his latest post just thirty seconds before. The profile picture was tiny and there was a chance it was a fake account, but when he clicked it and saw he had thirty-seven friends in common with the commenter, he couldn't deny who it was.

'My dad's just liked the post about us being able to freeze seven embryos, and he's put a thumbs up in the comments.' As Aidan called out again, he felt as if he was trying to convince his husband that an alien had landed in their front garden, because it sounded every bit as far-fetched.

'You're joking.' Jase came back through from the kitchen and watched as Aidan clicked on the commenter's name and went back into his dad's Facebook profile. They'd never been 'friends' online, any more than they were in real life, and Aidan had always suspected his father would be horrified to be linked to the account of his openly gay son. But now that he looked, a friend request had popped up on the bottom of the page too.

'My God, it's really him.' Jase put a hand on Aidan's shoulder and gave it a squeeze, which meant he knew he wasn't dreaming. 'I think it's a start.'

'I think it's a bloody miracle.' Aidan blinked again, still not certain if he could believe what was in front of his eyes, but at the same time knowing this wasn't the product of some elaborate scam. A part of his father, however tiny, had been able to express some happiness that Aidan and his husband might be a step closer to becoming parents. And if that was possible, then absolutely anything was.

* * *

The three weeks Isla had spent out in Florida were both the longest and shortest of her life. It had passed far too quickly, and she'd wanted to freeze time with her mother, and her sister's beautiful little family of four. But she'd also missed Reuben with a strength she wouldn't have believed possible, even though they'd spoken for at least half an hour, every single day. They'd had the sum total of three dates before she'd left, one of which had admittedly spanned the entire weekend before she'd flown out. But the length of time they'd been dating wasn't some kind of formula that could be equated with the depth of her feelings. They were out of her control, every bit as much as she'd expected they might be. Except, instead of being scary, that lack of control was exciting, and she couldn't wait to get back to him. The flight to Heathrow had been long enough, but now they had a night in a soulless airport hotel to recover, before starting the five-hour drive back to Port Kara.

'Do you think they keep a record of those photos they take when you do the electric scan of your passport?' Isla looked at her grandmother, as she loaded the last of the cases onto the luggage trolley.

'I hope not; I looked like the wreck of the Hesperus.' Joy wrinkled her nose. 'And frankly my love, you don't look much better!'

'Well thank you very much.' Isla laughed, because she knew she looked like she'd spent a rough night in hell. She had no idea what the wreck of the Hesperus was, but her grandmother had always used it to describe things that were in a pretty shoddy state. Isla had been quite surprised that the electronic passport system had even permitted her entry, as the mug shot they'd taken was so different from her carefully posed passport photo. Her hair looked like she had been plugged into the electricity, her skin seemed to have had all the moisture sucked out of it during the flight, and the bags under her eyes almost deserved their own spot on the baggage collection belt. How some people could step off an eight-hour flight looking even half-way decent was a complete mystery to Isla.

'Well, I've got nothing to declare, except for what an amazing time I've had.' Grandpa Bill winked as he pushed the trolley through customs and out into the arrivals hall.

'Someone's waving at you.' Isla couldn't see who her grand-mother was talking about at first. But then she spotted him, waving almost as frantically as she was trying to smooth down her hair.

'I don't believe it, it's Reuben.' The old Isla would have thought she needed to play it cool, and not give away just how thrilled she was to see him, in case it made her more vulnerable, but those days were gone. She didn't care what anyone thought about the wild-haired woman running towards him and into his arms.

'God, I've missed you.' He kissed her before she could even answer, but when she kissed him back it said far more than any response could have done. She was home, and there was nowhere else she'd rather be.

## 28

'Well that's it, we're PUPO.' Aidan clutched the scan picture in his hand, snapping a photograph of it to upload to their fertility journey story.

'Dare I ask what PUPO is?' Jase slipped an arm around his waist as he spoke, his face wreathed in smiles despite his obvious confusion. It had been the most momentous of days, after all.

'Pregnant until proven otherwise. Ellen has got two embryos on board, so she's pregnant. At least for now.'

'Do you think we're about to have the longest two-week wait of our lives?'

'Oh, it's guaranteed.' Aidan shrugged. 'And if it works, we'll then have the longest nine months of our lives. But, whatever happens, I'll never regret a second of this.'

'Me neither.' Jase squeezed his waist and Aidan sent up a silent thanks to whatever force it was that had brought this man into his life. Before they'd started trying for a baby, he wouldn't have believed it was possible to feel any closer to Jase, or to learn anything more about him. But the conversations they'd had, and the moments they'd shared, had deepened the love they had for one another as a result. Even if none of their attempts ultimately proved successful, he'd still consider himself the luckiest person in the world to have found Jase.

'I'd better upload this picture. I've had at least thirty messages already asking for an update.' Something else that Aidan could never have believed, was that so many people would be interested in their journey, and that strangers would be rooting for them, as well as all the people they were lucky enough to call friends. The selflessness that Isla and Ellen had shown had undoubtedly been the pinnacle, but they'd been shown so much kindness along the way, and it had restored Aidan's faith in human nature. 'Right that's it, the picture and update is on Insta and Facebook now.'

Aidan stopped dead as a Facebook notification popped up on his phone.

Sean Kennedy reacted to your post.

There was a love heart emoji next to the notification, and then another one appeared.

Sean Kennedy commented on your post.

Holding his breath, Aidan clicked on the notification.

Keeping everything crossed.

It wasn't the most gushing comment on the post, by any stretch of the imagination, but it meant the world to Aidan all the same. His relationship with his father was taking baby steps in the right direction, and whether or not he and Jase ever became parents, it was just one more reason he'd always be grateful they'd tried.

* * *

It was a glorious afternoon, and the sound of laughter drifted on the light August breeze. Isla had never been to Italy, and she'd certainly never experienced a family gathering there, but that's exactly what it felt like, being seated at a long table, on the terrace of Bocca Felice, overlooking Port Kara, with so many people she cared about. Aidan and Jase had arranged the lunch, and all of their family were there. Isla's grandparents had been invited too, along with Ellen and her family, and some of Aidan's closest friends from the hospital, including Danni and Esther. There was a celebratory atmosphere and, even though there was no way of knowing yet what the outcome of Ellen's embryo transfer would be, with another ten days to go, it felt as if there was some magic in the air.

Isla's consultant had been delighted with the results of her most recent blood tests, and it looked like the inhibitors were doing everything they should. The terror of her initial diagnosis had long since receded, and not just because of the test results. It was the people sitting around the table who had largely been responsible for that, and in a funny sort of way she was almost grateful for the diagnosis. Without it, she might never have learnt that keeping up a barrier did a far more successful job of keeping away the good things in life than the bad ones, and she might never have realised that love trumped everything else when it came to counting your blessings. As Aidan stood up, the chatter around the table gradually began to quieten, and he raised his glass in the air.

'I wanted to thank you all, not just for coming to join me and

Jase to celebrate getting this far in our journey, but for all the support you've given us along the way.' Aidan raised his glass higher still. 'Of course, we'd be nowhere without Isla and Ellen, and I'm sure they're just as grateful as we are, for the support their families have given them. It's a funny word, family, isn't it? I used to think it was all about the relationships you have with the people you're linked to by birth or upbringing, but if the last few months have taught me anything, I've realised that family can be so much more than that. Until recently, I thought that the phrase blood is thicker than water, meant that a blood tie would always trump any other kind. But I discovered it doesn't mean that at all. The real meaning is that the connections with the people you are closest to, form a tighter bond than anything else. I'm not going to put you off your linguine by explaining that it's got something to do with blood brothers and the waters of the womb, although it appears I just have.'

Everyone around the table laughed, and Isla leant closer to Reuben. 'What I'm trying to say, albeit very clumsily, after too many celebratory Chiantis, is that a found family can be even more special than one you're born into. In fact, by the very nature of the fact you've chosen it, I think it is. And I found my family, here, in Port Kara, and I love every single last one of you.'

As Aidan raised his glass again, Isla watched her grand-mother wipe away a tear, and she wasn't the only person around the table to do so. What Aidan had said put it perfectly, and as lucky as Isla was to have been born into the family she adored, she'd always be grateful for the family she'd found over the past year. If life really was measured in love, then she might just be the luckiest girl in the world. She was looking forward to the future now, with all the scary and wonderful things it might contain. One thing she knew for certain, was that she'd make the most of every last moment.

# ACKNOWLEDGEMENTS

I wanted to start with a huge thank you for all the support I've been given with *The Cornish Country Hospital* series so far. After the overwhelming success of *The Cornish Midwife* series, I was quite apprehensive that readers might not take to St Piran's, and the characters who work there, to their hearts in quite the same way. Thankfully, I couldn't have been more wrong and I'm so grateful to every single person who has left a review, spread the word about how much they're enjoying the series so far, and got in touch to tell me that they're loving the stories.

I'm absolutely delighted that you've chosen the third book in the series, and I really hope you've enjoyed this one too. As I always say, I'm not a medical professional, but I've done my best to ensure that the details are as accurate as possible. If you're one of the UK's wonderful medical professionals, I hope you'll forgive any details which draw on poetic licence to fit the plot. I've been very lucky to be able to call upon the personal experience of fertility treatment from a really good friend of mine, who I'll name here only as Julia, and I'm so grateful to her for sharing her story with me. So much so, that I've dedicated the book jointly to her, and to one of my oldest and dearest friends, Claire, who has a story of her own that I hope she'll write one day to share with you all. It would be the most beautiful book if she did, and I'll continue to nag her until she finally gives in!

I'm also very lucky to have another very good friend, Steve Dunn, who was a paramedic for twenty-five years and to whom I can go to for advice on medical matters when I need to. I've drawn on the expertise of another friend, Kate, a hospital consultant, who taught me that the only doctors who become Misters and Misses again, are the surgeons! As ever, I continue to seek support and advice in relation to maternity services from my brilliant friend, Beverley Hills.

I've drawn a little bit in this novel on my own cancer diagnosis more than ten years ago, which was very different to the one in this story, but nonetheless allowed me to experience some of the same hopes and fears as the characters. It taught me that tomorrow isn't promised, but the important thing is to try to make today count. I still have to remind myself of that from time to time, but I hope it's something readers can take away from this story, and we all need to follow Gwen's advice to go out and grab life! It's also the reason I finally decided to follow my own lifelong dream to be an author.

There are some characters in this story who are named because of a competition I ran on the Global Girls Online Book Club. A big thank you to Jackie Claridge-Wood for suggesting the name of Reuben, and Belinda Nemcich for suggesting Lexi, both of whom were named in honour of Jackie's and Belinda's family members. An extra special thanks goes to Helen Deutrom, for suggesting that I name a character after her late niece Angela, aka Chooky, whose mum, Teresa Boaden, allowed me the privilege of doing so. I don't think this is the last we'll see of Chooky in this series.

This is the point where I begin to thank all the other people who have helped get this book to publication. The first and biggest thanks has to go to the readers who choose my books, without whom I would not have a career. You've made so many of my childhood dreams come true, and I'm incredibly grateful to you.

At the end of *Finding Friends at the Cornish Country Hospital*, I wrote a long list of book reviewers and social media superheroes, who have played such a big part in bringing this new series to readers and spreading the word to others, including by regularly commenting on and sharing my posts, including all those listed as 'top fans' on my Facebook page, which is the place online – as an author – where I most feel like I'm surrounded by a found family of friends. I wanted to take this chance to thank as many people as possible again and, as such, my thanks go to Rachel Gilbey, Meena Kumari, Wendy Neels, Grace Power, Avril McCauley, Kay Love, Trish Ashe, Jean Norris, Bex Hiley, Shreena Morjaria, Pamela Spearing, Lorraine Joad, Joanne Edwards, Karen Callis, Tea Books, Jo Bowman, Jane Ward, Elizabeth Marhsall, Laura McKay, Michelle Marriott, Katerine Jane, Barbara Myers, Dawn Warren, Ann Vernon, Ann Stewart, Nicola Thorp, Karen Jean Wright, Lesley Brett, Adrienne Allan, Sarah Lizziebeth, Margaret Hardman, Vikki Thompson, Mark Brock, Suzanne Cowen, Debbie Marie, Sleigh, Melissa Khajehgeer, Sarah Steel, Laura Snaith, Sally Starley, Lizzie Philpot, Kerry Coltham, May Miller, Gillian Ives, Carrie Cox, Elspeth Pyper, Tracey Joyce, Lauren Hewitt, Julie Foster, Sharon Booth, Ros Carling, Deirdre Palmer, Maureen Bell, Caroline Day, Karen Miller, Tanya Godsell, Kate O'Neill, Janet Wolstenholme, Lin West, Audrey Galloway, Helen Phifer, Johanne Thompson, Beverley Hopper, Tegan Martyn, Anne Williams, Karen from My Reading Corner, Jane Hunt, Karen Hollis, @thishannahreads, Isabella Tartaruga, @Ginger_bookgeek, Scott aka Book Convos, Pamela from @bookslifeandeverything, Mandy Eatwell, Jo from @jaffareadstoo, Elaine from Splashes into Books, Connie Hill, @karen_loves_reading, @wendyreadsbooks, @bookishlaurenh, Jenn from @thecomfychair2, @jen_loves_reading, Ian Wilfred, @Annarella, @BookishJottings, @Jo_bee, Kirsty Oughton, @kel-mason, @TheWollyGeek, Barbara Wilkie, @bookslifethings, @Tiziana_L, @mum_and_me_reads, Just Katherine, @bookworm86, Sarah Miles aka Beauty Addict, Captured on Film, Leanne Bookstagram, @subtlebookish, Laura Marie Prince, @RayoReads, @sarah.k.reads, @twoladiesandabook, Vegan Book Blogger, @readwithjackalope, and @staceywh_17. Huge apologies if I've left anyone off the list, but I'm so grateful to everyone who takes the time to review or share my books and I promise to continue adding names to the list as the series progresses.

My thanks as ever go to the team at Boldwood Books, especially my amazing editor, Emily Ruston, my brilliant copy editor, Candida Bradford, and fabulous proofreader, Rachel Sargeant, all of whom shape my messy early drafts into something I can be proud of. I'm also hugely grateful to the rest of the team at Boldwood Books, who are now too numerous to list, but special mention must go to my marketing lead, Marcela Torres, and the Director of Sales and Marketing, Nia Beynon, as well as to the inimitable Amanda Ridout, for having the foresight to create such an amazing company to be published by.

As ever, I can't sign off without thanking my writing tribe, The Write Romantics, including my fellow Boldies Helen Rolfe, Jessica Redland, and Alex Weston, and to all the other authors I am lucky enough to call friends, especially Gemma Rogers, who is another fellow Boldie. Thanks too goes to another of my best friends, Jennie Dunn, for her support with the final read through.

Finally, as it forever will, my most heartfelt thank you goes to my husband, children and grandchildren. Everything I do is for you and, as Isla discovers in this story, if my life were to be measured in love, I know I'm one of the lucky ones.

# ABOUT THE AUTHOR

**Jo Bartlett** is the bestselling author of over nineteen women's fiction titles. She fits her writing in between her two day jobs as an educational consultant and university lecturer and lives with her family and three dogs on the Kent coast. Her first title for Boldwood is The Cornish Midwife – part of a twelve-book deal.

Sign up to Jo Bartlett's mailing list for a free short story

Follow Jo on social media here:

facebook.com/JoBartlettAuthor

x.com/J_B_Writer

instagram.com/jo_bartlett123

# ALSO BY JO BARTLETT

**The Cornish Midwife Series**

The Cornish Midwife

A Summer Wedding For The Cornish Midwife

A Winter's Wish For The Cornish Midwife

A Spring Surprise For The Cornish Midwife

A Leap of Faith For The Cornish Midwife

Mistletoe and Magic for the Cornish Midwife

A Change of Heart for the Cornish Midwife

Happy Ever After for the Cornish Midwife

**The Midwife Series**

The Midwife's Summer Wedding

The Midwife By The Sea

The Midwife's Winter Wish

The Midwife's Surprise Arrival

The Midwife's Leap of Faith

Mistletoe and Magic for the Midwife

The Midwife's Change of Heart

**Seabreeze Farm**

Welcome to Seabreeze Farm

Finding Family at Seabreeze Farm

One Last Summer at Seabreeze Farm

LOVE NOTES

LOVE IN EVERY CHAPTER

WHERE ALL YOUR ROMANCE
DREAMS COME TRUE!

THE HOME OF BESTSELLING
ROMANCE AND WOMEN'S
FICTION

 WARNING:
MAY CONTAIN SPICE

SIGN UP TO OUR
NEWSLETTER

https://bit.ly/Lovenotesnews

# Boldw∞d

Boldwood Books is an award-winning fiction
publishing company seeking out the best
stories from around the world.

**Find out more at www.boldwoodbooks.com**

Join our reader community for brilliant books,
competitions and offers!

Follow us
@BoldwoodBooks
@TheBoldBookClub

Sign up to our weekly
deals newsletter

https://bit.ly/BoldwoodBNewsletter